Dying for a Duke

By Emma V. Leech

****

Published by: Emma V. Leech.

Cover Art: Victoria Cooper
ASIN No.: B073RT8D2T

Table of Contents

Dying for a Duke

Chapter 1

"Never send to know for whom the bell tolls; it tolls for thee." - John Donne

Benedict Rutland, the Earl of Rothay, looked across the carriage at his mother, Lady Lucilla Rothay, and his eyes narrowed with suspicion. She was undoubtedly up to something.

The idea gave him a prickling sensation down the back of his neck and he adjusted his perfectly tied cravat with irritation. At the age of forty five and with five living children to her name, she really had no business looking as she did. She had been considered a diamond of the first water in her youth and in truth little had changed. She looked barely a day over thirty and was a magnet for trouble.

"What's disturbing you, mother?" Benedict asked, his nerves not soothed in the least by the way she leaped in her seat at the sound of his voice. Her wide aquamarine eyes widened yet further with alarm.

"W-what could be the matter, dearest?" she said, sounding nervous and terribly guilty. "I mean, apart from this dreadful funeral today and this awful black!" she said, plucking despairingly at the black crepe of her dress. "I shan't wear it a moment longer than I must," she added with a determined set to her jaw. "Anthony was always perfectly monstrous to me and I won't go about looking hagged to death on his account. If it wasn't bad enough when your father died!"

Benedict held back a sigh. There was no point in remonstrating. She had adored his father even though he'd been more than twenty years her senior, that much he knew. He had no doubt the black dresses brought back unhappy memories for her even though it had been ten years now since his father passed. "Yes, mother, but he was father's nephew. You must show respect."

She made a very unladylike noise of disgust and looked away from him. He didn't, however, believe for a moment it was the funeral that was making her twist her rings around her fingers and practically tie her black gloves in a knot.

"It's not that blasted poet is it?" he demanded. If it wasn't bad enough that the house was always full of dashing young blades on his sister's account - who had inherited her mother's extraordinary good looks - half of them were there to worship his mother. The young poet who was less than half her age was undoubtedly the worst, and the most determined.

Lucilla gave a gurgle of laughter, her aquamarine eyes alight with mischief. "Oh poor dear Ezra. He's such a lamb."

Benedict held his tongue against the comment that came to mind about serving him sliced with mint sauce. It wouldn't help.

Benedict had become the Earl of Rothay at the tender age of nineteen and found his family had been plunged into huge debt by both of his parents' gambling and frivolity. He discovered that they were both generous to a fault and spendthrift to a point that sickened him. He'd had a rude awakening when he found himself head of a large family who were all looking to him to make it alright, and without a feather to fly with. Only the timely death of his mother's youngest brother, his Uncle George, had saved them. George had never married and had made his fortune in India. He'd died a tragic death at far too young an age and had left everything to Benedict.

It seemed a terrible thing to Benedict that another tragedy was the source of their reprieve, but he'd had no time to spare on sentiment. Even his uncle's fortune, whilst it cleared their staggering debts, was not enough to support them all. But with some judicious investment and an iron fist on the family purse, Benedict had pulled them back from the brink. No amount of lectures or waving of horrifying bills in front of his mother's lovely face had the power to change her ways though. She would cry - prettily - in the face of his anger and beg forgiveness and then do it all over again.

He wondered what bills she was hiding now, and if that was the reason for her fidgets.

"How much, LuLu?" he asked, softening his tone with the pet name all of her children and close friends used for her.

Eyes of such startling innocence that every alarm bell rang a peal over him, blinked with astonishment. "Oh, it isn't money, Ben, dear," she said, biting her lip and looking down to rearrange the drapes of her dress into a more pleasing fall of material.

Benedict gave an inward groan of despair. "What then?" he demanded. "You'd best get it over with. You know you'll have to tell me in the end."

She swallowed visibly and looked up at him, her lovely face full of pleading. "You must see I didn't have a choice, dear. I mean he is my brother after all, and that poor girl. I can't imagine what her life must have been," she said, sighing and shaking her head.

"Oh good God, if this is to do with Uncle Edward, the answer is no! There never was such a shocking loose screw."

"Benedict!" his mother replied, clearly aghast and dismayed. "How can you say so? He's such a dear man, and such fun."

Benedict snorted in disgust. Uncle Edward was fun, that was true enough, he was also the most appalling rake with a dreadful reputation. "Wait a minute," he said as his flickering suspicions flamed brighter. "What girl? Don't tell me some woman has got her clutches into him?"

"Oh no, dear, not that." His mother cleared her throat and looked away from him and back to her rings, twisting the large diamond his father had given her the year before he died. "Only ... well you know he married that widow, and she had a daughter already. Well her mother died just a year or so after they married and so dearest Edward has brought the girl up single handed."

"And what, pray, does that have to do with us?" Benedict asked with a sinking feeling and a tone that made his mother's beautiful face blanch.

A stubborn look that boded ill flitted across her face and she crossed her arms. "Well, the poor creature has been following the drum nearly her whole life. She must be twenty or so by now and never had a come out! Can you imagine, Benedict? The poor creature trailing after the army for years during that dreadful war. My heart just bleeds for her."

"As does mine," Benedict replied, well aware that he sounded as though he didn't give a hoot which was far closer to the truth. "But I still don't see what affair it is of ours? What the devil have you done?"

"Why she's family, Benedict!" Lucilla exclaimed with reproach.

"No she isn't," he retorted. "She's my uncle's step-daughter."

"But Eddie positively dotes on her, darling. Loves her as his own child, he told me so. So you must see I couldn't refuse him."

"Oh God, no," he said, groaning and rubbing a hand over his face in despair. As if he didn't have enough with his eldest sister, Cecily, who at seventeen was set on giving him heart failure. Not to mention the dreadfully mischievous twins, Honesty and Patience, who were just fourteen and looking as though they would finish the job in a couple of years' time. Honesty and Patience, he thought with a snort of desperation. His parents had quite a gift for irony. At least young Jessamy didn't cause him too much worry except for falling out of trees and cheeking his tutor.

But now, on top of that he was to have another foolish young girl thrust under his protection who would no doubt need chaperoning and guarding from rakes and scoundrels. And that was without even considering his mother! It was the outside of enough.

"What, *exactly,"* he demanded with a tone that dripped ice. "Have you agreed to?"

"To ... to bring her out into society," Lucilla said in a rush, raising her chin with defiance. "And he's my brother, so I don't see why you must make a fuss."

"No, I don't doubt that," he replied with such a bitter snap to the words that his mother's eyes glittered and she looked away from him. He sighed and reached out his hand to her. She pouted for a moment before taking it.

"I haven't seen her since she was a child," she admitted. "But she was an adorable little thing. Blonde and blue-eyed, perfectly angelic, Benedict. I'm sure she'll be a sweet girl, and dear Eddie assures me she won't give us a moment's trouble."

Benedict mentally consigned his uncle to the devil but forced a smile to his lips. "I'm sure you're right, mother."

Lucilla sighed with pleasure. "Oh I am glad you aren't cross with me, Ben, darling. I do so hate it when you get on your high ropes."

Benedict gritted his teeth and with what he considered a heroic effort of will, said nothing.

"What is she called then," he asked. "This new family member we are to take to our bosoms?"

Lucilla gave him a sceptical look, rightly suspecting him of sarcasm. "Phoebe Skeffington-Fox."

Benedict snorted and his mother frowned. "That's my family name and a very old and distinguished one at that. I shan't allow you to mock it."

"I wouldn't dare, LuLu. So when is she arriving?" he asked, assuming he had a week or two at least to resign himself to the idea.

"Tomorrow," Lucilla said with a sparkling smile. "I declare, I'm so excited!"

"To ..." Benedict began and then snapped his mouth shut. Because really, what was the point?

"Have you considered, mother, that the family is in mourning and the season is over? We won't be able to present her before next year."

Lucilla waved her hand. "All the better," she said, beaming. "She'll have time to get to know people and accustom herself to polite society before having to face all that."

Benedict muttered dark thoughts under his breath as the carriage rocked to a stop and the door was opened. He walked down the steps and handed his mother out of the carriage, nodding at family members as they began to gather.

Looking around the sea of black, he searched for the head of their large and powerful family. At the age of seventy-eight, Sylvester, the fifth Duke of Denholm, was still a rather impressive figure, though he was a shadow of the man he had once been. All the Rutland men tended to be large and powerfully built and Sylvester had been a hulking bear of a man in his prime, both in character and build. But of all his descendants, Benedict resembled him the most.

Uncle Sylvester had always been a larger-than-life presence and someone to be relied upon. His own father had been fun and full of life, but never around when Benedict had needed him. Sylvester had taken him under his wing and treated him as his own son, better than he'd treated any of his true sons in fact.

"Ben!" his uncle boomed, holding out his hand to him. "Thank God! Get me away from these blasted toad eaters and fools will you, boy! Damned if I can stand another moment."

Benedict repressed a smile at the furious looks from his uncle's immediate family that happened to include the man's younger son and grandson. He gave Sylvester a reproving look and offered his arm. Sylvester limped away from the gathering and Benedict could feel the glowering stares burning a hole in his back.

"Can't you be civil for five minutes, you old goat?" he said, shaking his head at his uncle who just snorted.

"Damned if I will. Not much time left, shan't spend it talking to people I can't stomach."

"John is your son," he replied, with just a touch of disapproval. He found it hard to muster more than that as he himself couldn't stand the man. "And we are burying his older brother today. Perhaps you could be just a little more sympathetic."

"Bah!" Sylvester exclaimed. "We never could stand each other, everyone knows it. Don't expect me to weep over his coffin now. If there's one thing I can't abide, its liars and cheats. Anthony was both and there isn't a scrap of use in denying it. I didn't like Anthony and he didn't like me. He's dead and I'm sorry for it, but I can't pretend my heart is broken."

Benedict nodded, knowing it was true enough and then hesitated before he voiced the niggling doubt in his mind. "Didn't you think it a bit ... odd, though?"

Sylvester's shrewd green eyes looked into his, a glitter of satisfaction in the surprisingly deep emerald. "Too smoky by half," he muttered, nodding. "Glad you thought so too, my boy. I told 'em, but the coroner wouldn't have it. No evidence of foul play. Accidental death was their verdict." He gave Benedict a disgusted look. "Damned fools! No way Tony could have turned that blasted curricle on that road. I may not have liked him but he was a nonpareil. I've never seen a man like him for handling a whip."

"Nor me," Benedict replied, frowning. "But if it wasn't an accident?"

"Don't know," Sylvester replied with a sigh. "He had enemies did Anthony, a man like that always will. Never did know when to hold his blasted tongue."

Benedict hid a smile at that and looked up as the bells began to ring.

"Ah well," Sylvester said, sounding suddenly a touch melancholy. "Best get this over with then." He was silent for a moment as they walked to the church doors, hobbling on his gouty leg. "Get me out of here soon as you may, there's a good lad," he asked, his voice rather frailer than Benedict had ever heard it before. "Can't stand to see that wretched grandson of mine strutting about now he's a marquess."

"Of course, Uncle."

Sylvester nodded, satisfied. "Thank you for inviting me to stay with you," he added. "Must admit the idea of that gloomy house on my own wasn't a fond one. But be dashed pleased to see your mother. Looking in fine twig today I must say!"

Benedict chuckled and nodded as Sylvester's eyes took in his mother's lovely figure with an appreciative eye. "And she's very much looking forward to seeing you, Sir."

With a sigh Benedict steeled himself for the coming ordeal, and not just the funeral. God alone knew what chaos Sylvester and his mother could create together. With a smirk of satisfaction he wondered if Phoebe Skeffington-Fox had the slightest idea of what she had let herself in for.

Chapter 2

"What dire offence from am'rous causes springs,
What mighty contests rise from trivial things." - *Alexander Pope*

"She's here!" squealed Honesty who had been standing guard at the window with her twin, Patience, since early morning. "Oh I say, Jessamy, come and look at this, what a carriage!"

Benedict repressed a sigh as Jessamy scrambled onto the window seat beside his sisters.

"Oh, Ben, do come and see," called Jessamy, his big eyes popping in his head. "What a bang up turn out!"

Benedict's lips twitched but he frowned. "Will you three get down from there? What on earth shall Miss Skeffington-Fox think of you all if you stand there gaping like the circus has come to town?"

Scowling and muttering the children came away from the window, casting their big brother reproachful glances as they went to the front door to greet the new arrival. The footmen crossed the marble-clad entrance hall and flung open the doors of the house on Grosvenor Square.

Standing beside his mother to greet Miss Skeffington-Fox, Benedict could forgive his younger siblings their enthusiasm. The lady's shiny new chaise was drawn by four perfectly matched greys and the accompanying baggage and valises that attended her arrival were astonishing. It was quite beyond anything Benedict had seen in all his life. His instinctive disgust at such obvious expenditure was quite halted, however, at the sight of the lady herself. Dainty, gloved fingers accepted the footman's hand and a vision stepped down from the carriage.

For just a moment it was quite possible he forgot to breathe.

"Well I never," his mother whispered beside him. "But then I did say she was angelic."

Angelic was the only word that could possibly describe a face like that, Benedict thought, with a rare dash of whimsy. Her hair glinted in the summer sunshine like ripe corn and her lithe figure tripped down the stairs and presented them both with a delighted smile. That startling expression dimpled her cheeks and made her bright blue eyes glitter with vivacity. She seemed to exude life and laughter and Benedict's heart sank at the realisation. The last thing his family needed was more encouragement to be frivolous and vain after all his hard work to instil moral fibre into them. This spirited creature may look angelic, but he didn't have the slightest doubt that every lovely inch of her was trouble.

"Instinct tells me you must be Aunt LuLu," she exclaimed, running up to his mother and holding her hands out. "But I cannot believe it. You aren't nearly old enough to be Papa's sister! You look more like this gentleman's sister than my aunt!"

Predictably this drew a delighted peal of laughter from Lady Rothay.

"Incorrigible child!" she scolded. "When you must know very well this is my eldest son, The Earl of Rothay."

Benedict watched with misgiving as she dipped a low curtsey and looked up at him from under her long lashes. "I'm so pleased to meet you, my Lord Rothay." Her eyes were warm and full of humour as they looked upon him and he felt a stab of real fear. Trouble. She was *trouble*.

Benedict took her hand and greeted her with icy civility.

"Miss Skeffington-Fox," he replied, with dignity. "You are most welcome."

He felt the appalled look that his mother sent his way without having to see it but Miss Skeffington-Fox didn't seem in the least perturbed. In fact he was alarmed to see the flicker of a smile at those luscious, full lips, though it was quickly vanquished.

"Oh but we are cousins are we not, my Lord. You must, I beg you, call me Phoebe."

Benedict inclined his head a little but made no reply and did not echo her demand.

"I hope you will forgive my uncle's not receiving you. Yesterday's funeral was fatiguing for him. You understand that the family is still in mourning?"

"Perfectly," Phoebe replied with a sympathetic smile. "You have my condolences, my Lord."

Casting him one sharp look of disapproval, his mother quickly swept their guest up and into a flurry of introductions. Once done, Lady Rothay turned to escort her into the house, only Miss Skeffington-Fox halted on the steps and gave a shrill whistle through her teeth.

Everyone froze in shock and then gasped as two huge grey wolfhounds leapt down from the carriage and trotted meekly to her side. She looked up at the faces around her with surprise as she took in their mingled expressions ranging from appalled horror and awe.

"Oh dear," she said, laughing and not looking the least bit remorseful. "Have I shocked you? I'm afraid I will you know. Papa says I have the manners of a Light Bob, but then I would I suppose, having been brought up with them from the cradle."

Benedict sucked in a breath of astonishment. Good God, the girl was a hoyden to boot. What the devil were they to do with her?

Lady Rothay gave her an uncertain smile and Phoebe took her arm in an affectionate manner. "Oh, pray don't be angry with me, ma'am. I promise I shall do my best to behave. I'm not in the least stupid I promise you and will learn anything you wish to teach me."

"Oh, dear child," Lady Rothay murmured, covering her hand with her own. "As if I could ever be cross with you."

"And I'm so pleased to meet you too," piped up a soft voice.

Benedict watched in dismay as Cecily ran up to her and grasped her other hand. "I am so happy to have another sister closer to my own age," she added.

Phoebe tipped back her head and laughed. "Oh, you sweet thing, but I'm three and twenty, my dear."

This fact was exclaimed upon by all and Benedict's thoughts darkened further as he wondered why she hadn't married yet, *come out* be damned. Any woman who looked like that would never be short of offers.

In fact the picture made by his beautiful dark-haired sister and the lovely fair Miss Skeffington-Fox was quite breath-taking. With growing apprehension he foresaw the lines of love-struck young men queuing outside his door growing to epic proportions in the near future.

Phoebe laughed and kissed Cecily's cheek. "Oh, but aren't you a beauty! My goodness are we to come out together? We shall set the *ton* on their ears I think!"

And with that terrible prediction ringing in his own ears, Benedict followed them into the house.

They gathered in the drawing room where tea was brought and Jessamy immediately demanded the names of the two lofty giants who were flanking either side of Phoebe in the manner of Egyptian Sphinx. Phoebe grinned at the little boy whilst gently removing one large paw from the delicate hem of her cobalt blue sarsnet gown. Benedict refused to notice that the colour exactly matched her eyes.

"This handsome fellow here is Goliath," she replied stroking the wiry head with affection as the big creature stared adoringly up at her. "And this beautiful lady is his lovely wife, Delilah."

Benedict frowned with disapproval. Firstly it ought to be Samson surely, not Goliath, and they hardly seemed appropriate names for a young lady's pets. Certainly not Delilah!

He noticed too late that Phoebe was looking up at him with unconcealed amusement.

"You do not approve of my dogs, my Lord," she said. He noted that she didn't make it a question. He cleared his throat, embarrassed despite the fact that it was she who ought to be blushing.

"I doubt you seek my approval, Miss Skeffington-Fox."

To his growing annoyance the woman laughed at his slight. "Indeed not, my Lord. Especially as these were a gift to me from the Duke of Wellington. He named them you see," she added with a smile that was so full of devilry and satisfaction at having bested him that his temper was lit.

Jessamy looked up at her with undiluted awe in his eyes at this news. "You ... you know Old Nosey?" the boy breathed out in astonishment.

"Jessamy!" Benedict scolded him, making the boy jump. "His Grace the Duke of Wellington to you, my boy!" he said, perfectly aware he sounded like a pompous arse and a hypocrite too. Jessamy knew as well as he did that he often referred to the general by his nickname.

"Oh, I rather think the general likes his nicknames, when they are used with such affection," replied Phoebe, staring at him unblinking. There was a challenge in her eyes he didn't believe he'd misinterpreted.

"I bow to your greater knowledge of the man," he said, inclining his head without the merest trace of a smile.

"Yes," she said, nodding her head with every appearance of seriousness. "I should." Only the glimmer of amusement in her eyes betrayed that she was mocking him but it was only too visible.

The eyes of everyone in the room bore into him and he made his excuses, leaving the room with all haste.

He shut the door behind him with a muttered curse and wondered why he'd let the blasted woman rattle him so. She was clearly a baggage and no better than she ought to be. He would have to do his utmost to limit the damage she could wreak, most especially to Cecily who at seventeen, was at a most impressionable age.

He walked back to the entrance hall just as the footman was greeting Miss Theodora Pinchbeck, his betrothed. “Theodora,” he said with real relief as he took in the cool elegance of his wife to be. “I cannot tell you how glad I am to see you.”

Miss Pinchbeck was a good-looking rather than beautiful woman. She was tall and a little too slim with an angular face and a rather long nose that gave her a slightly horsey appearance to those unkind enough to remark it. She was, however, the epitome of good manners and grace and would never in her life whistle on the doorstep or bring two big ugly and ill-named dogs into a family’s house without a by your leave!

Miss Pinchbeck smiled at him. Her grey eyes were placid and showed none of the sparkling devilry of Miss Skeffington-Fox, for which he was heartily thankful.

She placed her gloved hand in his and lifted her cheek to be kissed.

“I take it your cousin has arrived?” she enquired with a slight quirk of one eyebrow.

“She has,” he replied with a grim expression. “And I’m afraid I shall have to introduce her to you. You won’t cry off will you?” he asked, smiling at her.

“I have made a promise, Benedict,” Miss Pinchbeck said with a serious little frown puckering her brow. “Your family is my family, for better or for worse.”

Benedict opened his mouth to explain he had only been joking but thought better of it.

“Worse, my dear,” he replied instead. “Most certainly worse.”

***

Phoebe looked up as Lord Rothay returned to the drawing room and felt pleased that she hadn't frightened him off so easily. She had been disappointed in his leaving, wondering if perhaps she had misjudged him. She prided herself on being a very good judge of character and had taken an instant liking to the earl because of rather than in spite of his frigid welcome. The trouble was that she could never resist a challenge - and Lord Rothay was most certainly a challenge. She could almost hear her maid Sarah Huckington's sigh of dismay. In this case, however, it was followed by her own as he was accompanied by a pinch faced young woman who looked her over with barely concealed contempt. She had just taken a sip of her tea when Lord Rothay entered and introduced Miss Pinchbeck. Her name was so vastly appropriate that Phoebe almost choked and had to set the cup down with some haste before it rattled to the floor.

"I do beg your pardon, Miss Pinchbeck," she replied, hoping her amusement was sufficiently hidden. From the lurking scowl in Lord Rothay's quite startling green eyes she gathered that this was not the case. "I am very pleased to meet you," she added with a demure smile.

"Miss Pinchbeck is my fiancée," Lord Rothay added, and she was certain she saw a glint of malice behind the words. Phoebe looked back at Miss Pinchbeck and repressed a smirk with difficulty.

"I felicitate you both," she said as she mentally shook her head over the match. What a disaster that would be!

Miss Pinchbeck murmured a dutifully polite reply and sat down. The heavy sighs that caught her ear from the twins was duly noted as a pall of restraint descended over the room. Phoebe glanced at her aunt who returned a pleading look but it seemed nothing could be done but endure. The next twenty minutes were inexorable and strained Phoebe's good manners, such as they were, to breaking point.

Benedict and Miss Pinchbeck dominated the conversation which was as dull and colourless as Miss Pinchbeck's dove grey silk dress. It was refined and elegant but had nothing of interest that might capture the eye, or cause offence. Phoebe thought she'd really rather cause offence than be accused of being dull.

Trying in desperation to turn the conversation from the depressing route it had taken into discussing the weather and the possibility of rain this afternoon, Phoebe seized her chance.

"What a lovely gown, Miss Pinchbeck," she said, trying her best to be friendly in the face of such obvious disapproval. "It's exquisitely cut. Who do you visit here in town?"

"Oh, nobody you would have heard of, Miss Skeffington-Fox," she replied with such a modest smile Phoebe had to bite her lip. "She is really not one of the shining lights of the *ton's* modistes you understand, but she suits my tastes."

Phoebe saw the look of approval that Benedict cast his betrothed and surmised that Miss Pinchbeck lived up to her name more completely that she had imagined. She was undoubtedly a penny pincher.

"I must tell you, Theodora, that Miss Skeffington-Fox here arrived with so many band boxes and valises we have been obliged to give over a whole room to their storage. "

Phoebe flushed as Miss Pinchbeck gave a disparaging titter of amusement and felt a rush of anger at his slight. How dare he? She had spent her whole life following her father from one rude posting to another. Admittedly there had been some glamorous parties and the like but for the most part she had lived in dangerous and meagre circumstances that Miss Pinch*mouth* wouldn't endure for a day. She had finally brushed the dust from her skirts and allowed herself the pleasure of shopping. And yes, she'd enjoyed it and spent a fortune, damn him.

"You disapprove of my spend thrift ways, no doubt?" she put to Lord Rothay, her words laced with a dangerous tone he would do well to note. But Lord Rothay did not yet know her.

"How you spend your father's allowance is no affair of mine, Miss Skeffington-Fox," he replied with a tight smile.

"I collect that I asked you to call me Phoebe, *Cousin Benedict,*" she said, enjoying the dark look in his eyes. "And it appears that you have made it your affair by commenting upon it."

An appalled hush fell over the room.

"Would anyone care for more tea?" Lady Rothay squeaked, clutching the teapot and sending Phoebe an imploring look.

"In fact it would seem that you imply that I am wasting my father's money," she persisted, ignoring Lady Rothay's futile attempt to divert her, the atmosphere in the room practically crackling now. "But you see I have rarely had the chance to buy such niceties as Miss Pinchbeck probably enjoys as a matter of course. I have spent my life in rather different circumstances than the safety and polish of refined society, so yes, I have been rather extravagant. Indeed my father positively forced me to ensure I spent every penny he sent my way to make up for the lifestyle I have lived until now."

She paused, noticing with deep satisfaction he looked dreadfully discomforted and knew he was on the point of begging her pardon. She'd be damned if she offered him the opportunity. Phoebe was already planning her dignified sweep out the room and hoped he suffered agonies of guilt over his presumption and ill manners. The thought pleased her enormously.

"In fact, Lord Rothay, I wouldn't have missed the past years for the world, despite the privations that were sometimes forced upon us. But then I am not, as you perhaps now perceive, the kind of woman who succumbs to fits of vapours or will allow herself to be bullied or talked down to. Now if you will forgive me it has been a rather fatiguing day and I think I shall go to bed." She turned to Lady Rothay. "Perhaps you would be so kind as to send a little tea and toast to my room, Aunt Lucilla? I don't think I could face dinner right now." She leaned down and kissed her aunt's cheek and whispered. "Forgive me," before giving her a saucy wink and sweeping out of the room just as she had planned.

Chapter 3

"It is one thing to show a man that he is in error, and another to put him in possession of truth." - John Locke.

"Tea and toast?" exclaimed her maid, Sarah Huckington, as she shook out the creases from a lovely butter yellow silk dress. "What on earth do you mean you asked for tea and toast? You'll be famished! You know you need to eat your dinner or you get in one of your tempers."

Phoebe turned from the dressing room table with a scowl. "I do not have tempers," she said, with a huff. "And it was worth it for the look on his face."

"Aye, well, it seems he may well have asked for a set down if what you say is true," Sarah replied with a nod as she reached for another gown.

"Oh it is, he was positively odious," Phoebe replied and turned back to the mirror to finish brushing her hair. "And he certainly got a set down," she added with relish.

Sarah straightened up and looked at her via the mirror. "Well you just keep out of his way, my lamb."

"Keep out of his way?" Phoebe looked back at her in astonishment. "Why on earth would I do that?"

Narrowing her eyes, Sarah crossed the room and snatched the hairbrush from her, brushing her long golden locks with rather more vigour than was required. "Now, little Bee, you just told me he was rude and overbearing and so full of puff you could hardly stand it. So tell me why you wouldn't stay away from a man you clearly can't stand."

"Can't stand?" Phoebe repeated, blinking at the woman who had been her nurse from infancy and the closest thing to a mother she'd ever known.

"Oh, do stop parroting me, child. You've spent the past half hour ranting about his faults. Are you telling me you don't hate him?"

"Of course I don't hate him," Phoebe replied laughing at the consternation in Sarah's eyes. She gave a heavy sigh. "I think he's wonderful."

Sarah threw her hands up in despair. "I swear, Miss Phoebe, I've known you since the cradle and I still don't understand you. You are the most contrary creature on God's green earth."

"Oh but, Sarah," she exclaimed, grabbing her hand before she returned to unpacking. "You haven't seen him. He's the biggest man I've ever seen. Such broad shoulders and dark hair and those eyes, oh, Sarah, they're green! Not a muddy sea green either, green like ... oh like emeralds I suppose."

Sarah snorted. "I've never known you lose your head over a pair of pretty eyes before, my lass, and Lord knows you've had enough of them looking at you with adoration. Goodness me, when I think of Captain Dreyton," she said with a deep sigh as her own eyes became a little misty.

Phoebe huffed. "Oh, don't start harping on about Captain Dreyton again, Sarah, I beg you. We would never have suited."

"And why ever not?"

Phoebe watched as Sarah got a mutinous look in her eyes, her arms crossed beneath a generous bosom. Poor Sarah. All she wanted was to see Phoebe safely married, she did worry so. She would never understand that Phoebe was looking for ... for ... well to be truthful she had no idea what she was looking for. But she couldn't help but feel she had found whatever it was in the odious Earl of Rothay. However unlikely that may seem.

"Give me one good reason why you shouldn't have married Captain Dreyton. And I want a good one mind," Sarah warned.

"Because he was too nice!"

Sarah stared back at her in outrage. "Well of all the bottle headed ... *too nice?* Well if that don't beat all," she muttered, turning back to the case and shaking out a deep green sarsnet with irritation. "Too nice! And now you're thinking of setting your cap at an ill-mannered brute who no doubt thinks you're a hoyden, though I'm not sure I blame him."

"He's betrothed."

Sarah dropped the dress in horror. "Now, Phoebe," she began with a warning note in her voice. "Don't you dare!"

Phoebe looked back at her with wide eyes. "Sarah, whatever can you be thinking?"

"Don't you dare go flirting and making up to a man who's already engaged to be married, my girl!"

Phoebe laughed and crossed the room to give Sarah a hug. "Oh as if? You know I never would! In any case I'm not going to do any such thing. In fact I'm going to make his life perfectly unbearable," she said with a grin. "Though if he happens to discover that his betrothed is joyless, miserly and unfeeling in the process I really can't be blamed for it."

Sarah covered her eyes with one hand. "Oh, Lordy," she said, a despairing edge to the words. "And here I was thinking I'd finally persuaded your father to send you out of danger."

Phoebe took her hand and towed her to the bed, patting the mattress to get her to sit down.

"Do stop fretting, Sarah, you know my schemes always work out famously in the end."

Sarah turned and looked at her, clasping her hand tightly. "But even if your wretched scheme works, my lamb. What would you be wanting with a man who's rude and unkind to you?"

Phoebe smiled and pictured the earl's glowering countenance in her mind's eye. "Oh, papa told me all about the family. The poor man became earl at nineteen when his father died and found the family was all but bankrupt. He was barely more than a boy, Sarah, and he had to take on a young family *and* try to save them from ruin. Can you imagine?"

Sarah made a tsking noise of sympathy and shook her head.

"Is it any wonder he's forgotten how to have fun and ... and looks for safety and ... and a dull life over facing all that uncertainty again?"

She looked up to find Sarah giving her an old-fashioned look. "And so?" she demanded. "How exactly is this scheme going to change all of that?"

Phoebe wrapped her arms about herself. "I'm going to teach him to be brave," she said with a smile.

***

The next morning Benedict found his mood had not improved from the previous evening. Despite Theodora's conviction he had been in the right and that Miss Skeffington-Fox was dreadfully outspoken and hadn't the slightest delicacy of mind, he could not help but feel a sense of guilt.

A hoyden she may be, but he had gone out of his way to provoke her for reasons he simply couldn't fathom. There was something about *Cousin Phoebe* that made him out of reason cross. Nevertheless he hadn't stopped to consider that she might have been excited to be in London and to soon be attending parties and balls in the manner that any young woman would enjoy. He hadn't really considered what kind of life she must have led up until now at all, despite his mother's words on the subject.

At all accounts it would appear that her rakish father had not set her a good example and had given her a deal too much freedom and a free tongue. Those things would need to be checked, he decided. She was obviously spoilt and wilfully independent and that was something he would not tolerate. But a guiding hand should bring her to heel soon enough. He believed himself more than equal to the task though he would no doubt have to be extremely patient over the coming weeks. However he was a fair man and he realised that he did owe her an apology. So with this in mind and the intention of being generous and charitable, he went down to breakfast.

Benedict paused half way down the stairs as his uncle's booming laughter filtered out from the breakfast parlour. Breakfast was generally a quiet affair. Benedict did not like noise or chatter first thing and most of the family trod carefully around him until he had left the breakfast parlour. Though as he was generally the first up this wasn't too much of a hardship. His uncle too was generally an early riser when he was on form, which he clearly was today. He had not expected to see Miss Skeffington-Fox at such an hour. Standing in the doorway, however, he looked upon a very jovial scene as his Uncle Sylvester waved a hand at him.

"Ben! Ben, my boy, I've just been speaking to your charming cousin. Where on earth have you been hiding her?" He beamed at Phoebe, his green eyes full of the dash and sparkle of a man half his age.

"Nowhere, Sir," Benedict replied, silently thanking God that this was the case. Though if he'd had a hand in her upbringing, she'd not be such a blasted nuisance. "Miss Skeffington-Fox has been with her father following Bonaparte's trail of destruction." Privately he wondered if Miss Skeffington-Fox had left a trail of her own.

"So she's been telling me," Sylvester replied nodding. "Thought you was something out of the ordinary first moment I set eyes on you, my girl. Not like those insipid misses we generally see round here. Bore you to tears they would."

Benedict bit back a retort, knowing damn well that his uncle did not approve of Miss Pinchbeck. As the man was a confirmed womaniser in his youth, Benedict had always been able to shrug off his comments. Unlike most of the men of his family Ben was not made in that mould and only wanted a woman who would be a stable and steadfast companion. Someone who knew how to behave and would never make him blush for them or gamble away their fortune, or whistle on the doorstep. Benedict glanced at Phoebe to see her biting her lip. With annoyance he realised she was trying not to laugh. Damn the chit, and he still had to apologise to her. Sylvester, who was totally oblivious to Benedict's chagrin, returned his attention to the diabolical blonde at his side.

"Now tell me, child," the old man demanded. "Did you really hold up a Bandito or are you bamming me?"

Benedict choked on his coffee.

"Oh no, your Grace," Phoebe replied, with her cornflower blue eyes wide and guileless. "I wouldn't do that. It's perfectly true."

"No, Phoebe," the duke replied with reproach. "If I have to tell you again to call me Sylvester, I shall be affronted you know."

Phoebe laughed and Benedict frowned as the sound seemed to wrap around him. It was warm and inviting, inviting him to join the fun.

"Very well, Sir ... I beg your pardon, Sylvester. But yes, I did though sadly the gun was empty. I had to bluff though you see - he was a most unsavoury character."

She shuddered and Benedict felt a strange jolt of concern. She was making light of it, turning it in to a delightful story to amuse his uncle. But what must she have felt if it was true? He felt a sudden and unwelcome desire to shield the wretch from any such dangers in the future. Though as she was unlikely to fall among Bandits in Grosvenor square, he wasn't sure why he should be concerned at all.

"But how did you hold him off if the gun was empty?" Sylvester demanded, watching as she picked up a second slice of plum cake.

"Well, he didn't know that," she said with a grin before popping a piece of cake into her mouth. She swallowed and looked back at the duke. "And besides, I'd hidden in the cellars where they'd stored the explosives and had the forethought to grab a box of matches before I went down. He'd have been very foolish to believe I wouldn't have struck that match, don't you think?"

"Good God!" Sylvester exclaimed, looking at Phoebe with a cross between astonishment and pure delight.

Benedict fought the need to put his head in his hands and groan. He could well believe the wretch set off explosions wherever her feet touched the ground.

"That settles it," Sylvester said, with the air of a man who was used to getting his own way. "You're all coming to Grizedale Court for the summer. Lady Rothay and the children and most certainly you, my girl! By Jove we shall have some larks!"

To Benedict's dismay Phoebe's eyes lit with excitement. "Oh, Sylvester, that would be perfectly wonderful!" She clapped her hands together and leapt out of her seat to kiss Sylvester's bristly cheek.

Clamping his teeth together with frustration, Benedict was almost certain the old man blushed.

"Oh thank you so much!" she exclaimed before she turned and met Benedict's dark gaze. "Only ..." she faltered, her joyous expression falling away so suddenly it would have been comical if he hadn't realised it was simply part of her evil genius. "Only ..." she said again, with the wistful tone of a child dreaming of a longed for treat.

"Only?" Sylvester barked in annoyance. He was not a man who liked to see his plans thwarted. "Only what?"

Phoebe stared unblinkingly back at Benedict before she turned her big blue eyes on the old man. "Perhaps Cousin Benedict wouldn't like it?"

If Sylvester missed the glimmer of devilry in her eyes as she delivered this performance, Benedict did not. The manipulative baggage! There was no possible way he could wriggle out of it without upsetting the old man who had clearly set his heart on the notion.

"Ben?" Sylvester repeated in astonishment. "Nonsense. Why should he? Ben loves Grizedale more than anyone, don't you, my boy?"

"Of course, Sir," Benedict replied through his teeth, glaring at the blonde harpy opposite him with loathing.

"There you are then," Sylvester replied, grinning broadly and stroking his bushy moustache with satisfaction. "All settled. Ben, get everyone packing up will you. We'll leave in the morning."

Benedict opened his mouth to say this was impossible at such short notice but had enough experience of his uncle in this mood to know it would be useless. If the duke said the household was to be packed up, the household would be packed up.

"Pass me that stick will you, my dear?" Sylvester asked, though Phoebe had already run to fetch it for him as the old man hauled himself to his feet. Benedict stood too but the old man shook off his helping hand. "Blasted gout!" he grumbled as Phoebe returned with the stick. "Still you're lucky I'm not a man half my age, Miss," he added, giving her a roguish smile.

Benedict watched as Phoebe's cheeks dimpled in an alarmingly endearing manner when she smiled at him. "Frankly I think I've been born far too late," she replied with a mournful expression.

"Ha!" the old man barked, clearly delighted that she would flirt with him. "Baggage," he muttered, but with such affection it was clear that no malice was intended. Phoebe then escorted him to the door and to Benedict's chagrin did not come back to the table.

Damn the woman. Now he would have to seek her out for the sole purpose of apologising when all he wanted to do was avoid her. Suddenly deciding he'd lost his appetite he pushed his plate away and decided to get it over with.

Chapter 4

Beneath her clear discerning eye the visionary shadows fly of folly's painted show:
She sees thro' ev'ry fair disguise, that all but VIRTUE'S solid joys are vanity and woe. - Elizabeth Carter.

To his intense frustration Phoebe managed to evade him for the rest of the day. As leaving at such short notice meant that he had much to keep him occupied, he had little time to dwell on the fact. To his frustration the woman seemed to invade his thoughts at the most annoying intervals and he spent most of the day feeling unaccountably cross. At least he had already planned to dine at his club so dinner would be avoided. There wouldn't be the slightest chance of getting her alone and apologising in private in any case. He blamed his simmering frustration on the fact that he did not enjoy being in the wrong.

Thanks to the unflagging work of his staff, Benedict found that the whole family was indeed ready to leave the next morning. A row of gleaming carriages waited outside the elegant town house though they wasted more than a little time discussing who would travel with whom. Sylvester, whose own comfort always came first, was adamant that Lady Rothay, Phoebe and Benedict would travel with him. He seemed frankly disinterested in how the rest of them organised themselves.

Though it was June, the day was overcast with a chill north wind blowing that made it feel rather more like March. Once certain that arrangements had been made to his satisfaction, Benedict was rather glad to get into the carriage and out of the cold. He found himself seated beside his uncle and opposite his mother and Miss Skeffington-Fox.

As uncharitable as his thoughts towards his new step cousin might be, Benedict had to concede that she looked ravishing. She wore a bright carmine red velvet pelisse, the tops of the sleeves caught up with rich silk military chain work. A charming velvet lined bonnet of the same shade framed her lovely face and cast her blonde locks an almost burnished gold. Limerick gloves and kid half boots completed the elegant picture and Benedict wished he was sitting beside her. At least then he wouldn't have to pay attention to ensure his gaze didn't steal back to take another look.

Despite his mother's attempts to draw him into polite conversation he managed to avoid being anything more than superficially entertaining for the first half of the journey. This didn't seem to be a problem, however, as the rest of the company were in fine spirits. Their convivial mood only seemed to blacken his own further, and it was with considerable relief that they drew up outside The Bull in Maidstone for some refreshment.

As Sylvester was only too eager to return to the comforts of his own home, this was a blessedly brief affair but did afford Benedict a moment alone with Phoebe.

She was walking outside of the inn as they waited for his mother and uncle to appear, apparently enjoying the weak sunshine that had begun to filter through the clouds.

"Miss Skeffington-Fox?" he called, drawing her attention to him and he strode towards her, determined that he should not be thwarted again. "May I have a moment of your time?"

"Of course, Cousin Benedict," she said, smiling at him, though that ever present challenge lurked in her eyes. And he knew damn well she only called him *Cousin Benedict* to rile him. Which it did.

"I would prefer that you call me Benedict, rather than insist on this ridiculous charade we are cousins when you know full well we're no such thing." The words shot out in irritation and he remembered with a stab of annoyance he was supposed to be apologising.

"Oh, are you disinheriting me?" she replied, blinking up at him with those big blue eyes.

He scowled at her and wondered just how many men had capitulated to whatever it was she demanded of them under the weight of that beautiful countenance. Well he would not be one of them. He ignored her question and ploughed on.

"I would like to apologise for my behaviour to you, Miss Skeffington-Fox," he began but she shook her head, stopping him in his tracks. Reaching out she tugged at his sleeve and then wagged her finger at him.

"Phoebe," she said with a reproving expression. "If you are Benedict, then I *must* be Phoebe."

"Very well," he said, taking a breath. "Phoebe, I would like to apologise for my rudeness."

"Why certainly," she replied, beaming at him, but then her lovely expression puckered a little, her blonde brows drawing together. "Only ... which particular rudeness were you referring to?"

Why the little ... Benedict clenched his jaw and his eyes fell, as she bit her full lower lip between white, even teeth. He knew she was laughing at him. The problem was she had a point, but he was damned if he'd apologise for the fact she made him furious every time she opened her perfectly lush mouth. He drew his eyes away from that distracting article with a shake of his head.

"I am apologising for making assumptions about how you spend your allowance. I hadn't considered the kind of life you must have led until now and that, perhaps such expenditure would be a novelty to you after such restrictions. It was ... unjust of me and I'm sorry for it."

There, damn her. He'd said it and she could find whatever she liked within the words to throw back in his face. She'd not hear another apology from him. But to his surprise her face softened and she smiled at him.

"Thank you," she said simply. "I confess you put me quite out of countenance for papa was forever demanding I should spend more money on my appearance. But what is the point when you are forever covered in dust or mud and surrounded by soldiers who spend their days fighting for their lives? It seemed obscene to be so taken up with such fripperies in the circumstances."

He frowned, looking at her with a dawning respect. He hadn't expected such an answer as that. "Yes," he replied, and discovered himself sounding almost approving. "I think you were quite right."

To his surprise she availed herself of his arm, though he hadn't volunteered it, and he found himself strolling along the lane with her.

"But I'm not going to pretend I didn't enjoy spending every penny on the contents of those cases," she added, with a more familiar twinkle in her eyes.

Benedict snorted. "I never doubted it for a moment." He glanced down at her to find she was staring up at him with a warm expression. "I think you enjoy most everything you do," he added. Damn, he hadn't meant to say that out loud, but he'd found himself staring down into eyes of such blue he felt he might drown in them if he wasn't very careful.

"I think perhaps I do," she replied, her voice soft. She didn't blink, her head raised up as it barely reached his shoulder, though she was tall for a woman. He looked away from her and noticed with relief that Sylvester and his mother were returning to the carriage.

"Time to go." He hurried her back to the carriage and handed her in, making a mental note to keep out of her company as much as was possible.

***

Phoebe's eyes widened as the imposing structure of Grizedale Court came into view.

"Knew you'd like it," Sylvester said with satisfaction, though she'd not said a word. Apparently her face was expressive enough though as she glanced back to find his bright green eyes trained on her.

"It's lovely," she said with complete honesty. "I've never seen anything so beautiful."

The old man beamed at her and she thought she saw a glimmer of approval in Benedict's eyes too. Ah, this was a way to reach him, perhaps. He loved the place.

"When was it built?" she asked him, unsurprised when he gave her the answer without hesitation.

"The earliest parts of it were built by King Ecgberht of Wessex in the ninth century but it was extensively added to in the sixteenth century. Sylvester's father remodelled the North front to a Palladian design in seventeen forty nine and grandfather commissioned Capability Brown to design the Park and gardens some fifty years ago. He also added the picture gallery which you really must see. It's quite wonderful."

Phoebe watched, enchanted as Benedict spoke about the Court. His whole face became animated, his eyes warmer and full of enthusiasm. It was such a startling change from the severe, proud man she had encountered up until now that she caught her breath. Yes, she saw the real Benedict now. This was who he really was if only he would remember it.

"I do hope you will give me a tour, Benedict," she said, knowing full well he'd be unable to refuse in front of his mother and uncle, no matter how badly he wanted to. The warmth fell from his eyes and his face shuttered up but he gave a curt nod.

"It would be my pleasure," he replied, sounding as though he'd rather stick pins in his eyes. Phoebe bit back a grin and waited for the carriage to rock to a stop.

Once Benedict had handed her down from the carriage Phoebe could only stand and stare. Though it wasn't only the magnificence of the building that struck her but the many staff and footmen who went about their business or stood looking aloof and rather formidable. The one exception to this was the butler who gave her a surprisingly warm smile as he welcomed her to Grizedale Court.

He was a tall man, perhaps in his fifties, with thick dark hair, greying at his temples

"Well, Keane?" Sylvester demanded of him. "How many damned parasites in residence, eh?"

Keane didn't blink at this description of his master's family and merely went on to list the guests. "Lord and Lady Rutland are here and Viscount ... I beg your pardon the *Marquess of Saltash* arrived a few moments ago with a Mr Wilfred Spalding."

Sylvester snorted in disgust and the way in which the butler pronounced this last name led Phoebe to believe that he in no way approved of the man. Lord Rutland must be Sylvester's youngest son, John, as the old man had given her a brief family tree the day before. The new marquess now, after his father's recent death, was his grandson, Harold. Neither man seemed to have gained Sylvester's affection much less his respect and he had advised her to keep out of their way.

A woman hurried out of the house at this point and ran to kiss Sylvester's cheek.

"Ah, there you are, Lizzie, want you to meet Phoebe Skeffington-Fox. A cousin of Ben's here."

Phoebe saw the slight grimace Benedict gave at this description but ignored it and smiled at the woman who was tall and slender with the family's trademark dark hair and green eyes, though hers were more hazel than the bright emerald of Sylvester and Benedict. She was perhaps thirty and had a nervous look to her, like a little rabbit that might hop away if startled, and was dressed all in pale lavender silk. She looked every inch the spinster that Phoebe knew her to be.

"Hello, Miss Skeffington-Fox," she said, looking a little dazed by Phoebe's glamorous scarlet ensemble. "I'm so pleased to meet you."

"And I you, Lady Elizabeth, though please do call me Phoebe, Skeffington-Fox is such a mouthful it's really very tiresome."

The lady looked relieved at this invitation and gave her a slightly more assured smile. "Well, only if you will please call me Lizzie, everybody does you see."

Phoebe did see and strongly suspected that Sylvester's granddaughter - Harold's sister - was put upon by all and sundry. Deciding that it was probably about time Lizzie had a champion she took her arm in a companionable manner and they walked into the house together.

Once more Phoebe had to stand and stare. Her first impression was of light and space which she hadn't expected in such a big old house. The hall was galleried and rose an impressive two stories to show a curved roof which was heavily decorated with intricate, white plaster mouldings. All around and up on the galleries were big white marble archways and the white stone balustrades following the white marble stairs and floor. The overriding effect of all that white marble reflected the light from the many windows until the whole room glittered, even in the weak sunshine of the late afternoon.

"Oh, how lovely," she said, turning in a circle and craning her neck to take in the many beautiful, gilt-framed paintings.

The tranquillity of the scene was disturbed by the clatter of nails on marble and a ferocious barking sound as five hunting dogs exploded into the hall from outside. The timing of this seemed unfortunate as a tall and rather exquisite looking young man had just descended the stairs and the dogs seemed to take exception to him. Uttering a shriek which Phoebe thought most unbecoming he cowered whilst the dogs circled him, growling until Benedict shouted at them. Instantly recognising a voice of authority they ducked their heads and walked towards him instead with a docile and chastised wag of their tails.

"Those damned dogs are a menace," cried the pretty young man on the stairs, pointing at the creatures with loathing. "Wretched things ought to be shot!"

"Touch my dogs and it will be the last thing you do, you impertinent cully!" boomed a furious voice entering from the same door the dogs had just made use of. Phoebe turned in astonishment, feeling she had fallen into the scene of a play. The man who was built on the same massive lines as Benedict was clearly Sylvester's son, John - Lord Rutland. Once again the thick dark hair and green eyes were in evidence though his face was florid and showed signs of excess that his thick waistline only echoed. There was nothing in his face that Phoebe found to like as he stared at his terrified nephew with pure loathing. She decided on the spot that Sylvester's advice to stay clear of him and Harold, who she took to be the coxcomb trembling on the stairs, was good advice indeed.

"If you can't control them," Harold continued, his voice rising to a shriek. "Then you shouldn't be surprised if someone takes matters into their own hands. They're dangerous, they should be put down!"

Phoebe caught Benedict's eye, who happened to be stroking the silky ears of one of these dangerous creatures as it gazed up at him with a worshipful expression. The lurking amusement in his gaze was obvious as was an obvious chagrin at the appalling behaviour of his family.

"I'll take matters into my hands and put you down before you lay a hand on my dogs, by God," John thundered as he stormed towards Harold who uttered a gasp of horror and ran to stand beside Sylvester.

"Enough!" Sylvester shouted, stamping the heavy oak stick he leaned on against the marble floor in fury. "How dare you make such a show of yourself in front of my guests."

"Well it would be a mercy killing, the damned little fribble makes me sick," John muttered. "But I beg your pardon," he added, rather ungraciously. At this point he noticed Phoebe and his bloodshot eyes brightened rather noticeably. "Pleased to meet you," he said, suddenly rather more urbane. "Don't be frightened of the dogs, they won't hurt you. Not if you're not a pathetic little weasel at any rate." He winked at her and she was relieved to note Benedict had come to stand beside her.

"You needn't fear for Miss Skeffington-Fox," he replied, greeting his cousin with a cool nod. "She owns two monstrous wolf hounds that should arrive at any moment."

John scowled at that. "Trained are they?" he demanded.

"Oh, indeed," Phoebe replied with the sweetest smile she could conjure. *"They* have perfect manners."

Benedict cleared his throat and rather hurriedly suggested as the hour was growing late that they all go and get ready for dinner.

Chapter 5

"WHILE here the poet points the charms
Which bless the perfect dame,
How unaffected beauty warms,
And wit preserves the flame." - David Garrick

Dinner was as horrifying as Benedict had expected, only lightened by the chagrin in Phoebe's eyes on the arrival of his betrothed. He scolded himself for his presumption of her interest in him, and the satisfaction he took in it. She was no doubt on the lookout for a rich husband and an earl would do just fine.

Theodora looked elegant and cool as ever; she always reminded him of an ancient marble statue, unchanging and rather aloof. He found it reassuring. She would never subject him to ridiculous arguments and passionate tempers or come to dinner looking so ... He risked a glance back at Phoebe and wished he hadn't as every man in the room was doing the same thing. He glared at his cousin, John, who was ogling her ample cleavage in full view of his wife, Jane. Though if he'd been married to Jane, he might be every bit as desperate. The woman had the face and figure of a bulldog, all square shoulders and compact strength in a short frame, and the personality to match.

As though drawn by some magnetic force he found himself looking at Phoebe once more. Dressed all in tulle over a pale pink satin she looked fragile and ethereal until you saw the glint in her blue eyes. Like a naughty fairy, he thought, finding his lips twitch at the thought and then chastising himself roundly for it. She was sitting beside Sylvester of course, who had made sure she and his mother, Lady Rothay were either side of him with no regard for the rest of them. Sylvester didn't give a hoot for manners and never had. The results of which were obvious in his son, John.

Phoebe gave a convulsive laugh that had all of the ladies looking at her with disapproval, even his mother looked a little shocked, and it was clear Sylvester had said something outrageous to her. Phoebe looked up and caught his eye, her expression rather defiant as he stared at her in annoyance. Couldn't she at least try to act with a little decorum? He glanced back across the table to find Theodora giving him a sympathetic look and found himself even more irate.

Dinner was interrupted by Keane entering and announcing the arrival of Lord Oliver Bradshaw. Benedict gave a sigh of relief as he looked upon one of his more agreeable relatives. Oliver's mother had been Sylvester's youngest sister and he and Benedict were relatively close in age, Benedict being two years older. Oliver had inherited his father's looks rather than the Rutland dark colouring and was handsome and blond with pale blue eyes. He was a little shorter than the lofty Rutland clan and less heavily built but he was a fine figure of a man and his reputation with the ladies was formidable. It was easy to see why, however, as he gave a charming and friendly smile to the ladies present.

There was a few moment's disorder whilst another place was laid for him and Sylvester took the opportunity to introduce Phoebe. Benedict stamped on an irrational surge of irritation as Oliver looked like all his Christmases had come at once. Having been seated beside Benedict, Oliver greeted him with a wide-eyed and eloquent question without ever saying a word.

"My mother's brother's step-daughter," he said in answer, managing to infuse the words with deep disapproval. That was of course a mistake as Oliver looked even more intrigued.

"Tell me more," Oliver demanded, his blue eyes twinkling with determination.

"Don't go getting any ideas, Ollie," Benedict warned him in an undertone. "She's a damned hoyden and a blasted nuisance but she's under my protection, and so you can take that gleeful look from your face."

Oliver looked at him in frustration. "Damn it, Ben, you never used to be such a dashed gloomy stick in the mud."

"Nevertheless," Benedict replied, who thought in his opinion it was about time Oliver stopped behaving like a school boy kicking up larks.

Finally the interminable meal came to an end and the ladies withdrew.

Benedict sipped his port and let the conversation wash over him. John was talking low and urgent to the old man and Sylvester sounded irritated as hell. No doubt the rumours about John's financial affairs were true then. Benedict had always thought him a fool so it was no surprise. He might be a terrific sportsman but he didn't have the sense he was born with when it came to business affairs. Benedict had tried to warn him about some spectacularly bad investments he'd made but had been told in no uncertain terms to mind his own business, so he had.

Harold and his friend, Mr Spalding, also had their heads together and Benedict frowned inwardly. He rather thought his cousin had got himself in over his head there. Although Harold was five years older than Benedict, he could never help but feel the man was his junior. There was something inherently childish about him, and not in a good way. He was spoilt and indolent and dressed like a blasted fop. At least mourning dress was forcing some taste upon him and they were being spared the outrageous colour combinations he often sported. Benedict remembered with a shudder of distaste a combination of canary yellow pantaloons and lilac striped waistcoat that had made him feel positively nauseated.

Mr Spalding, however, was undoubtedly a blood, and a very knowing one. Benedict knew the type. Probably from a decent family but with no money behind him. He'd no doubt latched onto Harold and shown him into the worst kind of gaming hells where they'd fleece him blind and Spalding would take a percentage. He had mentioned at dinner he'd hunted with the Quorn and dropped a couple of very distinguished names. But then he had a good if rather sly countenance. He dressed in the latest fashion but not to excess, his address was good and his manners exemplary. Though in present company anyone could shine, Benedict thought with a snort of amusement.

He looked up as Oliver came and sat beside him. "Why so glum, old man?" he demanded, clapping Benedict on the back. "If that cousin of yours don't give a man a reason to smile, I can't think of another."

"She's not my cousin," Benedict replied with a sigh of annoyance. "And I am engaged to be married."

"Good God, aren't we proper," Oliver said, tutting at him. "What did happen to you, Ben? We used to have such larks."

Benedict finished his port and set the glass down. "We're neither of us boys, Oliver. Sometimes one has to take responsibility."

To his surprise Oliver nodded. "Yes," he said, sounding rather serious. "I know that's true, but surely that doesn't mean you can't have a little fun now and then?"

Benedict got to his feet and looked down at him smiling. "Well only a little," he said, smirking as Oliver laughed and followed him to rejoin the ladies.

***

Phoebe repressed a sigh of utter boredom and cast her eyes at the door once again, praying that the men would return soon. So far she had navigated Lizzie's dull if well intentioned conversation, Theodora Pinchbeck's barely hidden insults, and Lady Jane Rutland's furious gaze. Though how it was her fault the woman's husband was a revolting Satyr, she couldn't at all see. Lady Rothay was an ally up to a point, but she couldn't afford to offend her soon-to-be daughter-in-law as she and her husband to be held the family's purse strings. In the end Phoebe had retreated to the far end of the room to sit with Cecily and the children, and could well understand why the oldest of Benedict's sisters preferred to stay with her younger siblings rather than join the adults.

"Are you sorry you came?" Cecily whispered to her in an undertone. "I shan't blame you if you are."

Phoebe grinned at her and shook her head. "Oh I'm not such a wet goose, Cecily, dear," she said. "It will take more than the Miss Pinchbecks of this world to dampen my spirits. Though," she added with a serious tone. "I could well understand how she could give you a fit of the dismals."

Cecily smothered a giggle of delight at having her brother's intended so described. "Oh dear," she said, looking contrite. "I know I shouldn't as she'll be my sister soon, but ... Oh, Phoebe, I try to like her I swear I do but she just takes the fun out of everything." She gave a heavy sigh and Phoebe frowned, surprised by just how bad things were. She'd believed she'd made a pretty sound judgement of Miss Pinchbeck's character but she wasn't blind to her own mistakes and would have been ready to be proved wrong. That she'd been correct and more than she'd realised was both a relief and a sorrow for she didn't like to see Cecily and the children looking so miserable.

"There'll be no bearing her once they're married," Honesty piped up, none too quietly either. Cecily hushed her and Honesty blushed and returned to the game of Spillikins she was playing with Patience and Jessamy.

"She's right though," Cecily whispered in an undertone. She gave a heavy sigh and looked dejected. "I was so looking forward to coming out next season but I know she'll find a way to spoil it."

Phoebe took her hand and squeezed it. "No she won't," she said, her tone determined. "I'll see to that."

If she'd been intent on removing Miss Pinchbeck for Benedict's sake - and she admitted for her own - she was now utterly committed for the sake of the family. If she had seen anything resembling love or affection pass between the two of them she would have hesitated and probably called a halt. But to her critical gaze there seemed to be nothing more than a polite understanding between them. She wondered what kind of life they would lead together and if Benedict had considered what their physical union might be like? Her father's voice came to mind as she considered the question, *"like bedding a dead fish I shouldn't wonder."* Her wicked Papa had always been candid in matters of sex and being raised by a rake had left her rather well prepared for dealing with them as she knew all of their tricks. A good thing for a pretty girl who was raised beside an army on the march, but she had kept her honour intact and received a flattering number of marriage proposals.

Dealing with a straight-laced, overbearing, morally rigid earl was outside of her experience, but she was a quick study. Once again she heard her father's merry laughter and knew he would egg her on as it was about time he was brought down a peg or two. Swallowing down a bubble of laughter herself she turned back to Cecily who was looking at her like her own personal saviour.

"Will you really, Phoebe?" she asked, her pretty green eyes wide. "I don't see how you can possibly stop her interfering though," she added with a dejected sigh.

"That's because you don't know me very well," Phoebe replied with a wink that made Cecily giggle again. "And I'll be sure to take you shopping and find the most spectacular gowns."

Cecily looked so enraptured by this idea that Phoebe thought she might actually cry with delight. This was abruptly called to a halt as Miss Pinchbeck bore down on them. She had clearly overheard this last remark.

"Ah yes, Miss Skeffington-Fox, I'm sure Cecily would adore to go shopping with you. You know all the most fashionable places no doubt. Though of course they may not be suitable for such a well brought up young lady as Miss Rothay. She has not seen the world in such a rough and ready manner as you."

Cecily gaped in horror at such an obvious attack but Phoebe was glad that Miss Pinchbeck had finally shown her true colours. It meant she could declare her intent.

She favoured Miss Pinchbeck with a little confused frown. “Oh, dear,” she said, blinking with an innocent expression. “Do you mean to say you find my dress unsuitable? I shall have to speak to Lady Rothay and ask her advice though it’s strange as it appears I go to all the same Modistes as she does. We were planning to take dear Cecily shopping together but if you think perhaps we are wrong to do so I shall speak with her about it immediately.” She made to get to her feet as Miss Pinchbeck blanched, her mouth tightening.

“Well,” she said, with a cool tone. “I’m sure if Lady Rothay approves I have nothing further to say about it.”

“No,” Phoebe said with a bright smile. “I don’t suppose you do.”

“Though her brother may have something to say on the matter,” she added with a malicious glitter in her eyes that showed she had every intention of making him interfere.

“Well let’s ask him,” Phoebe said, gaining Benedict’s attention with no difficulty as he came into the room with Sylvester leaning on his arm for support. With his uncle’s accord he strode towards them, frowning at the imperious manner she had waved her hand. “Now Benedict, I was just discussing the merits of a brother’s intervention in the matter of his younger sister’s dress for her coming out. Don’t you think you should be fully involved in choosing her wardrobe?”

“Good God, no,” he said, a look of utter revulsion on his face. “I don’t have the least interest or intention of interfering in that. My mother is more than capable of choosing anything she needs I assure you.”

“Yes,” Phoebe said, nodding as though this was sage advice indeed. “You see, Miss Pinchbeck, that’s exactly what I said.” Benedict looked from her to Miss Pinchbeck in surprise, realising there was some undertone he had been unaware of. “Only Miss Pinchbeck said neither Lady Rothay nor I was equipped to choose for such a well brought up young lady as Cecily.”

Miss Pinchbeck flushed a rather unbecoming shade of scarlet, her grey eyes glittering with fury. “You’ve twisted my words,” she cried in outrage.

“No she didn’t,” Cecily said with more bravery that Phoebe might have credited her with. “You said the Modistes that Phoebe visits are all well and good for a girl like her who’s seen the rough and tumble of the world but not for me. But mama goes to all the same places as Phoebe does!” To Phoebe’s delight the girl looked flushed and indignant and if he might have believed Phoebe of twisting the truth for her own ends, he didn’t doubt his sister.

Miss Pinchbeck flinched under the frowning gaze of her betrothed though he said nothing to her.

“I ... I think I shall go to bed,” she said, putting a hand to head. “I have a headache.”

“Yes,” Benedict said to her, with a rather cool tone. “I’m sure that accounts for it. I imagine you will feel better in the morning, Theodora.”

Miss Pinchbeck gave a taut nod and walked away from them.

“Now, now, little hell cat,” Sylvester said, his shrewd green eyes looking at her with delight. “At daggers drawn already, eh? I knew I was right about you.” He turned to Benedict and slapped his shoulder. “Girl’s got spirit, lad. I like to see it.” And with that ringing endorsement he left Benedict with Phoebe and Cecily. Cecily, no doubt sensing tension leapt to her feet to get her mama another cup of tea as her courage appeared to be all used up.

Phoebe looked up at Benedict and gave him a beatific smile to which he returned a cool, considering expression.

“Now then, Miss Skeffington-Fox,” said another male voice beside her.

Phoebe drew her attention away from the big glowering man staring down at her and to the rather handsome blond fellow who had arrived halfway through the meal. They had been introduced but the seating plan had not allowed for much conversation.

"Mr Bradshaw," she replied with a warm smile, noting with annoyance that both Harold and his friend Mr Spalding had followed him.

"Oh no, we don't stand on ceremony when Sylvester holds court do we, Ben?" he replied chuckling. "Call me Oliver, do."

"Yes, Cousin Phoebe," Harold replied with a smirk. "We are very informal here you see."

Phoebe dared a glance at Benedict and saw him raise one eyebrow just a fraction. Damn him. She wasn't, of course, Harold's cousin but she couldn't object to him using her given name in front of Benedict as she'd made such a fuss over him being *Cousin Benedict.*

"Skeffington-Fox," replied Mr Spalding, his voice quiet and his eyes roving over her, weighing her up in a manner she took exception to. "I once knew a man who spoke of a Captain Skeffington-Fox, fought a duel with him over some woman. The good Captain put a bullet in his shoulder, damn near killed him," he drawled, looking to see how this little nugget had gone down.

Phoebe blanched and glared at Mr Spalding in fury. The story about her father had been a dreadful scandal when she was quite a little girl. She drew a breath, fully prepared to rail at him for bringing such a subject up in polite conversation when she was saved by an unlikely ally.

"Shut your damned mouth, Spalding," Benedict said, his tone dripping ice. "I hardly think that is the kind of conversation for the drawing room, let alone disparaging a man who may or may not be this young woman's relation."

He held his arm out to Phoebe who took it with alacrity.

"Come, Miss Skeffington-Fox, you are looking a little flushed, but then it is rather stuffy in here."

"Yes, indeed, I could do with a little air," Phoebe agreed quite readily and allowed Benedict to escort her outside onto the terrace that overlooked the gardens.

Chapter 6

Heard melodies are sweet, but those unheard
Are sweeter; therefore, ye soft pipes, play on. - John Keats

The chill wind of earlier had died away and the night was mild if damp. Phoebe drew in a deep breath, finding she really had needed air and relishing the cool breeze that fluttered against her skin.

"Thank you," she said, smiling up at Benedict with gratitude. "You were very gallant."

Benedict's face darkened a little, his expression just visible in the deepening twilight. It was as though he hadn't realised or meant to be anything of the sort and was now regretting it.

"I don't like the man," he said, sounding gruff now. "He's far too knowing and ... insinuating. God knows what Harold was thinking of bringing him here."

Phoebe nodded. "Yes, he does seem rather a sly boots doesn't he?" Watching with amusement as Benedict frowned harder at the cant expression. "I imagine he fancies himself something of a rakehell," she added, blinking up at him with an innocent expression. "But he's really not got the touch has he? He's merely rude."

Benedict's jaw tightened perceptibly. "You should not speak so," he bit out. "Or you will give the impression of having had some experience with rakes. If you are in search of a husband, it won't help you."

Phoebe laughed and shook her head. "Oh but it is only you, Cousin Benedict, so I am in no danger and feel I can speak freely."

"Do you?" he bit out, sounding increasingly annoyed.

"Oh yes," she said, nodding with the utmost seriousness. "And after all you know very well my father has the most appalling reputation, but he's the dearest man. But then rakes often are, aren't they? I mean ... they wouldn't be half so successful if they were bad company."

"I must bow to your greater knowledge of the subject."

Phoebe gave an irrepressible burst of laughter. "Oh, how ungracious of you! Though I suppose I deserved it."

Benedict glowered at her. "You deserve a great deal more, Miss Skeffington-Fox but not being your father I am at a loss for how to proceed."

Leaning back against the wall, Phoebe tilted her head a little to observe him. "Oh dear, we're back to formality I see. Yes, I imagine you would take me in hand if you had the responsibility."

"I would," he agreed, his posture rigid. Phoebe thought she had never seen a man so utterly taut with annoyance, and she'd annoyed a fair few in her time.

"Yes, I think it's a good job you don't have that power," she muttered. "I imagine you would have spanked me."

Watching him as closely as she was, she didn't miss the tiny intake of breath or the way his eyes darkened at her words, though it was immediately followed by a look of disgust.

"This is not an ... *appropriate* conversation," he said, turning away from her. "And I demand you not to be so free with your tongue. You have indeed been encouraged towards the most outrageous freedoms in your speech and I must insist that you do not speak so in front of Cecily."

Phoebe glared at him, her own temper rising now. "I am not speaking to Cecily though, I am speaking to a grown man. Of course I should never speak so to a green young girl. But I am no such thing and I believed you to be a man of the world to whom I could speak without reserve. But I see I was mistaken, you are in fact ..."

She clamped her lips shut aware that her wretched temper had gotten the better of her, not for the first time.

"Oh don't stop there," Benedict said, his tone dark as he stepped closer, glowering down at her, using his massive bulk to intimidate. "What am I?"

It was the wrong thing to do as Phoebe wasn't easily intimidated and only found such masculine posturing a challenge. She raised her chin, staring at him with defiance. "You're a prig. You're so starched and unbending you must look down your nose at everyone. You wouldn't know how to have fun if your life depended on it and you've been determined to disapprove of me since before I even arrived! But you needn't worry, I promise that I'll give you plenty more reasons before either of us is very much older. Goodnight, my Lord Rothay."

Furious both with herself and him, she turned on her heel and left him standing alone on the terrace.

***

Benedict watched the infuriating young woman as she tossed her golden curls and stalked away from him and couldn't help but feel a grudging sense of admiration. When he'd stood over her, determined that she should be cowed by him, he'd expected that she would stutter and back down immediately. Though he felt guilt for using such tactics he had never known a woman who wouldn't give up any argument with him after little more than a look of displeasure on his face and a couple of cutting remarks. But then Phoebe Skeffington-Fox was unlike any woman he had ever known before, thank God! The thought of his sisters acting in such a way made his blood run cold. Yet he couldn't help but remember her rage with a smile as he pictured how she'd stood up to him and hadn't even looked the slightest bit discomforted. In truth she'd looked furious enough to wring his neck with those slender hands of hers. The little wretch.

But now her words came back to him with a frown and he felt his own anger bubble back to the surface. A prig! *Him?* Indeed he was no such thing. He'd never looked down at anyone in his life, it was monstrously unfair. And perhaps he had judged her on her father's reputation but he'd been spot on after all. Any woman who could look him in the eye and suggest he would like to spank her ...

He swallowed convulsively as an unwelcome and forceful surge of desire burst through him. It stole his breath and forced a decadent image of Miss Skeffington-Fox with her blonde hair in as much disarray as her skirts. Benedict hauled in a breath and banished the image from his mind. Damn the woman. With growing agitation he stalked back into the drawing room with the intention of downing a large drink and going early to bed - and putting Miss Skeffington-Fox firmly out of his mind for the rest of the summer.

***

His intentions to avoid Miss Skeffington-Fox did not get off to a good start. Summoned to the drawing room by his mother not long after breakfast he found Lady Rothay with his cousin Lizzie and Phoebe as well as the children and Miss Pinchbeck.

Miss Pinchbeck looked as though her manners were being tested to the utmost if the tight-lipped expression of disapproval was anything to go on. But if he'd believed Phoebe would evade his eyes after last night's row he was to be sorely disappointed. In fact she beamed at him as he strode in the room, completely ignoring the glower on his face or the fact he was trying as hard as he could to ignore her outside of a formally polite and chilly *good morning.* Her eyes were full of amusement and he couldn't help feeling that she was laughing at him because he was acting just like the prig she'd accused him of being. It didn't make him feel better.

"You wanted me, mother?" he demanded rather abruptly, wanting to be out of the blasted woman's presence as quickly as he could.

Lady Rothay frowned at him for a moment but nodded. "Yes, dear. Phoebe has heard all about Grizedale's armoury and was speaking of going to investigate it, but I said she simply must allow you to show her around. After all it is your area of expertise."

Benedict hesitated. As much as he wanted to get away from Phoebe it was true, the armoury and all the ancient weaponry it contained fascinated him. In fact he'd made quite a hobby of it in his youth and had spent a lot of his summer holidays cataloguing all of the items and researching them. The idea of sharing his knowledge with others, particularly someone who found it of interest was tempting. Besides, he could hardly refuse now as his mother well knew.

"Of course," he said, smiling at his mother and avoiding Phoebe's gleeful expression. "Theodora, will you be joining us?"

His fiancée grimaced with distaste. "No indeed. Ghastly things. I can't imagine how anyone can spend the morning looking at such blood thirsty objects, but please don't let me spoil your fun."

"Oh, we shan't," Phoebe said, with a bright smile as she took Benedict's arm and followed him out the room.

Benedict gritted his teeth and promised himself he would be meticulously polite. He'd have to be, seeing as Cecily the twins and young Jessamy were coming too.

The armoury was a vast oak panelled room with windows down one length and was dominated by *The Knight.*

"My what a splendid fellow," Phoebe said, looking astonished at the gleaming figure astride his ebony steed. The horse was in fact carved of wood and had been Benedict's idea when he was not much older than Jessamy. He had longed to see the knight and horse, both in full armour and so his uncle had commissioned the work. "And what a wonderful way to display him. I can almost see him galloping into battle."

"The armour is actually for jousting," Benedict said, but couldn't help but smile, pleased that she could see the figure in the same way he had hoped people would. "It dates from the fifteen seventies." He moved them on to a display cabinet where a large sword rested on a bed of scarlet silk. "This is the oldest piece we have," he said, quite unable to keep the pride from his voice. "It dates from nine hundred and fifty two AD. It's five foot five and three-quarter inches long and belonged to our ancestor. Guy of Denholm."

He looked around to find Phoebe staring at it with rapt fascination. "My word," she whispered. "What stories it could tell us."

Benedict nodded, finding it hard to look away from her lovely profile as she stared down into the glass covered case.

"Legend has it that the sword was given to Guy by King Eadwig to vanquish a monster."

He found himself smiling as she stared up at him wide eyed with surprise. "Not really?" she asked, though he could almost see the desire to be told about dragons and fanciful beasts burning in her eyes. The children had wandered away now, all of them having heard his stories before and they were quite alone beside the cabinet. It seemed a shame to disappoint her.

"Yes," he said, nodding quite seriously. "There is a cave not far from here, very deep and full of ancient paintings. The story says that a fierce three-headed monster lived in the cave and would only be placated by the sacrifice of a virgin every third Sunday."

Phoebe gaped at him and then burst out laughing. "Oh you wretch!" she exclaimed with delight. "You're bamming me."

Benedict's lips twitched just a little, unwilling to show her that he was really rather pleased by her reaction.

"Well," she said with a huff. "That serves me right for saying you had no sense of humour doesn't it." She looked up at him, a warm expression in her eyes that made him want to make her laugh again. "I owe you an apology I think," she said, her eyes suddenly growing serious. "I'm afraid my wretched tongue runs away with me sometimes and I say ... oh, the most outrageous things." She glanced up at him and he found she was looking a little dismayed. To his chagrin he discovered he didn't like to see such an expression on her face. "Well I'm afraid you know only too well. But I have a frightful temper you see and ... and well you were rather odious," she added, with a frown.

He gave a bark of laughter, torn between annoyance and delight. What would the dreadful creature say next? "I thought that apology was coming along rather too nicely," he said with a shake of his head. "And we'd gone almost a half hour in each other's company without you insulting me or goading my temper."

A touch of guilt slid into her eyes and she bit her lip for a moment. It was the most distracting sight and Benedict stood, rapt, watching the fine white teeth bite that full lower lip until she let it go again leaving her mouth reddened. "Is that what I do?" she asked, frowning.

He tore his eyes away from her lips. "You know damn well it is," he snorted, though not unkindly and drew her onto the next exhibit.

She was an interesting companion, he had to acknowledge that much as he showed her the Civil War collection and a series of crossbows, longbows and claymores. She seemed to share his fascination with history and the idea that these weapons had been carried by men like him, perhaps his own flesh and blood. Men who had fought and perhaps died for what they believed in with sword in hand. He brought her back to some of the smaller display cases and a piece he particularly admired.

It was a dagger though a very ornate one. "This is one of my favourite pieces," he admitted. "It's a Landsknecht dagger," he said, watching with interest as she bent to get a closer view.

"Ah, Ben, now don't tell me you're boring poor Phoebe with all this dreary history."

Benedict stiffened and found himself annoyed by the arrival of his cousin Oliver. Though in the country Oliver was still dressed in dashing style and made Benedict feel a tad dowdy in the less formal attire he preferred when at Grizedale.

"I wouldn't dream of it," Benedict replied, feeling suddenly constrained and wondering if he had misjudged Phoebe's enthusiasm. He was rewarded by a hand on his arm.

"Oh please go on, Ben," she asked, her blue eyes lively with interest. "It's been the most fascinating morning, truly."

Somehow he found he could overlook her too familiar use of his name and didn't remark upon it in the light of such genuine interest. He cleared his throat.

"Er ... very well then. Well like I said, this is a Landsknecht dagger. The Landsknecht were rather dashing mercenaries first formed in the fifteenth century. If you note the dagger is embellished with what is known as *puff and slash* wire work. They were noted for being rather flamboyant you see and the wire work was supposed to echo the fantastically puffed and slashed costumes of the era."

"How incredible," Phoebe said, clearly delighted. "To think of these dashing young men having weapons made to go with their outfits!"

Benedict chuckled and nodded. "It appears men can be every bit as frivolous as women. Not that we needed any proof," he added in an undertone, raising one eyebrow at Oliver.

"Well I say," Oliver said with a huff. "There's no need to pick on me because I said your weapon collection was dull!"

Their attention was taken as Harold and Wilfred Spalding entered the hall and sauntered over to where they were gathered. Benedict noted Phoebe's face lost any sense of amusement and found himself moving to stand beside her.

They came and stared down at the antique dagger and Wilfred seemed particularly struck by it. "A beautiful thing," he murmured. "Beautiful *and* deadly, an intriguing combination." He glanced up at Phoebe with a covetous look in his eyes and Benedict saw her step farther away from him. There was something about the man that made him want to throw him out the house. As it wasn't his right to do so, however, he contented himself with glaring at him.

"Must be worth a fortune, eh, Wilfred?" Harold said, staring at it with the same kind of expression that Wilfred had looked upon Phoebe with. "All that gold."

"Don't start spending your inheritance just yet, old boy," Oliver murmured in an undertone. "Rather vulgar."

Harold flushed and looked at Oliver with indignation blazing in his eyes. "Well it will be mine, at all accounts. The old boy's bound to fall off the perch soon, and then *I'll* be head of the family," he sneered.

There was an unpleasant silence that stretched across the expanse of the armoury. Benedict clenched his fists and denied himself the singular pleasure of boxing the fool's ears with great difficulty. How dare he speak in such a way about Sylvester.

"Well then, Cousin Phoebe," Harold said, stepping away from the cabinet. "How do you like the armoury? More history in this old place than you can shake a stick at you know."

"I've enjoyed looking at it very much," Phoebe said though her smile had become rather brittle. "Benedict is very knowledgeable," she added.

Harold made a disparaging noise. "Yes, anyone would think he was the heir the fuss he makes about the place."

"Watch your mouth," Benedict growled, and stepped closer to Harold who blanched. "I've a mind to take you outside and teach you some manners for that remark."

He was suddenly aware of a hand gripping his arm and looked down to find Phoebe's slim fingers wrapped around his wrist.

"Come on, Harry," Wilfred said with a smirk. "We'd best go before the brute lays you out cold."

If Harold objected to this slight to his masculinity, it wasn't apparent as he did nothing but stalk away in high dudgeon in his friend's wake.

"Such a little charmer, our Harold," Oliver said, shaking his head.

"I beg your pardon," Benedict said to Phoebe, as remorse for his behaviour flooded him. "I should not have let him goad me, particularly not in front of you. I do apologise."

"What on earth for?" Phoebe said looking revolted. "I'm only sorry you didn't plant him a facer. I would have."

Benedict gaped at her for a moment and then laughed- there was really no other answer.

Chapter 7

I am – yet what I am, none cares or knows:
My friends forsake me like a memory lost:
I am the self-consumer of my woes – John Clare

Phoebe spent the afternoon investigating the old house by herself and whiled away a pleasant hour strolling about the grand corridors and inventing ghost stories. The portraits of many generations of the family looked down at her, some more benignly than others. Many of them shared that sharp green-eyed gaze that seemed particular to the Rutland bloodline, though there were few who had the force of that emerald green nor the strength of character that seemed so obvious in both Sylvester and Benedict.

She smiled to herself as she looked out of the window at the lovely park lands designed by Capability Brown. It had been a revelation to see Benedict talking with such passion about the history behind the items in the armoury. She'd know there was passion within him, had sensed it from their first meeting. But he'd buried it far away and tried to forget it, along with the ability to laugh and smile and be a little foolish.

Her step-papa had told her that Benedict's father was a great character, full of fun and merry as a grig. In fact it sounded much like they were two of a kind though the late Earl had been more susceptible to dice than petticoats. She imagined that this was at the heart of it. That the burden of responsibility had fallen too heavily on Benedict's young shoulders and he'd carried it as best he could. But he'd lost a part of himself in the process, becoming too staid, too conservative and far too judgemental.

It wasn't too late though, she was sure of it. There had been a few moments this morning when he'd looked at him with something less than disapproval and the sensation had been ... most enjoyable.

She determined to make him do it again as soon as possible. Providing he wasn't so provoking as to make her lose her temper again.

She found now that she had come upon a pretty little saloon all decorated in yellow and gold and was drawn in to investigate. It wasn't a large room but bright and very cheerful and Phoebe thought she might return to sit and read a book here later. It had a very pleasant ambiance. Hearing a slight cough she turned in surprise to see that the Butler, Keane was in the room already.

"I didn't want to startle you, miss," he said, apologetically but she laughed and shook her head.

"Not at all. Am I disturbing you though?"

"Oh no, miss," he replied, smiling at her. "Only, his grace had lost a book he was reading and as he often sits in here in the mornings, it seemed the place to begin my search."

"Have you found it?"

Keane held out a small leather-bound volume in his gloved hand. "I have, thank you, miss."

Phoebe nodded and then realised that here might be a source of information about Benedict. "Have you been with the family a long time?"

"Oh yes, indeed," the man replied, looking really very proud at the fact. He was quite a handsome man she noted. Tall and well made, his nose had been broken at some point but this seemed to give him a more interesting aspect. He appeared precise in every aspect and she suspected he was the model of an efficient butler. "Man and boy in fact," he added. "My father was a footman here you see and I was born on the estate. I've been butler to the duke for ... well now, it must be over twenty-five years. I only wish it could be much more."

He looked suddenly ill at ease as though he didn't ought to have spoken so.

"If you don't mind my noting it, miss, there is something about you that loosens the tongue." There was laughter in his eyes and Phoebe returned it with a slight huff.

"Well, whatever it is I need more of it, I shall never get any gossip this way, shall I?" She chuckled. She grew serious though, turning to a question that seemed pertinent. "You ... wouldn't continue here once Sylvester passes?"

Keane's face darkened perceptibly and she wondered at the depth of feeling she saw there. "It wouldn't feel right, miss."

She nodded her understanding, aware that she had touched a nerve, and tried to lighten the mood by asking about the subject she was truly interested in.

"I imagine Benedict must have spent a lot of time here as a boy. He and Sylvester seem very close."

"Oh yes, miss," Keane replied, and she saw approval in his face now. "Lord Rothay, now there's a fine gentleman and the spit of his uncle at the same age you know." He paused, his mind's eye drifted off to a place in the past. "Though he's a much more ... sober character now," he added, with what Phoebe thought was admirable tact. "Not like when he was a boy though."

"Oh?" Phoebe demanded, grabbing onto this piece of information with delight. "Was he very naughty?"

"Naughty?" Keane repeated, his eyes wide. "He was a blessed nuisance." He snapped his mouth shut and gave her a reproachful look. "Now, miss, you've done it again and I never gossip."

"Oh," she huffed, bitterly disappointed. "Just as it was getting interesting."

"Well it isn't my place to speak of his lordship so," he said, a gentle rebuff that was softened further by the twinkle in his eyes. "Though if I was wishful of hearing tales of the young man, I should go and speak with his mother, myself," he added with a grin. "She's always happy to talk about her son and his devilry. Quite misses it too if you ask me. Reminds her of his late father. Ah, now there was a character ..."

He coughed and gave her an old-fashioned look.

"Now if you'll excuse me, Miss, I'd best get this back to his Grace before you get me into trouble."

"You're no fun, Keane," she said, pouting, and then laughed as he winked at her on his way out.

She lingered in the pretty room for a while before giving into the lure of the gardens. The weather had grown rather warmer today and soft cottony clouds scudded in a deep blue sky. The breeze plucked at her muslin skirts with a playful touch and she took a breath, pleased to be out in the open.

"Taking a stroll, Cuz?" sounded a voice from behind her.

She turned and smiled to see Oliver's friendly face as he walked towards her. He looked as dashing as ever, very much a man of fashion, and she couldn't help but admire the picture he made standing in front of the great house.

"I am, though you know perfectly well that I am not your cousin," she replied with a reproving smile.

"I know it. Ben was only too quick to make the point."

"I bet he was," she replied laughing. "I'm afraid I teased him rather about it."

He stopped beside her, his blue eyes frank and admiring. "About time someone teased Ben in my opinion," he replied, looking at her with warmth. "Though I'm more than happy to stand in if you feel the need to tease someone else."

Phoebe raised an eyebrow at him, finding she wasn't entirely displeased by his flirtatious manner. Of course he was the kind of man to flirt with any attractive female who fell into his path, but she didn't mind that. He seemed fun and light-hearted and those were characteristics she could value. "Oh, but you are aware of your short comings I think, Cousin Oliver," she said, lowering her voice to sound rather more sombre. "So there's no fun in it, you see." She spread her hands in a resigned manner and Oliver laughed at her in delight.

"Lordy, now I see how you can put Ben in such a stew! My short comings! Well of all the nerve," he replied, his eyes dancing with merriment.

"Well now you did invite me to tease you," she said, wagging her finger at him.

"I did too," he agreed, strolling along the gravelled path with her. He paused and held out his arm. "I hear the rose garden is just coming into bloom," he said, with a twinkle in his eyes. "Shall we go and inspect it?"

Phoebe glanced up at him, well aware that he meant to continue their flirtation. As handsome as he was, she wasn't interested in him. Benedict had caught her attention and in her eyes Oliver didn't compare. But he was well-mannered, pleasant company and she knew well enough how to keep a flirt at bay, and she didn't want to offend him. "Why not," she replied, smiling at him, and allowed him to lead her into the gardens.

By the time they returned to the house, arm in arm and with Phoebe laughing heartily over something Oliver had said, they found they were being observed.

"Oh dear, now we're for it," whispered Oliver to her as Miss Pinchbeck's disapproving countenance watched them approach the house. "What does Benedict see in her?" he demanded

"I'm sure I couldn't comment," Phoebe replied, her lips twitching with amusement.

"Dashed sure you could," Oliver said with a rumble of laughter.

"Oh stop," she scolded him, looking away from his amused expression. "You'll start me laughing and she'll know we're talking about her."

To Phoebe's relief Miss Pinchbeck did not wait their arrival but went into the house. Her escape was short lived, however, as the lady wasted no time in drawing her aside after lunch.

"I feel duty bound to give you a word of warning," she said, having asked Phoebe to step into the drawing room with her for a moment.

"Really?" Phoebe replied, with a little laugh. "How very thrilling."

Miss Pinchbeck walked to the window, one hand clasped in the other in front of her, her face cool and devoid of emotion. She was dressed once again in a lovely but severely cut gown in a sour, pale green. Phoebe thought it didn't suit her colouring but made her look rather sallow.

"It is no laughing matter, Miss Skeffington-Fox, and I would not interfere if it wasn't for the rather ... unfortunate circumstances of your upbringing."

"Oh, I see," Phoebe replied, as fury blazed to light. How dare she! "My unfortunate upbringing, of course," she repeated with a smile and a slight inclination of her head.

"As you are, as Lord Rothay said himself, in need of a guiding hand."

"Did he indeed," she replied, a dangerous note in her voice.

Well of all the odious ... Phoebe gritted her teeth and decided his lordship would be receiving a few choice words about discussing her with his fiancée.

"So I feel it my duty to give you some advice, that walking the gardens alone with a man is not at all proper. Particularly not one with the reputation of Lord Bradshaw." She turned back and looked at Phoebe, her expression one of supercilious contempt. "I don't doubt things were different when you spent your days following the army camp, my dear. But here in England people will make judgements about your behaviour, and I'm afraid no gentleman would ever wish to marry you if you insist on making a spectacle of yourself."

At this point Miss Pinchbeck illustrated her words by waving her hand in a general direction at Phoebe's person.

Phoebe clamped her jaw shut. It would be only too easy to engage in a satisfying row that would vent her spleen, but Miss Pinchbeck deserved so much more. So instead she simply got to her feet and gave her a benign smile. "Thank you so much for your advice, Miss Pinchbeck. I assure you I will put it to excellent use."

She noted the surprise in the woman's eyes and smiled inwardly. She had obviously been expecting Phoebe to make a scene and would then have run to tell Benedict how she had thrown all of her well-meaning advice back in her face. Well Phoebe had met Miss Pinchbeck's kind before and had her measure. It didn't dilute her fury, however, and she strode away in a white rage and headed for the library. Perhaps an hour or two lost in a good book would calm her nerves and stop her from returning to wring *dear* Theodora's blasted neck.

Entering the library she closed the door behind her and took a deep breath to steady herself before heading for the shelves. It was a vast and well-stocked room with shelves that ran floor to ceiling and a number of comfortable chairs in which to curl up in peace. Except fate had decided peace was something Phoebe wasn't going to experience today.

"Well, well, Cousin Phoebe, what a delight."

Phoebe turned with a startled shriek as the voice had sounded in her ear. To her dismay she found herself face to face with Harold. But far worse than that was the fact that he had clearly been drinking and had a gleam in his eyes that she did not in the least approve of.

"Harold," she said, trying to move away from him and finding herself cornered. "You gave me a fright."

"Shall I give you another?" he asked, a deeply unpleasant smile flickering over his mouth. He might have been considered a handsome man by some but Phoebe found his features too feminine and there was a slightly febrile look in his eyes that made her wonder about his sanity. "Though I suspect a dashing sort like you isn't easily frightened."

He lunged for her as Phoebe screamed and tried to push him away. He may have been built on far more slender lines than Benedict but he was strong none the less. Phoebe found herself trapped in his embrace, her arms crushed in front of her against his chest.

"Let me go, Harold. Let me go and I won't tell Sylvester ..." The threat fell on deaf ears and her words were cut off by Harold forcing his mouth against hers.

Phoebe struggled and tried to pull her hands free to no avail. Stamping on his foot with the heel of her shoe made him curse for a moment but she was just forced harder against the bookshelves. With revulsion she felt his excitement as his hips pressed against her and she tried to get her knee into a position where it could do the most damage.

As it happened, this wasn't necessary as Harold was almost lifted from his feet by a hand grasping the back of his coat, and he flew unceremoniously to the ground.

"Get up, you damned snake," Benedict roared as Harold looked up at him in horror.

"B-but, Ben," Harold stammered, holding his hands out in front of him. "It was just a misunderstanding, that's all ..."

"Oh!" Phoebe stalked forward and delivered him a kick in the side. "You appalling, odious, little toad," she cried. "You attacked me!"

"What is going on here?"

Everyone looked up as Wilfred Spalding strode into the room and Phoebe noted that Harold looked even more afraid.

"Harold, you've been drinking," Mr Spalding said in disgust as Harold scrambled to his feet. He looked around at Phoebe and Benedict. "I don't know what he did but I'm sure he'll apologise, when he's sober. Come along, Harold."

Harold appeared to be only too keen to comply with this order but found himself suddenly hampered by Benedict's large hand closing around his throat and ramming him against the book shelves.

"Not so fast, you little weasel. I've had just about enough of you and your insinuating ways, and your appalling manners, so I give you fair warning. You look at this or any other young lady with malice again, and you'll have me to answer to. Do I make myself clear?"

"P-perfectly," Harold replied, though his words were constricted by the iron grip of the huge man holding his throat.

Benedict let him go, his expression one of utter disgust, and with the deepest relief Phoebe watched the two men leave the room.

Chapter 8

The serpent of the field, by art
And spells, is won from harming;
But that which coils around the heart,
Oh! who hath power of charming? - Lord Byron

Benedict took a breath to try to dispel the murderous rage that was still thrumming in his blood. It wasn't helped when he turned back to look at Phoebe. She held her arms about herself and he could see she was trembling.

"S-sorry," she said, giving him a tremulous smile. "I ..." Whatever she'd been about to say seemed to escape her as she gave a faint sob and covered her mouth with her hand.

"Phoebe!" It seemed the most natural thing in the world to cross the room and take her in his arms. "It's alright now," he crooned, smoothing his hand over her hair and finding it just as soft and silky as he had imagined it might be. She wrapped her arms around him, clinging tightly and he took another deep breath, though the reasoning behind it seemed to have changed. His breath caught entirely as she looked up at him, her blue eyes wide and glittering.

"I'm sorry," she said, trying to smile again. "I'm not usually such ... such a wet g-goose," she stammered.

"You had a dreadful fright," he replied, gazing down at her and fighting the longing to kiss her lovely mouth. He pulled his gaze away in horror as he reminded himself of the ordeal she had just suffered. "Come and sit down," he said, his voice sounding a little too loud suddenly. She seemed just as unwilling to release her hold on him as he was to force her to move away but he made himself remember his position.

He sat her down and went to fetch her a small glass of brandy which he pressed into her hand.

"Drink it slowly," he advised. "It's very strong."

To his chagrin, she drank it down in two large swallows and handed him the glass back with a trembling hand. "May I have another please," she said, her voice quiet as she looked up at him with a rather sheepish expression.

He nodded and took the glass from her. Once he'd given her another, smaller measure he sat down in the chair opposite her.

"Are you alright?"

She had curled herself into the big armchair she was sat in, her pretty muslin skirts tucked around her ankles. Her hair had tumbled loose during her struggle with Harold and fell about her shoulders. She looked young, and very vulnerable. He felt a strange sensation ripple through his chest which was swiftly followed by feelings of such protectiveness that he wanted to go and rip Harold limb from limb.

"I'm fine," she said, nodding and looking anything but. "I'll just finish this and I'll be more the thing, I'm sure," she added.

The urge to cross the small space between them and take her in his arms again was so fierce he could almost taste it. Damn it. He had no right to such emotions. He was engaged to Theodora. With a burst of annoyance he thought that his fiancée would never have found herself in such a position. She would never make him feel this ... this ... out of control. He was angry all at once, and not just at Harold.

"You need to stay away from Harold," he said, his voice rather harsher than he intended. "He's weak and volatile and you ..." he waved his hand at her feeling unable to describe just what it was he was looking at. "You present a great ... temptation to him."

Phoebe stared back at him and the temperature in the room seemed to plummet in the light of her expression.

"I beg your pardon," she said, her voice very quiet. "Are you ... are you saying this is *my* fault?"

Benedict opened his mouth and closed it again. "I ... No ... I didn't ..."

"Because," she said, getting to her feet. "That is very much what it sounded like."

She glared down at him and he could see she was trembling still, but he didn't think it was fear this time.

"So should I perhaps keep to my room and not come out while he's allowed to wander at will?" she demanded, her voice growing rather strident. "Oh perhaps I can come out as long as I make no effort to look attractive in case he happens to catch a glimpse of me?"

"Phoebe," he began, wondering how this had gone so horribly wrong. "I didn't mean it like that but ... but you're very beautiful. You'd be a temptation to any man and ... and you shouldn't allow yourself to be in a situation where you're alone with one."

Her face grew white with rage. "You've been speaking to Miss Pinchbeck. That ... that ..."

Benedict stood and caught hold of her hands. "She said you'd been walking with Oliver alone, yes. She only meant to help you, to guide you, you see. I think perhaps your father has not told you about the dangers of such behaviour. Of course there is no harm in it most of the time, though your reputation might suffer, but Harold is another matter. He's not right, Phoebe, he's dangerous."

She pulled her hands from his grasp, looking at him in disgust. "I have been avoiding him," she shouted. "I came in here to get a book and I didn't know he was already in the room. He crept up on me, Benedict. I was just looking for a book and he attacked me!" she cried and his heart felt bruised at the look in her eyes. "But I'm alone with you aren't I. Am I doing wrong now? Should I not be here? Will you hurt me now because I've given you the opportunity?"

"No!" he shouted, appalled that she could think it. "No, of course not. I could never ... I would never hurt you. No sane, decent man would." He reached out and put his hand to her face, looking down at her with his heart in his throat. "Forgive me. I ... I've made a mess of this I know. I didn't mean ..." He swallowed, wanting so badly to kiss her that it was an ache beneath his skin. "I don't seem to be able to say the right thing when I'm with you."

"No," she said, the bitterness in her tone unmistakable. "You don't."

He dropped his hand and she stepped away from him. "If you'll excuse me, I would like to go to my room."

He nodded, unsure if he felt relief or desperation that he hadn't acted upon his feelings.

"I'll escort you."

She gave a snort of disgust but didn't forbid him to follow her so he walked along the corridor at her side and up the stairs. As they passed Harold's room their gazes met as a furious argument could be heard on the other side. The words were muffled but it sounded like Mr Spalding was very angry indeed. Not being the kind to listen at keyholes Benedict didn't pause until he had seen Phoebe safely to her door.

"I'm sorry if I upset you," he said, avoiding her gaze. "It was far from my intention."

Phoebe said nothing in reply but walked into her room and closed the door behind her.

Benedict stood staring at it for a moment not knowing what it was he was feeling. It was as though he'd been turned inside out and put together in a haphazard fashion. Things that had seemed so black and white just days ago no longer had the same clarity. His emotions were blurring the lines and that he could not allow.

He stalked away from her door feeling that somehow Phoebe was to blame. Everything had been fine before she'd turned up. His life was comfortable and well-ordered, his younger siblings all financially secure. It had taken him a decade to do it but they were safe and he was a wealthy man. His personal life was satisfactory. Except suddenly it wasn't. The overwhelming desire he'd just experienced for Phoebe had unsettled him more than he cared to admit.

Desire had never played a part in his courtship of Theodora. In fact he wondered what she would do if he displayed such behaviour to her. Regrettably his thoughts then wandered to what Phoebe might have done if he'd acted on those feelings and kissed her. Would she have been shocked? Would she perhaps have encouraged him? The thought made him catch his breath.

Footsteps ahead of him brought him back to his senses as he noticed Mr Spalding hurrying down the stairs ahead of him.

"Wait there," he demanded, quickening his step.

Spalding looked up at him from the floor below, his expression impatient.

"Lord Rothay?" he replied. "What can I do for you?"

"I'd like a word please," Benedict said, the tone of his voice brooking no argument as he gestured for Mr Spalding to go into the drawing room.

Spalding did not look like he welcomed the interview but neither did he prevaricate.

"How can I help you, my Lord," he asked as Benedict closed the door behind them.

Relieved to find the room empty, Benedict went and poured himself a large brandy, offering one to Mr Spalding who shook his head. Taking a large sip of his drink, he observed the man with a critical air. He was dressed in the height of fashion but with none of the excesses or frills or nauseating patterns which made Harold look so foolish. But there was a sly look in his eyes, a considering look as if bets were being taken that Benedict disliked intensely.

"I see no point in beating about the bush, Spalding, so I'll come to the point," he said, watching the man to see his reaction. "Harold is in debt, serious debt. It's been my opinion that he's being blackmailed and has been for some months now."

"Is that right?" Spalding said, his facial expressions making all the exclamations of surprise that simply didn't reach his eyes.

"It is," Benedict replied, his tone dark. "I have bailed him out on two separate occasions now but enough is enough. So I am telling you as I have told him. There will not be a third time. So if that is your intention I suggest you go and find another fat pigeon to pluck. My uncle may be elderly but he is in good health and fine spirits. He may easily, and I sincerely hope he does, live another ten years, perhaps more. So any thoughts that Harold may have of coming into his inheritance in the near future are far and wide of the mark. Have I made myself plain?"

"Abundantly," Spalding said, his eyes full of rage. "Though I am at a loss as to why you are speaking to me about such matters."

"Are you?" Benedict said, knowing his expression was as grim as his words sounded. "Well I don't think I am far from the mark. So I tell you now, you'll not get another penny, do you hear?"

Both men started as the doors that led out onto the terrace opened and Oliver walked in. He looked surprised to see them.

"Oh, I do beg your pardon," he said with a smooth smile. "I didn't mean to interrupt."

"You're not," Benedict replied, wondering how long he'd been standing on the terrace and what he'd heard.

He walked out and closed the door on the two men and headed into the gardens. Deciding the only thing that could undo the knots of tension in his shoulders was a long walk he set out at a brisk pace and wondered just how far he would need to go before Phoebe's lovely face faded from his mind.

***

The next morning Phoebe sat in the sunshine, the scent of roses on the warm air of the summer's morning soothing to her jangled nerves. She had been so desperately angry with Benedict yesterday and even knowing that he hadn't really meant the words the way they had sounded did not make her feel better.

Harold's actions had been appalling and frightening and she would take great care not to be in his company alone again. Frankly she never, ever, wanted to see him again. But Benedict had frustrated her. She had seen the anger in his eyes, he'd looked very much like he wanted to kill Harold and was more than prepared to do it. The passionate nature she had suspected dwelt within him had been only too apparent. But then he had retreated into his usual demeanour and become the priggish Earl all over again and she'd wanted to slap his smug face.

"Hello there," called a cheerful voice, and Phoebe looked up to see Oliver strolling towards her. "I wondered if I'd find you outside and here you are." He stood and put his hands up, as though framing her for a painting. "And what a lovely picture you make, like the goddess of summer, surrounded by roses."

Phoebe sighed inwardly, she wasn't sure she was in the mood for Oliver's particular brand of charm but she wasn't enjoying her own company much either.

"That didn't impress you one bit did it?" Oliver said with a frown of consternation.

She laughed despite herself. "Oh, dear. I am sorry. You see, I'm not in the mood to be flirted with so I'm going to be very bad company I'm afraid."

"Oh, well that's put a spoke in my wheel hasn't it." He stood grinning at her and then moved closer so she made room for him to sit down. "Now then, my unhappy rose, what has happened to make you mope about the gardens? You don't strike me as a girl who has fits of the sullens so someone has upset you."

Phoebe cast him a grateful look and then sat back against the bench with a sigh of frustration. “Yes they have,” she admitted. “More than one person truth be told.”

“Who is he?” he demanded with a theatrical tone. “Tell me now and I shall vanquish the dastardly villain.”

Laughing at his ridiculous posturing Phoebe shook her head. “Oh don’t be so absurd,” she said in great amusement. “But thank you, I feel much better now.”

“Good,” he said, nodding and giving her a sideways glance. “But you still haven’t told me who upset you.”

She gave a sigh and shook her head. “I shouldn’t be sitting here alone with you, you know,” she said, instead of expanding on the other events of the day before. “I am putting myself and my reputation in the gravest danger.” She looked back at him with a solemn expression which he returned with one of comical shock.

“No!” he exclaimed. “With me?”

Phoebe nodded, her eyebrows raised. “Oh, yes. Miss Pinchbeck gave me a thundering scold for it, I assure you. Apparently no decent man would have me.”

Oliver snorted and gave a loud bark of laughter. “Shouldn’t think you’d give a decent fellow the time of day, myself,” he chuckled.

Phoebe gave him a rueful glance and sighed. “No,” she said, sounding a touch despairing. “You may well be right.”

The two of them laughed and then stopped abruptly as Benedict’s glowering figure cast a shadow over them. Standing against the sun as he was, it was impossible to see the expression on his face but Phoebe was quite certain he was scowling.

“Right, well, things to do,” Oliver said brightly.

Phoebe glared at him. “Coward,” she hissed as he leapt to his feet, leaving her with a mischievous wink.

"Checking up on me, my Lord?" Phoebe demanded as Benedict moved around to sit beside her. She discovered his expression to be every bit as annoyed as she had imagined it to be.

"Of course not," he said, snapping at her. "I merely wanted to assure myself that you were quite well and had suffered no ill effects from yesterday's fright." His green eyes were full of irritation which somehow gave her great satisfaction. "But as I see you are in spirits as ever, I shall leave you alone."

He said this, but still made no move to leave her.

"Please don't let me detain you, my Lord," she said, her voice cool. "I wouldn't want Miss Pinchbeck to be concerned about you spending time alone with such a scandalous woman."

"Phoebe, stop it!" he said, and his voice had an altogether different tone now.

She turned and looked at him but he'd turned his head away from her.

"Stop what?" she asked, intrigued as to what was bothering him.

"Stop, *my Lord*ing me for starters," he replied in frustration. "You forced your way into possession of my given name despite offending every expression of good manners so don't give it up now!"

"Well, I see you have sought me out only to give me further insult," she said, getting to her feet. "In which case I shall bid you a good morning." She turned away from him and began to walk towards the edge of a woodland path.

"Phoebe!" he called. "Phoebe, don't walk away from me."

But Phoebe was enjoying herself far too much to give into him now. There had been something in his voice that had caught her attention and she didn't intend to let it go.

Hurrying on further into the woodland she knew he was following her but looked back for a second to confirm the fact and promptly tripped. Righting herself by clutching the tree trunk she had stumbled into, she looked down to see what had caught her foot. A man's arm was laid across the path, draped carelessly, the rest of his body lying in the shadow of a lovely beech tree. The dagger sticking from his chest was still altogether too visible, however.

Phoebe stumbled again in shock and screamed.

Benedict was beside her a bare moment later. "Oh my God," he exclaimed and then pulled Phoebe against him, her face cradled against his shoulder. "Don't look, love."

He held her tightly for a moment until she caught her breath and looked up at him.

"I-it's Harold isn't it?" she stammered and watched as he nodded.

"Yes," he said, his voice dull. "It's Harold."

Chapter 9

The level sunshine glimmers with green light.
Oh! 'tis a quiet spirit-healing nook!
Which all, methinks, would love; but chiefly he,
The humble man, who, in his youthful years,
Knew just so much of folly, as had made
His early manhood more securely wise! - Coleridge

Benedict sat with Sylvester until the old man fell asleep. The doctor had brought him a draught to calm him earlier, but Sylvester had refused to take it until things had been arranged to his satisfaction. As a close friend of the Chief Magistrate and having already voiced suspicions about the verity of his eldest son's death, it shouldn't be too long before London's Bow Street Runners came to investigate the scene at his request.

Sylvester had dispatched the letter as soon as the appalling events had sunk in and it was clear that Harold had been murdered. With luck they might get someone here by late tomorrow afternoon

Harold's body had been taken to the family's chapel until the Magistrate's people had come to investigate. That the dagger lodged in his chest had been the very one he'd admired in the armoury did not escape his attention and made chills run down his spine. Was that just coincidence? If a weapon needed to be found quickly, the armoury was the obvious place to go and the Landsknecht dagger an obvious choice as most of the other exhibits were too large and unwieldy to be carried discreetly.

He may have had no love for his cousin but the idea that someone had killed him in such a violent fashion made Benedict ill at ease. That the murderer was likely still under this roof, perhaps even a member of the family ... nausea roiled in his stomach.

He left Sylvester's room and walked down the corridor until he found himself outside Phoebe's room. The poor young woman must rue the day she came to them. First Harold attacked her and the next she trips over his dead body. That she'd lived most of her life under very uncertain and dangerous circumstances did not make him feel any happier. Giving a soft knock at the door he waited until her maid opened it.

"I'm sorry to disturb you, Mrs Huckington, I wanted to enquire if Miss Skeffington-Fox was well after her ordeal?"

The maid snorted and opened the door a little wider. "And how do you imagine she is, my Lord? What a lot of nasty goings on. I'm sure I don't mean to speak ill of the dead but I don't know if he might have deserved it, treating my innocent lamb in such a fashion."

Hearing Phoebe described as an innocent lamb was something that Benedict took with remarkable composure, mainly because his protective instincts seemed to be running in overdrive. Phoebe may act in a manner that led people to draw the wrong conclusions of her, and her tongue might be shockingly loose. However he felt that her maid had the right of it despite his own allegations to her face. She was an innocent in every way that counted and he would make sure she came through this unharmed.

"If there is anything I can do ..." he began and then trailed off, aware that he really had no business here. He ought to be with Miss Pinchbeck, making sure she was not too distressed. The idea of Theodora showing any kind of emotion was hard to imagine, however.

"I'll let you know, my Lord, don't you worry and you can rely on old Sarah to guard her like a lion." She gave a sniff and shook her head, muttering to herself. "No one hurts my girl and gets away with it" She looked up as if remembering he was there, adding, "I'll tell her you've been asking after her too."

Benedict nodded and walked away. He was told by Miss Pinchbeck's maid that she had retired to bed with a headache and suppressing uncharitable feelings of relief, made his way downstairs. At least Theodora wasn't the kind to give into fits of the vapours and hysteria. Though to be fair, neither had Phoebe. She had been distraught at first of course, but she had rallied quickly and seen immediately what must be done as clearly as he had.

Knowing full well he was far from ready for sleep, he settled himself in the library with a generous measure of brandy and tried to cudgel his brain into figuring out who could be responsible for such a reprehensible crime.

***

Phoebe sighed and stared at the ceiling. Whenever she closed her eyes she was greeted with visions of Harold's horrified, glassy-eyed stare. She'd never sleep at this rate.

Deciding that the past hour's tossing and turning was only making matters worse she got up and decided a large brandy might do the trick. She could of course have woken Sarah, but she hated to disturb her maid for such a trifling matter. It seemed a shabby thing to do when she was quite capable of fetching it herself. She slipped into a rather lovely dressing gown which was composed of many layers of diaphanous material dyed in varying shades of green and tucked her feet into matching satin slippers.

Thus attired she took hold of a candle and stepped silently out into the corridor. She had almost gained the bottom step of the staircase when it suddenly dawned on her that there was every possibility that the murderer was still at large ... and possibly even still in the house. She paused as that appalling notion sunk in and then scolded herself for being so fanciful. Taking a breath she scurried across the darkened hall and opened the door of the library as quietly as she was able.

To her relief a lamp was still lit and she was just walking across to the waiting decanter when she stopped in her tracks. Benedict sat asleep in one of the wing back chairs. His long limbs were cast with negligent grace before him, his head tipped back showing a strong jawline and neck where his cravat had been tugged undone. The white silk hung about his neck and seeing him look anything less than perfectly attired roused a strangely protective feeling in her heart. She stepped a little closer, taking care not to wake him and looked down at the sweep of thick, dark lashes against his skin. His mouth was open just a little and he looked somehow vulnerable despite his great size. For a moment Phoebe just stared, too transfixed to move as she wondered what that sensual mouth might feel like against her own.

She felt her skin flush at the idea of it. Strangely despite her father's shocking reputation she was as her maid had suggested, an innocent. The thing with having a rake for a step-father, she reflected, was that he knew all the tricks that could be employed on a naïve young woman and had been quick to teach his new daughter how to evade and protect herself from them. So although she was by no means innocent of what could pass between a man and a woman, and was probably aware to a shocking degree of what those pleasures could involve, in actual experience she had none whatsoever. That fact had never troubled her over much before, but here, now, alone with Benedict, the desire to know what she was missing became hard to ignore.

The decanter was on the side table next to him. Kneeling down beside his chair she took a glass and poured herself a measure. The chink of glass against glass as she replaced the stopper roused the sleeping giant beside her as she had hoped it might.

She sipped at her drink, watching as his eyes flickered open, the deep green glinting in the candle light as he focused on her. For just a moment he smiled and gave a sigh of content and then his eyes opened fully and he sat up.

"Phoebe!" he exclaimed, looking down at her in horror. "What the devil are you doing?"

"I couldn't sleep," she said with a shrug. "Every time I closed my eyes I saw ..." She gave an involuntary shudder. "Well you know what. But in any case I decided a glass of brandy might be just the thing. I didn't know you were sleeping in here did I?" she added with a sniff before looking at him with a frown. "What are you doing here?"

"The same as you I imagine," he replied with a tart look as he got to his feet.

"Well it worked then," she said, laughing at him. "You were fast asleep."

He sighed, looking rather annoyed with her. "As you should be, so take your drink and get to bed. You really didn't ought to be wandering about alone at night in the circumstances, especially not ..."

Phoebe had stood whilst he was giving this little lecture and the outfit she was wearing seemed to come to his attention with some force.

"Especially not dressed like that," he finished, his voice sounding a little rough.

"Oh," she said, holding out the fine material with one hand and looking up at him. "Don't you like it?"

She watched as he opened and closed his mouth. "It's ... very lovely," he said, apparently with some difficulty. He stepped away from her with some speed and moved over to stand by the empty fireplace. "You shouldn't be here," he added, sounding cross again, though he didn't look at her. "Imagine how it would look if anyone was to walk in on us."

Phoebe frowned at him and stepped closer. "How would it look?" she asked, giving him her most innocent expression and then smiling in a rather devilish fashion. "Oh," she breathed, taking another step closer. "You mean that people will believe this is a romantic tryst and that you've set out to seduce me?"

She watched with growing amusement as the colour flared in his cheeks. "Anyone who knows us will more likely believe it was the other way around," he snapped, his eyes flashing with irritation.

Phoebe teetered on the edge of losing her temper for a moment before deciding on a different course of punishment for that particular remark. Instead of taking him to task for such an ungentlemanly comment, she slid her hand over his chest. She heard his sharp intake of breath with a strange feeling of power as his eyes darkened.

"Oh," she said quietly, looking up at him, standing so close their bodies almost touched. "Do you think I could seduce you then? I had thought you disliked me too much for that."

His breathing was heavy now, the massive chest beneath her hand rising and falling with some speed. "I ... I never said I didn't like you."

Phoebe laughed at that, smoothing her hand up and down in a rhythmic motion, feeling the sensuous silk of his waistcoat, warmed by his body, gliding beneath her fingertips. "You didn't need to say it in so many words," she whispered, watching the intriguing battle that seemed to be going on behind his eyes with fascination. "So do you mean to say that you do like me after all?"

There was a heavy pause. "No," he gritted out. "You're ... you're ..."

Licking her lips in a provocative manner Phoebe stepped closer still so that she was pressed against him. "I'm what?" she demanded, sounding just as breathless as he did.

"Oh God," he murmured, and reached out a hand to touch her face and then froze as they heard footsteps crossing the hall outside.

Before Phoebe had time to react he hauled her across the room and pushed her into a narrow space between two of the floor to ceiling bookcases. Pulling at one of the ornate wooden carvings on the panelling, Phoebe watched in astonishment as a narrow door swung open at his command. It revealed a very small gap, just big enough for one man, perhaps. But as voices could be heard alongside the turning of a handle, the two of them slid into it and closed the door behind them.

The only way for them to possibly fit meant that their bodies were crammed into the tiny space and pressed tightly together. Phoebe could hear her own heart beating in her ears and she didn't think it was just the nearness of their discovery that had done it. She was certain Benedict had been going to kiss her. Her contemplation of the subject was halted, however, as the library door closed and the men's voices became audible.

"You have access to it, man, don't tell me you don't," said a familiar and obviously angry voice. "You have ten days and then my patience is at an end and you'll face the consequences."

"That's John!" she whispered to Benedict who pressed his finger to her lips. Unable to do anything else she stood quietly, resting her head against his chest.

Another man replied, his voice fainter, less distinct as he was obviously further from them. "I won't do it," the voice said. "It isn't right."

There was an outraged bark of laughter. "You dare to tell me what's right? You've betrayed this family's trust badly enough already. There's no point in pretending there's any honour in you now." There was a pause and Phoebe thought that John must have walked closer to the man he was threatening. "Do as I say or I'll tell Sylvester everything, and then where will you be?"

The rest of the conversation was too muffled to hear and a moment later the door closed and the footsteps receded again.

"John's blackmailing someone," Phoebe said in alarm. "And he's next in line for the title now Harold is gone."

"I know that!" Benedict replied, sounding impatient. "I just can't believe that John ..." She felt him shake his head in the darkness. "Well let us hope the runners can get to the bottom of it. I just pray to God none of the family is responsible."

"Did you recognise the other voice?" she asked, suddenly very aware that the men had gone and neither one of them had made any attempt to leave their cramped hiding place.

"No. It was too indistinct."

She fell silent for a moment and simply enjoyed the feeling of Benedict's warmth and strength. His arms were wrapped around her and she could hear his heart thundering in his chest as her head rested against him. She felt she could stay here like this for the rest of the night and be perfectly content.

"What are you going to say to the runners when they come, Ben?" she asked, feeling anxious for him all of a sudden.

"What do you mean?"

She hesitated, wondering how to put it. "Well ... it's just that the knife that was used ... You were telling us all about it and you had a row with Harold because of it, and ... and then you ... after he attacked me ... You rather looked like you wanted to kill him, you see. And I don't doubt that dreadful Mr Spalding will be quick to point it out. And you are also one step closer to the title now ... It might not look good."

He was silent for a while and she realised this angle had perhaps not occurred to him before. "Do you think I killed Harold?" he demanded.

She looked up at him though she could see nothing in the darkness. Instead she reached up her hand and laid it against his cheek. "No. Oh, no," she said. "I know you couldn't do such a thing."

He turned his head a little and she felt the warmth of his breath as it gusted over her hand.

"I could," he said, his voice rough. "I damn well wanted to when I saw him ..."

She caught her breath at the anger in his voice. "But you didn't."

"No," he replied. "I didn't." He reached up and his hand covered hers against his face. Hardly daring to breathe she waited as he turned his face towards her palm. She was so terribly aware of his mouth, that his lips waited just a breath away from her skin ... But he dropped her hand, his voice terse. "We'd better get out of here before anyone else turns up."

The moment was gone and she could not help but mourn its passing. Unwilling to leave her alone, Benedict escorted her back to her room where Phoebe realised she still hadn't managed to get her glass of brandy. With a sigh of frustration she lay on her bed and spent the rest of the night wide awake and remembering the moments pressed close to him in the dark.

Chapter 10

I met a lady in the meads
Full beautiful, a faery's child;
Her hair was long, her foot was light,
And her eyes were wild. - Keats

The next morning Phoebe looked out of her bedroom window to see Benedict's large frame striding down towards the picturesque lake that dominated much of the outlook in front of the Court. Deciding that last night had been a missed opportunity and having spent much of her sleepless night considering who the murderer was, she realised this was a good time to find him alone.

She didn't doubt that he would try to avoid her from now on after the unspoken passion of last night, and that she couldn't allow. So deciding to forgo breakfast she dressed for a morning walk. She arranged for her wolf hounds to be brought to her from the stables where they were staying for the moment and was hurrying outside when Sylvester emerged from the library. The old man looked grey and worn and her heart went out to him.

"Oh, Sylvester," she said, crossing the hall and taking his hand. "I'm so terribly sorry."

Sylvester shrugged but his green eyes were filled with sorrow. "Thank you, my dear," he said, his voice low. "Truth is I never liked the boy. Far too spoilt he was but ... but I never thought to see ..."

He shook his head and sighed. "Thought I might go and sit in the rose garden for a bit. Always cheers me up when they're in bloom. Reminds me of the late duchess you see. She planted them all ... seems like yesterday," he added with a wistful edge to his voice.

They paused as one of the stable lads appeared from the back of the house with Goliath and Delilah, and Phoebe was forced to make a fuss of them for a moment as the big animals danced around her with unrestrained joy. Once they were settled, she turned back to Sylvester.

"Shall I come and sit with you in the garden?" she offered, not wanting to abandon him.

"No, no," he said, his voice gruff and a little of his more teasing manner back in place. "You go after Benedict," he added with a wink.

Phoebe flushed and shook her head. "Oh but ... I was only ..."

Sylvester snorted with amusement as the footman opened the front door and was silent until it closed again behind them.

"Don't try to pull the wool over *my* eyes, young lady," he rumbled with a wicked glint flashing in the green. "I know exactly what you *were only ...*" He laughed then and patted her hand. "But don't go thinking I don't approve because I do," he whispered, though his voice was surprisingly fierce. "That Pinchbeck creature ..." He gave a visible shudder and shook his head. "She don't like me you know. Tried a time or two to come between me and Ben she has." His eyes took on a furious look that reminded her forcibly of his nephew.

"Thank God he's too loyal for that kind of behaviour. She can't wait for me to turn up my toes though. But I shan't a while yet, to spite her if nothing else. She'll make him miserable as sin, only the foolish boy can't see it. I've tried to tell him," he added, stamping his walking stick against the pathway in frustration. "She'll suck every ounce of happiness from his life and turn his children into joyless prigs too, you mark my words. But you can't tell Benedict anything; he has to come to it by himself." He stopped then and turned to Phoebe, raising her hand to his lips and giving it a gentle kiss.

"But you, my dear, with your spirit and vivacity, you are exactly what that foolish fellow needs to stop him turning into a dull and boring old man too consumed with propriety to remember to live, if only you could make him see it."

Phoebe smiled at him, feeling something of a lump in her throat at such praise. "I promise to do everything I can," she said, feeling suddenly rather emotional.

"You love him," Sylvester said, looking at her with approval and nodding, though Phoebe didn't feel quite up to answering that yet. "No you don't need to tell me yay or nay. I can see it in your eyes. It's new perhaps, but it's there and God willing he doesn't do anything to kill it before it has the chance to grow." They had reached the rose garden now and Sylvester chose a sunny bench with a lovely view over the best of the blooms. "Run along with you now, my dear," he said with a smile. "I'll just sit here for a bit on my own if you don't mind."

Phoebe bent down and gave the old man a fond kiss on his bristly cheek and then set off in pursuit of her quarry, happy in the knowledge that she at least had the duke's blessing to do so.

***

Benedict threw another stone, watching it bounce across the surface of the great lake. He had done this more times than he could count as a boy and he experienced a dreadful longing to return to the innocence of those days. He and Oliver had spent many happy days building camps and exploring, fishing for their own supper and sleeping under the stars. It was only looking back at it now. However, that he realised how gilded and unspoiled his childhood had been. Sylvester had played a great part in achieving that too.

The poor old man had looked so worn and fragile last night that it had hurt Benedict's heart to see it. This affair must be sorted out as quickly and quietly as possible. The scandal that could cling to their names after this would be dreadful if it couldn't be kept quiet.

And he must do nothing to add to that scandal. Like being found in a compromising situation with Phoebe. He swallowed as he remembered waking and finding her beside him last night. For a moment he'd believed he was dreaming, seeing her swathed in that lovely nightgown. She'd looked like a wood nymph all dressed in green and with her golden hair tumbling about her shoulders. Desire, so fierce he could taste it, rushed through his blood and he put his head in his hands with a groan of misery. Damn her. Why did she have to come and ... and turn his life upside down. It just wasn't fair.

He'd tried so hard to bury that side of himself, the reckless, careless creature that had gloried in the pleasures of life. His father had initiated him into his world when he was a very young man and Benedict, full of idol worship for his fun loving, charismatic father had leapt in feet first. Gambling, carousing and women, everything had been at his fingertips and Benedict had been quick to glory in every and any aspect of it he could find. Until his father had died and the thoughtlessness of that behaviour was brought home to him in stark clarity.

He had sworn then that all of that was behind him. He had cut himself off from that decadent world and remodelled himself into the solid and dependable kind of man that his family would always be able to rely on. Never would they have the shame of being dunned by their creditors, of the gossips tittering about the fact they were within days of the bank foreclosing on them. Never again would he let any of his family down with such feckless behaviour.

Never would he fall for some beautiful, bird witted female like his mother either. He adored her it was true and she was the most loving and wonderful mother any child could wish for. But she had as much sense of economy as a child with a sovereign and was just as adept at bringing scandal down on their heads as his father had ever been.

That was why Theodora had appealed so strongly. The model of repressed English femininity, she had never stirred passionate thoughts in him, and would never countenance anything that could cause the merest lift of an eyebrow from society. She had seemed like the perfect wife and he had been quick to propose. There was no love there, no romance, but at the time that had seemed a blessing. Now though ...

"Hello there."

A jolt shot through his heart at the sound of Phoebe's voice and he couldn't for the life of him decide if the feeling was ecstatic or furious. To add to his turmoil, she was clearly alone, with only the blasted dogs for company.

"I thought we agreed it was both inappropriate and dangerous for you to be out walking alone."

Phoebe's blonde brows drew together and she shook her head. "No, Ben dear, we didn't. *You* said it was inappropriate and dangerous but I didn't take any notice you see."

He gave a snort of despair and shook his head. "You do surprise me."

Phoebe grinned at him and sat beside him on the bench, far too close for his nerves which all flared to life at her proximity. She wore a charming walking dress of pale lilac muslin with a darker, lilac silk spencer. Her chip straw bonnet had a wide brim and was trimmed with the same lilac silk as the spencer and he found himself staring into the bluest of blue eyes and wondering how he would ever look away.

"You shouldn't be here," he said, his voice rough as he reluctantly forced himself to glare at the gardens instead.

"Why ever not?" she demanded, sounding cross. He huffed at her in annoyance and her voice was full of mischief when she next spoke. "Oh, I see," she said her voice soft as she slipped her hand through his arm. "Everyone will think it's another tryst."

He turned to glare at her and disengaged her arm from his. "It cannot be *another* tryst as there has never been one to begin with," he said with such hauteur that he just sounded like a pompous fool even to his own ears.

Phoebe pursed her lips for a moment before asking, “Hasn’t there?”

He caught his breath at the implication and remembered those moments pressed tightly together in the darkness of the priest’s hole. “No,” he replied, though his voice sounded a lot less steady than he was comfortable with.

“Well,” she said sighing. “There nearly was.”

Benedict shot to his feet. The temptation to take her into his arms and show her what a tryst with him would really be like was almost too much to bear. There would certainly be no argument about whether it had or hadn’t been ...

“Was there something you wanted, Miss Skeffington-Fox?” he demanded.

She looked up at him and sighed, clearly just as frustrated by his behaviour as he was himself. But it wouldn’t do. He was engaged to be married and there was no escaping that fact.

“Well several things really,” she said with a huff. “But if you insist on being so dull, then I wanted to speak to you about last night. Don’t you think that conversation was rather incriminating for Lord Rutland?”

Benedict frowned and knew her thoughts were only echoing his own. “It does look bad,” he admitted.

“What else do you know about him?” Phoebe asked, her blue eyes alight with determination.

Benedict paced for a moment, unsure of whether or not to speak to Phoebe about his suspicions. But he needed to speak to someone and, her reckless behaviour notwithstanding, he felt she was trustworthy.

"Neither Sylvester nor I believed Tony's death, that's his older brother, was an accident. Which means that it would appear, on the surface at least, that someone is after the title. I believe John is in debt," he said, glancing up at her. "I knew things were bad for him but ... I'm beginning to think they could be more than bad. Sylvester won't lend him any more money because he was against the investments that John made in the first place. He warned him ... we both warned him, but he's so damned pig-headed and arrogant."

"A family trait it appears," Phoebe murmured.

Benedict paused to give her a dark look before carrying on. "It is possible that John could have killed Harold. You heard him when Harold threatened his dogs; there was no love lost there."

"But how would that help him now?" Phoebe queried, her brow wrinkled in the most adorable fashion as she frowned at him. "I mean he still wouldn't inherit until Sylvester ... Oh!" she exclaimed, putting her hand to her mouth. "You don't think ..."

Benedict shook his head. "I can't believe he'd hurt Sylvester. I don't like John it's true and the two of them are always at logger heads but ... there is loyalty there, even if there isn't affection. Besides, it *could* help him now," he added. "The Denholm fortune is vast and if he's to be the next duke, it would give him breathing space. Everyone knows Sylvester is getting old, and anyone who doesn't know him might believe he'll fall off his perch at any time now. It would certainly make it worth any creditors hanging on."

"So you do think it was John then?" she pressed.

Benedict shrugged. "I don't know. That devil Spalding had some hold over Harold. I know he was blackmailing him but then why kill the golden goose ... unless ..."

He felt suddenly ill and looked down a moment later as Phoebe's small hand slipped into his. "What is it, Ben? You've gone positively white."

"I've bailed Harold out twice now," he said, hearing the guilt in his own voice. "But I took Spalding aside and told him there wouldn't be a third time. If there was no one else that Harold could turn to ..."

"Oh, Ben," she chided, though her voice was gentle. "You can't be held responsible for everyone's shortcomings you know. You paid his debts twice over and there was no obligation on your part. Why didn't his father help him?"

"His father refused, said he was a frivolous good for nothing and wouldn't give him a penny. He would inherit from his father's death of course, but the man's affairs seem to be in such a tangle. And he was too afraid of Sylvester to ask him," he added, curling his fingers around Phoebe's hand and wishing he had the strength to let it go.

"Well then," Phoebe said, looking up at him and giving his hand a squeeze. "You're not his father, Benedict. You know a blackmailer wouldn't just give up and walk away once he had his claws in him. He'd bleed him until he was dry. It would have to have stopped, eventually."

"Well it's stopped now alright," Benedict replied with a grim expression.

"Yes," Phoebe said, sounding a little less sure of herself now. "And I can't say why or who did it, Ben. But there is one thing I do know, that it was none of your doing. You have no reason to reproach yourself for Harold's death. He was a nasty, selfish little toad and as much as I pity the way he ended, he made his own bed. You didn't put him in it."

She sounded really rather fierce and he found himself staring down at her again, feeling the warmth of her hand in his. He wasn't used to having someone champion his cause. He had always had to standalone and protect everyone else from debt and scandal. It was a rare and rather wonderful feeling to hear someone defending him, even if it was only from himself.

"You're so sure of yourself, aren't you?" he murmured, touching a thick blond curl of her hair with his free hand.

"No, Ben," she whispered. "I'm not. Truly."

He felt his heart pick up, all too aware that the look in her eyes and the breathless quality of her voice was pure invitation. She wanted him to kiss her, she wanted him badly. His throat was suddenly dry and he swallowed.

"How did we get to Ben suddenly?" he demanded, reminding himself severely that his fiancée was back at the house.

He felt her sigh and he dropped his hand. "I thought perhaps you might not mind me calling you that way," she said, her voice dull as she turned away from him.

"Not even Theodora calls me Ben," he added with some force. She was taking things too far, too fast.

"Well that hardly surprises me," she retorted with equal annoyance.

"You shouldn't be here," he said, shaking his head and trying to hold on to his anger. She needed to leave now, she needed to stay away from him. Her behaviour was outrageous. "You shouldn't seek me out, alone. It's ... it's ..."

"It's what?" she demanded.

Benedict gritted his teeth and pushed at the desperate desire that wanted nothing more than to tumble her to the ground and kiss that furious look from her face. "I'm engaged to Miss Pinchbeck, Phoebe, and there is no changing that fact."

"You could change it," she said, her eyes flashing with challenge. "If you wanted to badly enough."

"Then I suppose I don't want to badly enough!" he flung back at her, though his skin was aching so badly to touch her he knew he had never spoken a greater lie aloud.

She started as though she'd been slapped and he was immediately contrite. He closed his eyes and took a breath. "Forgive me," he said, his voice taut and full of things that must remain unsaid. "I made a promise, Phoebe. That means something, to me at least."

She was quiet for a long time but when she spoke again her words surprised him.

"If it was John who killed Harold, why was he blackmailing the man in the library?"

He looked at her, feeling somehow hurt that she had said nothing about his words. Perhaps he had only wanted to be persuaded that something between them was possible? God, how he wished it was possible.

"I ... don't know," he replied at last, not wanting to think about Harold or John or any of the bloody mess they were plunging into. The investigative officer should be here in response to Sylvester's letter soon, but in the light of Phoebe's words about his own possible motivation that thought was less than comforting.

"Is John a talkative drunk?" she asked next, forcing him to raise his eyebrows at her. She shrugged at him in response. "I just wondered if he might let something slip given the right inducement."

Benedict frowned and nodded. "He's not what you'd call discreet that's for sure."

Phoebe pursed her lips as though considering this and got to her feet. "Very well, I shan't bother you any further. I wouldn't want to compromise you after all," she added with a tight smile.

Benedict winced as she gave a shrill whistle and the two big wolf hounds bounded back towards her from wherever they'd been hunting. With a heavy sigh he watched her lovely figure retreat back along the path to the house and wondered what the bloody hell he was supposed to do now.

Chapter 11

Tho' veiled in spires of myrtle-wreath,
Love is a sword that cuts its sheath,
And thro' the clefts, itself has made,
We spy the flashes of the Blade!
But thro' the clefts, itself has made,
We likewise see Love's flashing blade,
By rust consumed or snapt in twain:
And only Hilt and Stump remain. - Coleridge

Phoebe dressed early for dinner and headed down stairs. It had not escaped her notice that John enjoyed a drink by himself before the ordeal of the family meal. She felt entirely in sympathy with him about that much at least. The idea of spending time with Miss Pinchbeck was not a soothing one and her last meeting with Benedict hadn't been as hopeful as she may have wished.

She felt sure he was regretting his betrothal to the wretched woman but he was far too honourable to back out on his promise. Besides, knowing the Pinchbeck woman she'd probably sue him for breach of promise. In which case the only thing to do would be to make her cry off. That was going to be far more difficult. Benedict was a catch, especially for the Pinchbecks of the world. She was perilously close to being left on the shelf. She was attractive, Phoebe had to admit that much, but it was in such a cold and aloof manner. There was nothing soft or giving about her, and she strongly doubted there ever would be. Her heart squeezed in her chest at Benedict throwing his life away on a woman like that. Just thinking about what kind of mother she would be to his children made unwelcome tears spring to her eyes.

Giving herself a sound scolding she realised this way of thinking was getting her nowhere and would give her a fit of the dismals if she didn't stop immediately. So taking a deep breath she gathered her nerves and searched out Lord Rutland.

She found him in the library as she had thought she might, with a large drink in hand. It didn't look like his first.

"Oh," she said, affecting surprise. "Hello, my Lord. I was looking for Lizzie."

John snorted and shook his head, his eyes roving over Phoebe in a manner that made her skin prickle with disgust. "That silly creature! She won't be down until the bell's sounded I assure you." He walked over to the decanter and lifted another glass. "Come and have a drink with me. Haven't had the chance to speak with you yet."

Phoebe made out as though she was hesitant, dithering in the doorway.

"Oh, come on," he laughed, his eyes glittering a little too brightly. "I won't bite." He began to pour the drink and then winked at her. "Unless I'm invited to," he added with a leer.

With real misgiving, Phoebe closed the door behind her and prayed Benedict was as punctual as he usually was. She noted that he had poured her a large brandy, which was highly inappropriate for a young, unmarried lady.

She took it from his hand, shuddering slightly as he deliberately delayed releasing the glass, their fingers touching.

"There now, just what the doctor ordered."

Phoebe forced a smile. "After the past few days, yes," she admitted. "Poor Harold." She glanced up at him and saw his eyes narrow.

"Poor nothing," he said with real animosity. "The man was a fool and a fop. He's no doubt got debts to his eyeballs and someone decided he'd had enough."

"But they'd never get their money once he was dead," Phoebe pointed out, watching him closely.

"Then maybe it was more personal, God knows there must be a fair few people in the world wanted him dead, spiteful little rattlepate that he was. He was forever gossiping and spreading scandal."

"I heard the runner had arrived?" she asked, and saw his face darken, a frown of what might be concern furrowing his ruddy face.

"Yes, damn him. A Mister Formby," he said with a sneer. "Don't know what Sylvester was thinking of, involving someone outside of the family. Poking about in our affairs. Asked me all manner of impertinent questions. Told him I wouldn't stand for it." He looked belligerent now and had drawn himself up to his full and considerable height, his face flushing further with indignation. "Should sort these things out ourselves. Now there'll be some God awful scandal when the whole thing could have been dealt with quietly."

"But his grandson was murdered," she replied, really rather shocked. But then if John had murdered Harold he would have hoped the whole thing would be hushed up nice and quiet. "And," she pressed, feeling her heart thud a little harder. "Sylvester thought his eldest son's death was no accident too, so you see ..."

John frowned at that. "Gammon," he replied, shaking his head. "Tony was a neck or nothing chap and so I told Sylvester. Always told him he'd kill himself driving like he did, and so he has."

"It ... doesn't look good though," she said, her voice sounding far less careless and rather more terrified than she might have hoped. "For you."

John made a disgusted noise. "What piffle, and I told *Mr* Formby the same," he said, pouring himself out another drink. "Tony died by accident and whilst I wouldn't have lost any sleep over Harold's death it was none of my doing. Besides, according to their estimation of the time he died I wasn't even on the estate. Went to visit an old friend in Rye and stayed overnight. Fellow will vouch for me, no question. I didn't get back here until after all the hullabaloo began." He gave her a smug nod, his eyes narrowing spitefully. "Ben though, he took himself off for a long walk after a fight with Harold, according to Mr Spalding. Ready to kill him there and then by all accounts." He downed his drink and moved closer to Phoebe who tried to back up.

"Seems like you've set the cat among the pigeons there, my pretty. Didn't like Harold paying you court did he, eh?"

Phoebe looked at him in disgust. "Harold did not *pay me court,* as you so charmingly put it. He attacked me!"

"Oh, come, come," he said, his voice low and he moved closer still. "If you lead a fellow on you have to accept the consequences."

"I did no such thing!" she exclaimed, and ducked under his arm, making for the door. Sadly for her, big and unwieldy the man may have been, he wasn't slow. His huge hand grasped her arm and pulled her back to him, manhandling her into a rough embrace.

"What, like seeking me out alone, hmm? I know your type," he murmured, his brandy-soaked breath hot against her face. "You like to pretend innocence but really you want it rough, don't you? Yes, I know."

Phoebe's scream was muffled as he pressed his fleshy mouth against hers but this time she lost no time in connecting her knee to Lord Rutland's most sensitive flesh with as much force as possible.

"What the devil!"

John's howl of agony was almost drowned out by Benedict's curse as Phoebe stumbled away from John and fell against him with an unsteady yelp.

"What is going on here?"

To her dismay Phoebe saw she had quite an audience. A white-faced Lizzie, John's wife Lady Rutland and a supercilious-looking Miss Pinchbeck all looked on in horror.

"She tried to seduce me, Jane," John blustered, staring at his wife who promptly turned on her heel and left the room.

"How dare you!" Phoebe yelled and crossed the room to slap his face.

"Well, my dear," Miss Pinchbeck said with such a deal of smugness in her voice that Phoebe wanted to give her the same treatment. "I did warn you about your behaviour I believe."

"Miss Pinchbeck!" Lizzie exclaimed as Benedict made a furious noise and glared at his fiancée.

"Yes, you could tell she invited his overtures by the way he was howling in pain!" Benedict retorted with furious indignation.

Phoebe almost sagged with relief. She didn't give a damn what anyone else thought as long as Ben believed her.

"And it isn't the first time either," Lizzie said in disgust, looking at John with such loathing that Phoebe was quite startled. "I've lost count of the number of maids we've lost to his wandering hands. Oh poor Phoebe," she said, with real compassion before she turned on John with fury. "You nasty, despicable man! You just want to ruin everything for everyone. I do *so* hate you!" And with that parting shot she turned and ran from the room.

John looked a little taken aback himself but he had an unlikely ally.

"But she's here alone with him," Miss Pinchbeck pointed out with obvious satisfaction. "What else would the man have thought other than that she was throwing herself in his path? No doubt the title of Duke of Denholm cast its lures her way and she thought to take advantage of that."

"Theodora!"

To Phoebe's intense satisfaction Ben was staring at his betrothed as though he'd never really seen her before. Miss Pinchbeck had jolted with surprise at his outrage but now looked back at him with perfect composure.

"She's tried for you, my Lord," she said her voice even. "Why not move on when that pathetic attempt failed?"

Phoebe gasped and took an involuntary step backwards, away from the closeness of Benedict. She had known what kind of woman Miss Pinchbeck was but she was still surprised. Quite apart from the ignominy of being spoken about in such a way, she was shocked that the woman was so stupid. To behave in such a manner in front of Ben was sure to alienate him. A man who so despised scandal and scenes would not be thrilled to discover his future wife so ready to leap into the fray and add fuel to the fire.

Besides which Phoebe felt a fair measure of guilt. Rightly or wrongly she *had* tried to take Ben from her. Suddenly she felt very tired and rather foolish. This had been a ridiculous idea.

"If you'll excuse me," she said, trying for dignity but hearing her voice tremble in an alarming manner. "I think I'd prefer you to dissect my character out of my hearing."

Running for the door she snatched it open and headed for the stairs. She was almost at the top when she heard Ben's voice behind her.

"Phoebe!"

She didn't stop, too close to tears to withstand another of his lectures. She had no doubt he thought her a dreadful creature, no matter if he believed she hadn't been leading Lord Rutland on.

Phoebe had opened her bedroom door and was about to close it when Ben caught up with her. Pushing through he closed it behind him.

"Please go away," she begged, breathing hard to try to still the hot tears of mortification that were even now burning her eyes.

"Not until I'm sure you are unhurt," he replied, his voice so gentle that a sob rose to her throat.

She nodded and stepped away from him, turning her back. "I'm fine. It was foolish of me, I know it was. But I was only trying to help."

There was a heavy sigh and she started as his fingers closed over hers. "I know that, you idiotic creature. But it was more than foolish, it was damned dangerous." His voice was rough now and she looked up at him in surprise. "Promise me you'll not do anything like that ever again, Phoebe. If ... if he'd have hurt you we really might have had another murder on our hands."

She blinked faster but the tears fell just the same and she ran to him, wrapping her arms about his waist.

"Oh, Ben," she sobbed. "I'm so sorry, and it was all for nothing. I don't think he can have done it. He wasn't even here. He was with a friend in Rye who'll vouch for him."

There was a moment's pause and then Ben put his arms around her. "Unless he's paying someone to cover for him."

"Oh," she said looking up. "I hadn't thought of that."

Benedict shook his head. "Either way, I had a very disagreeable interview with Mr Formby this morning and I get the distinct feeling he believes I am involved in this up to my neck. So please ... *please* stay out of trouble, Phoebe. At least until this mess is cleared up."

Phoebe sniffed and nodded, remembering herself and their earlier argument. She let go of him and moved away, putting some distance between them. "I'm sorry, Benedict. I'm afraid I've given you a deal of trouble. I ... I'll try not to from now on."

She was more than surprised when Benedict closed that distance once more and took her hand again. "You've given me more trouble than I've ever known my whole life," he said, but his eyes were smiling at her. "So I don't see why you should stop now."

He was staring down at her and Phoebe felt her breath catch in her throat. "Benedict," she whispered, hardly daring to believe in the emotion she saw there. “If ... if you truly want to marry Miss Pinchbeck I ... I’ll leave you alone, I promise I will.”

Benedict swallowed and his face shuttered up. “It has little to do with want now, Phoebe,” he said, his voice soft as his thumb stroked her palm in small, caressing circles. “You must see ... it’s impossible. There is nothing I can do. No matter what I might wish for.”

“But she’s odious and cruel and ...” Phoebe bit her lip as tears sprung to her eyes, knowing she shouldn’t say such things.

“Please, love, please don’t cry,” he begged her, looking torn. “I’ve been a fool, I know I have. Sylvester tried to tell me ...” He took a breath and raised her hand to his lips, kissing the fingers with a tender brush of his lips. “Forgive me,” he whispered and turned to leave the room. She watched as he hesitated at the door. “If there was a way, Phoebe, I’d take it. I swear I would.”

And with that he left her alone.

Chapter 12

Oh! lift me as a wave, a leaf, a cloud!
I fall upon the thorns of life! I bleed! - Shelley

The funeral was a strange affair as far as Phoebe was concerned. Apart from the unsettling Mr Spalding there didn't appear to be anyone there with a good word to say about Harold. His mother looked distraught of course, but according to Lizzie she always looked that way. Lizzie was surprisingly vocal on the subject in fact. Since her little outburst in front of John she seemed to have decided that Phoebe should be taken into her confidence. She had never been close to her brother, Harold. At five years older than her he had bullied her without mercy as a child and as adults the best she had hoped for was to be ignored.

She turned to look at Phoebe, her hazel-green eyes full of sadness.

"Mother *is* devastated," she admitted, with a shrug. "Of course she is, but ... I never believe she really *feels* anything. I've never believed she really gave two hoots about us other than the fact that Harold was the heir and therefore of value. I think it's the loss of the title that bothers her the most." She looked immediately contrite and flushed. "I shouldn't say such wicked things."

"Don't be foolish," Phoebe said with a smile as she slipped her arm through Lizzie's. "We're friends now and you can say whatever you wish to me, I assure you I won't be the least bit shocked."

Lizzie gave her a rueful grin though there was something of a sparkle in her eyes now. "No," she said, giving Phoebe's hand a squeeze. "I don't believe you would be."

The rest of the day passed quietly and Phoebe had no opportunity to see Benedict. She told herself perhaps that was for the best, for now at least. She hadn't the slightest intention of giving up on him, however. And was more determined than ever to rid him of the wretched Pinchbeck woman no matter what happened between them.

The afternoon was pleasant though as her newfound friendship with Lizzie deepened. They actually had a fair amount of thoughts and ideas in common if not experiences. Lizzie was endlessly fascinated by Phoebe's life following the army in her step-father's wake and wanted nothing more than to hear anything that Phoebe would tell her. In return, and in the spirit of confiding female friends, Lizzie admitted that she had a Beau, but that the family would never approve of her marrying him for reasons she wouldn't divulge.

"So, you see," she said with a heartfelt sigh. "I know just how you feel." She smiled when Phoebe gave her a quizzical look. "About dear Ben," she said, patting Phoebe's hand as she blushed. Good Lord, did everyone know?

"I can see you're in love with him. And little wonder," she added. "He's about the only decent man in the family. Well apart from Grandpapa of course. He's a darling."

"Yes." Phoebe grinned, more than happy to agree with that statement. "Sylvester is a darling."

"And Ben?" she pressed as they took another turn about the rose garden.

"And Ben ..." Phoebe sighed. "Oh, Ben is engaged to that horrid creature and far too honourable to do anything to get rid of her."

Lizzie nodded. "Yes, I thought that was it." She stopped and stared over the lovely landscape that took in acres of fields and woodland and the vast lake, and in the far distance the pale, silvery line of the sea on the horizon. "Life is cruel sometimes isn't it?"

"Yes," Phoebe replied, looking out at the sea and sighing. "Yes it is."

***

Surprisingly everyone seemed in rather better spirits at dinnertime. Perhaps it was just that they'd had enough of doom and gloom and bickering. Mr Spalding had left after the funeral once the runner had done interviewing him. A fact which everyone was more than pleased about, but Phoebe didn't think that alone would account for the good humour around the table. That Lord John Rutland and his wife were also dining out was another perk. But she thought perhaps the lurking presence of the runner, Mr Formby, was making even this disparate family close ranks. He'd been poking into everyone's affairs by all accounts and setting up everyone's bristles. Phoebe was due to speak to him tomorrow.

Oliver was also in fine form tonight and was flirting outrageously with both her and Lizzie who was looking very well this evening. She seemed to Phoebe to be suddenly a little more sure of herself. Phoebe hoped she wasn't being conceited in believing she may have had a hand in that. Whatever it was that accounted for the good mood of all present she was thankful for it.

Of course Miss Pinchbeck was still there to cast her disapproving sneer over every humorous remark, apparently believing there was still no call for levity. It was something Phoebe heartily disagreed with. Having seen the war at far closer quarters than anyone else around the table she knew the value of humour. She had seen the soldiers laughing and joking outrageously after a particularly gruelling day and knew full well it wasn't that they didn't care about their fallen comrades. It was their way of coping and reminding themselves they still lived. Phoebe wondered if Miss Pinchbeck had ever felt truly alive.

Grief also clearly gave people an appetite as everyone ate a hearty meal. Sylvester was in fine form, so much so that he'd asked the children to sit with him, joking and teasing them. Jessamy was clearly full of pride at this and the affection between him and the old man was a joy to see. He was getting a little over-excited perhaps, to the point where even Lady Rothay, who was very relaxed about such things, reprimanded him, albeit gently, for making such a row.

The desserts came in, including stewed pears with allspice and delicate little shortbread biscuits and a jam roly poly which happened to be Sylvester's favourite.

The old man smacked his lips with deep appreciation as he scraped the last of the jammy remains from his bowl. To her amusement Jessamy was equally concerned with cleaning his bowl with great care and looked rather bereft as he noted the serving dish was bare of seconds. He glanced around and saw that Phoebe, who was in truth struggling, had barely touched her own. He gave her a beatific grin which made her laugh.

"I say, cuz, can I have that?" he demanded. Without even waiting for her answer, clearly believing her indulgent smile enough of a reply, he leapt up from his chair to circle the huge table.

"Jessamy!" Miss Pinchbeck said, her voice sharp and deep with disapproval. "Show some manners. What are you thinking? You do not get up in the middle of a meal, certainly not to seek out someone else's leftovers."

Phoebe sent Miss Pinchbeck a furious glance but before she could open her mouth, to her surprise Lizzie stepped in.

"Isn't it good to see a boy enjoying his food, Phoebe?" she said, looking squarely at the woman opposite her.

"Indeed, Lizzie," Phoebe replied, enjoying herself enormously as she handed the bowl to Jessamy.

Unfortunately this defence of his character and the attentions of his rather unconventional great uncle had given the boy a little too much spirit. Jessamy, with all the aplomb of a boy of eleven, stuck his tongue out at Miss Pinchbeck.

The wretched woman gasped as though she had been struck and Phoebe's heart sank.

"Jessamy," Benedict said, his tone severe. "You will apologise to Miss Pinchbeck and you will go to your room."

For just a moment Jessamy's face fell as he realised he wouldn't be able to eat his coveted dessert. But with eyes the same shade as both his great uncle's and his big brother's flashing with indignation he decided to stand his ground.

"I shan't," he said, with perfect calm. "I'll go to my room and I beg your pardon for being rude, Benedict. But she's an interfering, miserable old pinch penny and I'm not the least bit sorry."

Benedict's face darkened with fury. "Jessamy, you will apologise or I swear I'll thrash you so can't sit for a week."

Jessamy folded his arms, his face white with anger. "Go ahead," he yelled. "I'll never apologise. She makes everyone miserable, and if you marry her I'll come and live with Uncle Sylvester and never see you again."

Phoebe sucked in a breath. As much as she was proud of Jessamy by not being cowed by the awful woman he had been dreadfully rude and he was giving Benedict no option but to punish him. Of course Benedict's wretched temper had flared and he'd reacted too strongly and now things could only escalate. She had to intervene before things got out of hand.

"Oh dear," she said, laughing a little. "You know this reminds me of that story I heard about you, Benedict." She gave him a hard look, willing him to remember how he had been as a lad which according to his mother was devilish to the core. "In fact you behaved far worse than Jessamy here and got nothing more than a scolding. Isn't that right, Lady Rothay?"

Benedict's mother's eyes flashed with gratitude as she nodded. "Yes, indeed. I was never so mortified. Do you remember, Ben dear? We were having the Archdeacon to dinner and a number of dignified guests. A shocking dull affair to be sure, but Ben enlivened it by stealing into the kitchens and eating most of the deserts and then being violently ill in the Archdeacon's lap before we'd even finished the first course. He refused point blank to apologise and ran from the room."

Phoebe bit her lip as Ben flushed though she wasn't sure if it was embarrassment or anger this time.

"The Archdeacon never came again," Lady Rothay mused with a considering expression. "I was never more glad of anything," she added with a mischievous glint in her eyes. "I sent Ben to bed with some mint tea and told him not to eat the desserts before they'd appeared at the table in the future."

"No thrashing then?" Phoebe asked, holding back her laughter with difficulty.

"No indeed," Lady Rothay said in disgust. "No one has ever laid a finger on my darling boys," she said with some heat. "And nor shall they," she added with a dangerous note to her voice as she looked over at her eldest son.

"Perhaps therein lies the problem," Miss Pinchbeck said, her voice cold and she laid her perfectly folded napkin on the table.

"Oh, Ben!" Phoebe cried in undisguised delight. "Did you hear? Your fiancée thinks you badly brought up."

Benedict glared at her, his eyes narrowed, though she was certain she saw his lips twitch a little. Oliver and his uncle were less restrained, however, and roared with laughter.

"By Jove, Phoebe, I shouldn't like to pull caps with you, what a rejoinder!" Sylvester said, chortling with undisguised delight. "Now, now, Miss Pinchbeck, do you retire or shall you come about?"

Miss Pinchbeck's face was taut and furious, her mouth pulled into a tight little moue of displeasure. "I'm afraid, I have not been brought up with the kind of manners that would allow me to cross swords with Miss Skeffington-Fox, sir, and I feel I have been made mock of enough for one evening so I shall retire gracefully." She turned to Benedict, her expression devoid of emotion. "My lord, forgive me if my manners have offended you but I pray no child of ours will ever behave in such a fashion. I was never more offended. Good evening."

Once she'd left the room, Jessamy burst out laughing and threw his arms around Phoebe. "Oh I knew from the start you were a right one!" he exclaimed.

Phoebe laughed and shook her head and put her dessert bowl in his hands. "Oh do be quiet, Jessamy. You were monstrously rude as you well know."

He looked a little crestfallen at this and nodded. "I know and I do beg pardon to everyone else. I will try to behave I promise. But she looks at me like ... like ..."

"Yes, I *know*," Phoebe said with a soothing pat on his arm. "But now do go and sit down and finish *my* dessert and try to behave like a young gentleman."

Benedict cuffed him round the ear as he passed his big brother's chair and Jessamy grinned at him. "Wretch," Benedict said before glancing back at Phoebe. "Both of you," he added under his breath.

***

Later that evening Benedict retired to the library and poured himself a drink. Sitting with the crystal glass in his hand, legs stretched out in comfort, he sighed. He'd got himself in the most damnable fix and he could see no way out of it. By God but he'd been a fool. The worst of it was that even young Jessamy had seen it before he had. He realised now that the whole family had tried to warn him, some more forcibly than others, but only now was he beginning to see Theodora in her true colours. The thought of spending the rest of his days married to the woman made his blood run cold.

He remembered Jessamy's defiant words at the table with a mixture of chagrin and amusement. He also felt more than a little guilty. Phoebe had been right to remind him of his own appalling behaviour as a boy. He'd been far more badly behaved than Jessamy had ever been and yet he'd always been so hard on the boy. Perhaps because he saw some of his own spirit there and was afraid he too could follow in their father's footsteps if he wasn't held in check.

But he had been holding him back too hard and that was far more likely to make the boy rebel. He knew that his little brother had become rather afraid of him over the past year or so - since Miss Pinchbeck had arrived in fact - and the guilt he felt grew as he realised he'd been more influenced by her than he had realised.

He gritted his teeth and wondered what kind of weak-willed fellow he was to have been so taken in. Well no more. He could not cry off their marriage, perhaps, but he was damned if he'd let Theodora run roughshod over his family. He would have to take her to task, and if she disliked it ... Well, he was only too willing to release her from their betrothal.

The pretty clock on the mantel chimed midnight but still Benedict didn't move. The old house stilled and grew quiet now all the servants had retired and he told himself he just didn't feel like going to bed. He closed his eyes with a sigh and laid his head back. That was the only reason.

It was twenty past the hour when the door slowly opened and he looked up to see a vision of such beauty in the doorway that he was certain his heart stopped in his chest. It restarted with a crash and beat with a furious rhythm as he realised the recklessness of her actions.

"Phoebe!" he exclaimed as she stole into the room and closed the door behind her with care. Once again that diaphanous dressing gown taunted him with the idea of what lay beneath its gauzy layers as she set down the candle she carried. "What the devil are you playing at?"

She smiled at him, her eyes alight with expectation. "I rather thought that was obvious, Ben, dear."

He cursed under his breath as desire burned under his skin, making his flesh prickle with the need to touch her, to reach out and pull her into his arms ... to make her his.

"Did you listen to nothing I said yesterday?" he demanded, his voice rough as he got to his feet and put some distance between them. He reminded himself in the strongest terms that he was a gentleman and despite her provocative and provoking nature, Phoebe was an innocent.

"Why yes, of course I did," she said, laughing at him. "Why do you think I'm here?" she added, sounding so utterly reasonable he ground his teeth in frustration.

"Phoebe I'm going to be married to Theodora, like it or not."

Phoebe sighed and toyed with the fragile layers of her gown in a most distracting manner. "Yes, Ben, I know," she said, her voice low. "But now I know that you *dislike* it excessively, and so ... here I am."

She walked towards him, her expression bold and unafraid and he swallowed hard, willing her to stop and turn around for he didn't think he could deny her.

"Phoebe," he said, trying to convey a warning in his voice and unsure if she was simply too innocent to hear it or too committed to her action to take note. "Phoebe, please ... go back to bed ..." His voice seemed to crack a little on that last word and he cleared his throat but suddenly she was right in front of him, staring up at him with such trust in her blue eyes that he was quite undone. He reached out a hand and traced the contours of her beautiful face. "Love, you're killing me here. Have pity."

Her mouth curved into a wide smile and his breath caught in his throat. "I'm afraid I can give no quarter, my Lord," she said, reaching up and winding her arms about his neck. "I love you, you see." She tugged at his head and before he had fully comprehended her words he found himself bending to close the space between them.

Her lips were warm and soft and so enchantingly sweet that he was utterly lost. His arms slipped around her curvaceous form and pulled her tight as he savoured the taste of her. She softened in his arms, becoming pliant and melting into his embrace, perfectly secure in her trust of him. The idea filtered through the haze of lust that was demanding he lay her down on the floor and show her just how things could be between them and pierced him with guilt.

She loved him.

She loved him and she trusted him to do the right thing.

Currently he was committed to marry another and was prime suspect in a murder case. If there was ever a worse object for her affections, he'd be hard pressed to think of one. He had to put an end to this, for good. He had no right to kiss her, to feel the way he did. None at all. He could take everything she was offering him and ruin her so very easily ... but he'd never forgive himself.

He pushed her away from him with such force that she stumbled a little.

"Ben?" she demanded, her voice a little tremulous. "W-what's the matter?"

"Everything," he said, his voice dark with anger, though she didn't realise that fury was entirely for his own revolting behaviour. "This is totally inappropriate. You must leave this room, *now.*"

"I won't!" she exclaimed. "I don't want to. You don't want me to!" she added, her eyes full of the bold surety he so admired.

Benedict faltered, there was such hurt in her eyes and he wanted so much to explain but ... she would always find a way to get around him, to tempt him with that lovely smile and that daring heart of hers. He would never be able to keep refusing her. He had to make it so that she no longer wanted him.

"Of course I don't want to," he said, his voice harsh though he kept his tone low. "To be sought out alone by a beautiful woman, what man in his right mind would want to refuse? But I am not such a low creature as John, nor Harold and I hope I have enough dignity not to be tempted into such careless conduct by any shameless petticoat who casts her lures my way."

Phoebe gasped and Benedict felt he may as well have struck her, the pain of his words was so obviously visible. For a moment she just stared at him. The force of her hand striking his cheek was almost welcome, the sting of her displeasure momentarily distracting him from the regret that appeared to be crushing his heart with more force than he'd thought possible.

But before he could give into the weakness that was begging him to explain his words, she had turned and run from the room and left him very much alone.

Chapter 13

O rose, thou art sick!
The invisible worm,
That flies in the night,
In the howling storm,
Has found out thy bed
Of crimson joy,
And his dark secret love
Does thy life destroy. - William Blake

Benedict could hardly be surprised that Phoebe ignored him at breakfast but it still made him heartsick. He reminded himself he was doing it for her sake but even such noble intentions couldn't stop his mind wandering back to that soul-searing kiss. He wondered if he'd ever be the same again, now that he knew what such things could feel like if love entered the equation.

Phoebe, though still as beautiful as ever, looked pale and tired and very fragile as she left the room after eating nothing at all and sipping at a cup of tea with little enthusiasm. Benedict didn't think it was just her coming interview with the punctilious Mr Formby that was making her look so very worn. She clearly hadn't slept and he well knew why.

He closed his eyes for a moment, willing God to help him and make it all come right. But God hadn't answered him when his father had died and left a frightened young man in charge of a young family with debts up to his neck. Only his own actions had saved them and so they would now. He would do the right thing as he had vowed to himself in the days after that fateful time in his youth. He would protect those he loved. Even if they hated him for it.

Swallowing down the bitter taste in his mouth he turned to Miss Pinchbeck. Her severe countenance was dark as she frowned at

Honesty and Patience who were giggling together over some silly joke they'd shared. The twins looked happy and innocent to his eyes and careless of the worries and hardships of the world. As far as he was concerned the longer he could keep that look in their eyes the more successful he would count himself as their guardian. How could Theodora look upon such unaffected pleasure and find herself displeased?

Perhaps he could change her, he reasoned. She had changed him after all, without even noticing it he had found himself becoming every bit as severe and joyless as she was. If that was possible, surely the reverse could be true?

"Would you like to walk in the gardens this morning, Theodora," he asked, forcing himself to smile as though the idea pleased him.

To his relief there was pleasure in her eyes as she turned to him and nodded.

"A lovely idea, my Lord," she replied, returning his smile though he felt he was speaking with an acquaintance rather than his future wife. "If you would give me a moment."

"Of course," he said, hearing the politeness between them now as something to be saddened by. Such a short time ago he would have believed it quite right and proper but ... Phoebe had changed that. She had changed everything.

They had taken a turn around the gardens with Benedict racking his brain for a topic of conversation when Theodora saved him the trouble.

"You were quite right to tell Jessamy you would cane him last night," she said, her voice full of conviction that her ideas were the righteous and correct way of going about things. "You know what they say, spare the rod and spoil the child. He's becoming wild I'm afraid. Quite out of control."

"I think that is something of an exaggeration," Benedict replied, doing his best to hold his temper in check.

"Nonsense. You saw as well as I did and your instincts told you to follow the exact same course of action that I would subscribe to. It just shows how like-minded we are," she added, sublimely ignorant to the torrent of feelings that were crashing about in his heart. "Our children will never behave with such an obvious lack of decorum. Any child of ours will be polite to his betters and know just what to say or how to act in any circumstance. I shall see to that," she added, with a tone that made a jolt of fear prickle down his spine.

"They sound like very dull dogs," he replied, an edge to his voice he could not disguise.

"Oh," Theodora said, laughing at him. "I know you are only funning, Benedict. You abhor bad manners just as much as I do. You know we have spoken of it often, so you can't pretend that you don't."

Benedict frowned knowing this much was true. "In adults for sure," he said, as he tried to take the first steps to gentling the brittle creature by his side. "And indeed I should hate for any child of ours to be downright rude of course. But ... isn't a certain liveliness of spirit, a vivacity that seeks out adventure and acts with daring, isn't that something to be admired, applauded even? I should indeed hope any child I fathered to be full of the same reckless spirit that I had as a boy. Of course it must be tempered and guided over time, but ... not erased, Theodora."

The look that she favoured him with chilled the blood in his veins. "Of course you will have ideas upon the subject," she said, as though she was indulging a particularly slow child. "But men never really understand the necessities of bringing up a child in the same way as a woman. Of course the children will be in my care, so you need not have any concern about their upbringing. You may rest assured that they will be well mannered and never give you cause for embarrassment. Further than that please do not trouble yourself with what are, after all, female concerns."

Benedict looked down into grey eyes that seemed to hold no shred of warmth or empathy and knew that he would never succeed. She was incapable of the gentler emotions, more than that she did not want to acknowledge that there was even a need for them.

"Theodora," he said, his heart thudding a little too hard. "Do you not think perhaps that our ideas are not so similar as we had once thought? In truth the way you describe our children fills me with horror," he admitted, knowing he must be candid. "My childhood was an idyllic, golden time that I look back at with great affection and nostalgia. In truth I was far from a well-behaved child. I assure you that Jessamy is an angel compared to the scrapes I got into. But I was not a wicked child either and I flatter myself that I did not turn out so very badly. I would want any son of mine to have that kind of freedom and I would not allow you to take it from him."

"I see," she replied, her tone frigid. "But I know of course who to blame for such ideas."

"There is no one to blame, Theodora," he snapped, his temper growing brittle. "Except perhaps myself for entering into a betrothal with a woman I did not really understand." He could not regret the words once they were out, but he knew at once that it meant nothing to her.

Her eyes narrowed and she looked back at him with all the icy contempt he knew she felt for the rest of the world. "Say what you will, my Lord. Nothing has changed and our children will be brought up in a manner that reflects their station in life. Now if you will excuse me I have much to do."

Benedict watched her go with an empty feeling in his chest. He would never be free of her. He was condemned to a joyless marriage and he was damned if he'd ever bring children into that equation. So there wouldn't be any. The idea made him feel hollow inside as though all the joy had been sucked out of the world. And he had no one to blame but himself.

***

Phoebe watched as Mr Formby checked his notebook. He was a short, sparse man with a narrow, slightly foxy face and a scattering of grey hair around an otherwise bald head. He was perhaps in his late forties and his appearance was on the shabby side with a worn coat and boots she was certain must have holes in they were so abused. A carelessly tied cravat completed the ensemble and she could well see why a man as judgemental as Lord Rutland had held him in such contempt.

His eyes, however, were bright and beady and she doubted much got past him. She had tried buttering him up with her most coquettish smile but had soon realised this was not the correct approach to take. They had already spent some time detailing her movements during the period the murder had taken place and now the man was silent, apparently lost in thought.

He tapped his pencil against his notepad with a slight frown between his eyes.

"And the death of the Marquess of Saltash?" He glanced back at his notepad to check the name. "Anthony Rutland," he said, though Phoebe wasn't sure what the question was supposed to be.

"What about it?" she replied, shrugging. "I didn't know him and it happened before I arrived in England. I'm afraid I have nothing to say on the matter."

"And the rest of the family, what do they say?" he demanded, sitting back in his chair and watching her like a blackbird with a beetle.

Phoebe sighed but thought she should say what she knew to be true. "I know that Sylvester, the Duke of Denholm that is, and Lord Rothay believed it was no accident," she said, holding his gaze. "Both of them said the man was something of a nonesuch. He was a member of the Four Horse Club and there was no visible reason why he should have over turned his curricle on the stretch of road he was discovered on."

"So they believe it was foul play."

She nodded, sure that this would be what they would say if they were here. "Yes, I would say so. Lord Rutland, however, is strongly of the opinion that it was an accident."

His head tilted a little to one side and the birdlike impression he'd given Phoebe only intensified. He scratched at his chin, his expression thoughtful.

"There is a deal of talk, about you, Miss Skeffington-Fox," he said, though there appeared to be no judgement in his eyes. "There are those in the family who think ill of you I believe."

Phoebe gave a snort of laughter. "You don't say," she replied with a dry tone. "I don't doubt I have been accused of nothing short of murder. Let me see ..." she said tapping a finger to her mouth. "Miss Pinchbeck, Lord and Lady Rutland and ... Mr Spalding ..."

She held her wrists out to him. "Am I to be tried on their evidence," she demanded in a deep voice, pleased by the amused twinkle she saw in his eyes.

"No, miss," he replied, his lips twitching just slightly. "However there are those who believe you may be the catalyst to murder." He looked back at his notebook, taking some time to peruse the pages which Phoebe was certain he was doing to unsettle her. She couldn't say it wasn't working. "Are you having ... a *romantic* relationship with Lord Rothay?" he asked, with remarkable nonchalance.

"Well," she said, with a little shock and more approval. "At least you're candid. I can't abide veiled comments and allusions where I'm never quite certain what I'm talking about." She took a breath, wondering what to say. "You have been candid with me and so I shall repay you in kind," she said, praying she was doing right to put her trust in this man. "I am in love with Lord Rothay." She looked at him, expecting surprise at least but his face was unreadable. "He is betrothed, however ill-advised the subsequent marriage may be," she added with considerable heat. "And I assure you he is far too honourable to do anything to embarrass his future bride." This last was said with obvious frustration but thankfully he didn't comment upon it.

"I see," he mused. "That is indeed ... candid."

Phoebe gave a curt nod and smoothed down the drapes of her sprigged muslin dress.

Mr Formby consulted his wretched notebook again and scribbled down a few notes before looking back at her. "People are saying that Lord Rothay killed Harold out of jealousy, because he was flirting with you."

"Fustian!" she threw back at him. "Those *people* are nothing but spiteful busybodies with nothing better to do than gossip. Far more likely that whoever told you that is guilty of murder and saying it to deflect attention to poor Lord Rothay."

Mr Formby's lips quirked into a smile. "I'll bear that in mind, Miss," he replied with a wry tone. "So it is your considered opinion that Lord Rothay is innocent of the charges against him."

"Completely," she said, with as much conviction as she could put into one word.

"But then you are in love with him," he added, lifting one grizzled eyebrow.

"True," she admitted. "But it's still the truth nonetheless, even if you don't believe it."

"Oh I believe *you* believe it, miss," he replied, glancing back at his book again before smiling at her. She wasn't entirely sure that was an encouraging statement but there was little else she could say. "If I may venture to say so," he continued, his beady eyes watchful as he spoke. "You seem like a young lady of strong opinions. So in your view, who did murder Harold?"

Phoebe started, having been ill-prepared for such a question, but as the question *had* been put to her ... "I had thought Lord Rutland a prime candidate," she admitted. "He's obnoxious and has a foul temper, he clearly had no affection for Harold either. But then he has that annoying alibi."

"Most annoying," Mr Formby said, nodding, his eyes glittering with something that may have been amusement but she wasn't sure.

"Though he may have paid someone for it of course. But then there is Mr Spalding," she said. "Another vile creature and I understand Lord Rothay believed he was blackmailing Harold. But if he was I don't see what was to be gained by killing him. But perhaps you have information about him that I don't?" she queried, narrowing her eyes at him.

"Perhaps," he replied, though he offered no further comment to her vexation.

"Well then," she said, taking a deep breath. "The obvious conclusion if not Lord Rutland and knowing that Lord Rothay is innocent as I do …" She offered him her brightest smile at that comment. "Then the next in line for the title is the obvious perpetrator."

"Ah," he said, nodding with a sage expression, returning his gaze to flip through the pages of his notepad. "Well assuming we are not speaking of young Master Jessamy who is actually next, then Lord Oliver Bradshaw," he replied at length.

Phoebe frowned and nodded. "Yes. He seems the most likely candidate, only ..."

"Only?" he echoed, leaning forward in his chair.

"Only I hope it isn't," she replied with a sigh. "You see he's very charming and such fun ..."

"You'd be surprised how often murderers are, miss," he said with a smile of understanding. "The successful ones at any rate. Well I think that will be all for now."

He got to his feet and Phoebe stood as he held out his hand to her.

“Thank you kindly for your patience, Miss Skeffington-Fox.”

“You’re most welcome, Mr Formby,” she replied, returning his smile.

“If I may say so I’ve enjoyed speaking to you.” His face darkened a little as he withdrew his hand. “I only hope I don’t have to disappoint you in the near future.”

“Oh,” she said, her stomach clenching with anxiety. “You ... You still believe Lord Rothay is guilty then?”

He shrugged, his eyes full of sympathy. “It’s not always my belief in the matter that gets a conviction, miss. It’s the evidence that speaks in the end, not me.”

Chapter 14

Is very life by consciousness unbounded?
And all the thoughts, pains, joys of mortal breath,
A war-embrace of wrestling Life and Death? - Coleridge

Phoebe practically ran outside, hauling in lungfuls of clean, fresh air. She may have been furious and hurt with Benedict, but whatever the outcome of their forlorn love affair, if you could even call it that, she would not let them hang an innocent man.

She set forth for the rose garden, having found, as Sylvester did, that it was a good place to soothe ruffled nerves. She wasn't the only one.

"Hello, Phoebe," Lizzie said, looking up with real pleasure. "How did it go with Mr Formby?"

Phoebe sighed and flopped down beside her. "I don't know," she admitted. "But it's not looking good for Benedict."

"Oh, Phoebe," she said, her voice full of concern. "Whatever are we to do?"

"I don't know that either," Phoebe wailed. "And I had the most dreadful row with Ben and made such a fool of myself."

Lizzie gave her an indulgent smile. "Oh come now, don't be such a goose. I can see the man is besotted with you, so I can't believe that to be true."

Phoebe looked at her and frowned. "You really think so?" she demanded. "I mean I had believed it, but last night he ... was very angry with me." She flushed and looked away as she remembered his words to her.

"You tried to seduce him?" Lizzie guessed and Phoebe started with surprise. She would never have believed that Lizzie of all people would talk about such things with her. Especially not with such clear sympathy in her eyes. "Never judge a book by its cover, my dear," she said with such understanding that Phoebe let out a breath.

"Yes," she admitted. "Yes I did and ... and he was furious with me."

Lizzie chuckled and shook her head, taking Phoebe's hand and squeezing it. "Well of course he was, you gudgeon. You were stealing his control and putting him in a position where he would be responsible for ruining you. Imagine if someone had discovered you, or in a few months' time once he was married to that awful woman you discovered you were with child ... what then?"

Phoebe let go of a breath she didn't know she'd been holding. "He ... he was very cruel to me."

"I don't doubt it," Lizzie replied, nodding. "He no doubt believed it was best that you hate him. That way you'll stay out of his way and he'll not be tempted again."

"Oh," Phoebe said as her words found their mark and she sighed with relief. "What a fool I was. I should have seen that ... I should have realised."

"Don't be so hard on yourself." Lizzie laughed. "You never see things clearly when you're in love believe me."

Phoebe glanced back at her. "How come you saw it all so clearly, Lizzie," she asked, her voice soft.

"Because I have stood where you stand now, and it took me many miserable months to figure it all out and reach a ... *satisfactory* conclusion," she replied with a mischievous twinkle in her eyes.

"Lizzie!" Phoebe exclaimed, both shocked and delighted.

"There now," Lizzie said with great satisfaction. "I'm not the little scatterbrained, old maid you believed when you first arrived, am I?"

"Oh, I never!" Phoebe objected.

"Oh ho, what a plumper." Lizzie grinned at her with a good-natured amount of teasing in her eyes.

"Well ..." Phoebe acknowledged. "I did think perhaps you were rather put upon."

"And so I am," Lizzie replied, nodding. "But sometimes it's better if people see what they expect to see, because then ... it stops them looking any closer."

She winked at Phoebe who laughed and realised that she had greatly underestimated her friend.

They talked a while longer before heading inside for lunch. If Benedict was surprised that she had got over her fit of the sullens so quickly he said nothing. She made it clear, however, that his little ploy hadn't worked in the slightest by favouring him with a warm look and her most inviting smile. That he hadn't been able to look away seemed to her a good sign.

After lunch Phoebe headed back outside. It was a lovely warm summer's day with a gentle breeze that blew the laden boughs of the fruit trees as she strolled through the orchard. Hearing squealing and laughter on the other side of the gate that led into the fields beyond the orchard and gardens, she went to investigate.

She found Jessamy and the twins Patience and Honesty involved in a game of rounders.

"Phoebe!" Jessamy exclaimed, clearly delighted. "You'll play won't you. Cecily just wants to sit in the shade and look pretty," he said in clear disgust.

Phoebe glanced with amusement to where he'd pointed to see Cecily arranged in a very picturesque setting. She did indeed look very lovely in her summer bonnet tied with a pink ribbon and her skirts artfully arranged about her. "Well," Phoebe replied with a smile. "You must admit she does it very well."

Jessamy made a revolted noise and rolled his eyes. "Oh but you're not so bird witted are you, cuz?" he demanded with pleading in his expression.

"Now how can I refuse such a delightful invitation?" Phoebe chuckled and took off her own bonnet putting it into Cecily's keeping.

She took the bat from Jessamy and watched as he strode back to bowl. The twins spread out on either side to field.

To her delight she hit the ball squarely and it flew across the field. Jessamy started shrieking at Honesty to run as Phoebe gathered up her skirts and belted for the first post. First second and third were all made and she took the decision to run for the last when she saw Jessamy running towards her ball in hand. With a yelp of dismay she ran faster and made the fourth but was going too fast to stop in time to avoid Benedict who had just arrived on the scene.

"Ooof!" was a very unladylike sound perhaps but Benedict was every bit as solid as he looked and she was quite winded.

"Phoebe!" he exclaimed. "Whatever will you be at next?"

She looked up feeling rather cross and expecting to see disapproval in his eyes and was slightly wrong-footed when she discovered he was laughing at her.

"What?" she demanded. "I just got a rounder."

"So I see," he replied, his green eyes alight with approval. She realised his hands were still at her waist where he had reached out to steady her. She thought it was perhaps only the children's presence that made him remove them. He was silent for a moment, looking around at the pink-cheeked faces of the children who were watching him anxiously, obviously afraid he would put a stop to their game. "Can I play?" he asked.

The beaming looks and shouts of joy made a warm feeling glow in her chest and it only grew as Benedict stripped off his coat and waistcoat and rolled up his sleeves. He looked back at her, his eyes full of warmth.

"Thank you," he said, his voice quiet.

"Whatever for?" she said in surprise as he picked up the bat.

"For reminding me what's important," he said, before walking off and taking his place to bat.

The game grew in excitement and volume over the next half hour or so when Oliver arrived, his eyes growing wide as he saw Phoebe picking up her skirts and running hell for leather to the final post before Ben caught her out. She was too slow this time and Ben gave a shout of triumph as he tapped the ball against the post.

"Out!" he yelled with obvious glee.

"Oh!" Phoebe huffed with annoyance and pouted at him as she walked back to the start.

"I say, bad show, old man," Oliver said shaking his head. "Not good *ton*, taking out a lady."

"Piffle," Ben replied succinctly. "She's a hoyden. I've been trying to get her out since I got here but she moves like lightning."

Phoebe poked her tongue out at him to illustrate the accuracy of this statement and Oliver laughed. To her surprise he started peeling off his exquisitely cut coat and rather beautiful waistcoat.

"Are you playing?" she demanded in surprise.

"Well, of course, my dearest cousin. Someone has to defend your honour after all."

Benedict snorted at that and Phoebe glowered at him whilst trying not to laugh.

"Wretch," she threw back at him before she handed the bat to Oliver. "For my knight in shining armour," she said with great solemnity.

Oliver bowed and made a magnificent leg before taking the bat and swinging back and forth like a sword. "To battle!" he cried.

Phoebe watched the continuing play with great amusement as the men became increasingly competitive. They had changed positions by now and Oliver was bowling, Ben standing up with the bat. Oliver, Phoebe and Honesty were in one team with Ben, Jessamy and Patience in the other. Currently the score sat at 10 rounders to Oliver's team and nine and a half to Ben's. Ben was now last up and everything depended on his score.

"Come on, Ben!" Jessamy yelled with obvious excitement, cheering his big brother on with such enthusiasm that Phoebe felt quite a lump in her throat. The two of them had seemed so distant when she first arrived with Jessamy obviously rather in awe and even a bit afraid of his eldest sibling. To see him now, cheering him on with such obvious hero worship was enough to make her eyes prickle with emotion. If she'd done nothing else, if Ben really could never be hers ... at least she'd achieved this much.

Oliver bowled a rather vicious and fast ball which Phoebe watched with trepidation until Ben hit it with a resounding crack.

Oliver cursed, yelling at Honesty, rather too forcefully in Phoebe's opinion, to move herself. He ran towards the girl, snatching the proffered ball from her hand and belting back as fast as he could as Ben bore down on the fourth post. Oliver, though, seemed in no mood to be a good sport and practically tackled Ben to the ground. Ben was caught off guard, obviously not expecting such a forceful blow and went down like a felled tree, hitting his head hard as he landed.

"Ben!" Phoebe exclaimed, running to him. She sank to her knees in the dusty field to find Ben out cold. Her heart clenched with terror and she patted his face. "Ben, Ben!" she cried in increasing agitation. To her profound relief Ben groaned and blinked his eyes.

"What hit me?" he murmured as Phoebe turned to glare at Oliver who had the grace to at least look a little sheepish.

"Sorry, Ben," he replied, giving them both a crooked grin. "I got carried away."

"I should say so!" Phoebe replied with heat. Despite his boyish grin she was really very angry with him. There was no place for such behaviour in what had been a friendly family game and she found her estimation of his character sinking rapidly. "I don't know what you could have been thinking."

The children were looking on anxiously and Phoebe held out her hand to reassure them. "It's quite alright. Ben is fine, aren't you?" she added with a touch of anxiety.

Ben nodded and chuckled and touched his hand to the lump on his head with tentative fingers. "I'll live," he replied, wincing as he investigated the wound.

"Oh, Ben!" Phoebe said in dismay. "There is a lump the size of an egg on your head."

"Well I've been told before I've a remarkably thick skull so no harm done." He winked at her and Phoebe laughed.

"Well I think that is quite enough excitement for one afternoon," she said, feeling in desperate need of a cold drink and a wash. "Come along, children, back to the house. Time to get cleaned up for dinner."

The children groaned but in a good-natured fashion as everyone was hot and dusty and very ready for a drink themselves. Phoebe watched them all trailing along with real affection and wished, Oliver's behaviour notwithstanding, that life could be like this all the time.

Chapter 15

I ne'er was struck before that hour
With love so sudden and so sweet.
Her face it bloomed like a sweet flower
And stole my heart away complete. - John Clare

"But you admit you paid the man's debts?"

Ben glowered at Mr Formby. He knew the man was only doing his job but he'd been stuck in the library answering the same damn questions over and over for the past hour and his patience was wearing thin.

"Yes," he replied, his tone more than a little terse. "Harold came to me on two separate occasions to ask for help. He said he was in trouble, gambling debts, and if he didn't pay up, the men he owed money to would not be pleasant to deal with."

"Did he believe his life was in danger?" Formby persisted, his brow furrowed.

Ben considered the question. "I didn't believe that was the case at the time," he admitted. "Harold was forever crying wolf as a child and he'd make the most God awful fuss over the most trifling of injuries. If he scraped his knees as a boy you'd have thought he'd broken both legs from the fuss he made. So no I thought perhaps there was a risk they might work him over a little but I didn't believe he was in real physical danger."

"But you gave him the money anyway?"

"Yes, of course!" Ben snapped as his patience deserted him. "He was my cousin, damn it. I may not have liked him much but I wouldn't let him get into that kind of trouble if it was in my power to help."

"Very philanthropic of you," Mr Formby mused, chewing at the end of his pencil with a thoughtful expression. "Unless of course the money you gave him was because he was blackmailing you?"

"What?" Ben exclaimed. "How utterly preposterous!"

Mr Formby shrugged. "We can see from your bank accounts that the amounts you stated were withdrawn when you said. We only have your word, however, as to the motivation behind that generosity. Perhaps Harold had some information on you that you didn't want to become public."

Ben stood and towered over Mr Formby his fists clenched. "My reputation is beyond reproach," he replied his voice icy with fury. "And you are welcome to investigate any aspect of my life as you see fit. I assure you, you'll find nothing."

Mr Formby looked up at him, his face perfectly placid. "Well now, my Lord, that's not entirely true is it. I'd find Miss Skeffington-Fox for starters."

Benedict blanched before his temper reasserted itself. "Leave the young lady out of this," he said, the fury in his tone perfectly audible. "She is innocent and has nothing to do with anything that has happened here."

Mr Formby pursed his lips, staring at Ben with a considering expression. "I'm afraid I can't do that, my Lord," he said, though the smile he gave seemed to be genuine with regret. "She is involved as much as you are our and she is in love with you."

"What!" Ben exclaimed, feeling any remaining colour drain from his face even as his heart squeezed at the words. "Who ..."

"She did, sir," Formby replied his tone a little softer now. "Sat there bold as brass and told me so herself."

Ben sat down rather too quickly and put his head in his hands.

"She's not involved at all I tell you," he said, clenching his fingers in his hair. "Despite what ... what her manner might indicate, she's an innocent. There has been nothing between us I assure you and ... and neither of us had anything to do with the murders, dammit!" he shouted.

Mr Formby gave a sigh and sat back in his chair. "I'll be straight with you, my Lord. I've spoken to every member of staff and family here and of anyone it could be, I'd really rather you and the young lady weren't involved."

"But?" Benedict said, his voice heavy with foreboding.

"But." Formby agreed, his expression grave. "It doesn't look good for you, sir. On recent investigation it has been found that the curricle the Marquess of Saltash drove had been tampered with. He was indeed murdered. We know that you visited the marquess the day before he died and would have had ample opportunity to make good any sabotage attempts you had in mind. We know you had a particular interest in the weapon that killed Lord Harold Rutland and that you were angered by his thoughts of selling it when he inherited the dukedom. We know that you have paid Harold Rutland two large amounts of money and only have your word that he wasn't blackmailing you. We have more than one account of the fact that you had argued violently with him and threatened to harm him - Lord Oliver Bradshaw was quite vocal on the subject I might add," he said, his bright eyes narrowing with intelligence that Benedict prayed was sympathetic to his cause.

"Furthermore Harold Rutland had flirted with and attacked a young lady who has admitted to being in love with you, and to whom I suspect you return such feelings. You also had ample opportunity for the deed as you were apparently walking alone in the gardens at the time the murder likely took place. We know too that of all the family you love Grizedale Court very deeply and that his grace has always wished you were the true heir. Need I go on ..."

"No," Benedict replied, a cold feeling settling in his stomach. "No need."

"Do you have anything to say?"

Ben snorted and shook his head. "Other than the fact I am totally innocent? What the devil do you expect me to say?"

"My Lord," Formby said, his voice grim. "I have to tell you that it is only your uncle's close friendship with the Chief Magistrate that is keeping you at liberty for the moment alongside my own instinct that you are not my man. I *must* return to London by the end of this week, however. Then I will be obliged to give my evidence, and my feelings on the matter will neither be here nor there. Do you understand?"

Benedict nodded. "Perfectly, Mr Formby. I thank you for your honesty and for believing me despite the evidence."

Mr Formby stood as Benedict got to his feet and held out his hand. "If you have any evidence to implicate anyone else, now would be a good time," he said with a wry smile before he bid Benedict goodbye and left him alone.

For the first time since all of this had begun Benedict considered the very real possibility that he might hang for crimes he hadn't committed. Tugging at his cravat he believed he felt the noose tightening around his neck and took a deep breath before snatching up the brandy decanter. He poured out a large measure and downed it before repeating the process twice more. The alcohol burned down his throat and pooled in his belly, the molten heat having little effect on the solid ice that seemed lodged in his gut.

What in God's name was he to do?

He found himself outside in the gardens, a feeling of utter despair washing over him. He could always run of course. The war was over with France now and he spoke the language tolerably enough. Or perhaps America ... He could run away from it all. He and Phoebe could marry and run away together; she would come with him he felt sure.

And yet how could he drag her into a life where his name would be forever tainted by the worst kind of scandal? Where he would never be able to settle for fear of the past catching up with him? It was unthinkable.

He wandered through the gardens, not seeing anything but a short, bleak future that ended with him climbing a wooden scaffold.

"Benedict?"

The soft voice filtered through the depths of his gloom like a shaft of sunlight despite the impossibility of being with her. His heart gave a little leap in his chest as he turned and saw her. Dressed in a sunny yellow gown of silk and tulle with her blonde curls shining she looked like summer personified.

"Hello, love," he said, his voice low.

She ran to him, her eyes filled with concern. "Ben, what is it? What's happened? You look white as a sheet."

He shook his head and tried to smile at her but somehow his face seemed to have forgotten the action and he couldn't make it work.

"Nothing, nothing," he said, trying to chase the concern from her eyes but failing miserably as her anxiety clearly deepened.

"Ben," she said, sounding a little hurt. "Please tell me and stop being so foolish. Haven't you realised by now that I'm not so easily chased away? No matter how vile you are to me," she added with a reproachful look.

"Oh God, Phoebe." Benedict put his head in his hands. Could he do nothing right? How was it that he was likely to be hanged for murder but even Phoebe could see through his only attempt at real deception? "I'm so sorry, love," he said, dropping his hands to his sides and feeling utterly exhausted. "I was trying to protect you though."

"I know that now," she said, smiling at him and stepping closer. Damn him but he didn't have the strength to push her away again. She slipped her hand into his and he took it willingly, caressing her soft fingers with his thumb. "But there's no need. Don't you see,

Ben. I love you. I would face anything with you. Even ... even if you needed to leave here. I'd run with you, you know that don't you?"

Benedict felt his throat grow tight as he looked down at her lovely face, a face that could grace Almack's or any grand ballroom of the *ton* and be acknowledged as a diamond of the first water. She would have eligible offers of marriage from all corners of the country without even lifting a finger to achieve them because she was beautiful inside and out. How could he deny her that?

"Phoebe, don't be foolish," he said, squeezing her fingers. "I can't run. A guilty man would run and I'm innocent. I'll go to the scaffold innocent if I must but I will not drag you into this so for God's sake don't ask me to."

"But, darling," she whispered, reaching up and putting her hand against his cheek. "I am in this, whatever it is. I may not be your wife in law but here," she said, placing his hand over her heart. "In here it makes no difference. For better or for worse, Ben. I won't let you chase me away again. You may be as obnoxious and odious as you possibly can and it won't make a jot of difference you know." She smiled at him, mischief twinkling in those lovely blue eyes. "After all, you were perfectly vile to me when we first met and I still fell in love with you."

He laughed despite himself, despite the desperation of his situation, despite accusations of murder and a fiancée that made his blood run cold he laughed and couldn't deny the joy that this woman brought him. No matter how bad things got, if she loved him, if she believed in him ... surely there was always hope.

He pulled her close, too tired of fighting his feelings for her. Tilting her head back he pushed the pretty bonnet from her head and pressed his lips against hers. She coiled around him like the wild honeysuckle climbing the trees at the edge of the woodland and he basked in her love. Whatever happened, he knew what it was now, to love and be loved. But then he realised that he had never told her how he felt before though she had declared herself more than once.

"Phoebe," he said, hoping she could see the sincerity in his eyes. "I don't know what's going to happen to me. I don't know how this is going to end, and ... and it may be that I'll say things that you won't like again to protect you, to keep you safe, darling."

She made a sound of protest and he pressed a finger to her lips, silencing her.

"Listen to me please. Whatever happens, whatever I may say or do over the coming days please remember this and keep the words in your heart for me. I love you, Phoebe. I love your ridiculous name and your outrageous tongue and all the wilful, shocking things you do and say and wear ... I love you without reservation. You've reminded me what it is to love and be alive and ... and to find the joy in life. I will never, ever forget that fact. I will love you until my dying day whether that be coming soon or when we are both old and grey. You're everything I never expected and didn't know I needed, love, and I'm so very grateful for you."

Phoebe sobbed and flung herself into his arms, and he held her tight. Relieved that for once he had found the right words to give her. The right words to show her how precious she was to him. No matter what the future held.

Chapter 16

Love conquers all things, so we too shall yield to love. - Virgil

After Benedict had persuaded Phoebe to return to the house before someone found them alone together, he had walked the grounds a little longer before returning to the house for dinner.

The meal passed without incident for once though Phoebe was remarkably quiet. Perhaps that was why, he thought with a rueful grin. He did notice, however, that Theodora seemed to be making some effort to be pleasant which was something. Her efforts were falling on stony ground for the moment, which was hardly surprising, but she seemed undaunted. To the point when after dinner she invited the children to play cards with her. Benedict sent Jessamy a stern look, forcing him to accept the offer.

"Yes, of course, Miss Pinchbeck, thank you," he said with great politeness if not sincerity.

While they waited for her to return with the cards, Jessamy sidled up to Phoebe with a scowl.

"What's she playing at?" he grumbled, with as much discretion as he was capable of, which meant the whole room heard him.

"Perhaps she is trying to make amends," Benedict said, wondering if perhaps now she'd had time to consider his words, they had actually taken hold.

Jessamy, the twins, Phoebe, Lizzie, Cecily and even his mother looked back at him as though he'd grown a second head.

"Well ... no, perhaps not," he added, with a sigh. But if that wasn't the case what was she up to?

"Perhaps she's realised if she pushes too hard, Benedict would rather run away with someone else," Honesty said with a devilish grin, as though she had heard his thoughts and replied with all the candour her name would imply.

"Honesty!" Benedict scolded her, truly shocked that his little sister could be aware of such possible goings on, let alone comment on them. Any further conjecture was happily put to an end as Theodora returned.

It was truly painful to watch her try to interact with the children. She simply didn't know how to speak to them without condescension and her attempts at humour were just ... well, not funny. The longer he spent with her, the harder he found it to rationalise his proposing to her. He must have been out of his mind.

***

Phoebe left everyone playing cards and went to get some air on the terrace. She knew she was foolish to hope that Benedict would join her; he would never be so obvious in front of everyone. But she still turned her head with a hopeful smile as she heard footsteps behind her.

"Oh, hello, Oliver," she said, trying hard to keep the smile in place.

"Well that's an overjoyed reaction if ever I heard one," he said with a grimace.

She laughed and shook her head, turning back to look at the twilight as it crept over the lovely gardens of Grizedale. "Forgive me, I am pleased truly. Just a little pre-occupied." There was a pleasant breeze tonight that freshened the warm air and she fancied she could smell the sea upon it as it fluttered around her skirts. She had a sudden longing to escape, to run away and walk barefoot on a sandy beach with the waves foaming around her toes and, of course, with Benedict by her side.

"I suppose murder will do that to you," he said, his tone thoughtful.

"It's just so awful, not knowing," she replied, shaking her head. "And for someone to be so desperate or so very wicked. I don't understand it."

He laughed then and it was a rather darker sound than she'd heard from him before. "Who can say what goes on in the mind of a killer," he replied, leaning on the balustrade beside her. "Or how desperate a man must be. It could be me of course," he said winking at her.

"Oh, Oliver, don't," she replied feeling really rather ill. "Don't joke about it."

"I'm sorry," he said, reaching out and taking her hand. "Truly, that was in bad taste. Though it seems I am indeed a suspect."

"Oh, don't worry, Ben has the edge on you there," she said, not bothering to disguise the bitterness in her voice.

Oliver was silent for a moment. "Phoebe, please, don't take this the wrong way but ... have a care around Ben won't you."

"What?" she demanded, incredulous as she turned to stare at him.

He looked hesitant as though he wasn't sure whether to speak or not.

"It's just ... I love Ben like a brother, you must see that but ... well he's got a shocking temper. He's really put the wind up me a time or two when we've fallen out. Handy with his fists too. I just ... I still don't think Tony was murdered, that's not him but ... I could see him killing Harold in the spur of the moment."

Phoebe gaped at him, a cold feeling shivering over her skin.

"V-very well, Oliver, I will take care I assure you." She took a breath and smiled at him. "If you'll excuse me, I think I'll retire now. I think all that running about this afternoon has caught up with me. Goodnight."

Phoebe turned and walked away, trying not to look as if she was hurrying and with a feeling of deep foreboding growing within her.

***

The next morning Phoebe found herself desperate to talk to Benedict and unload the burden of her suspicions. But neither he nor Oliver were present for breakfast. Oliver had apparently left to go into town and would be away a few days. Lord Rutland glowered at her and left the room as she entered and his wife always breakfasted in her room so she found only Lizzie, Lady Rothay, and the children who were just getting up to leave and cause mischief. Sylvester had apparently long since finished, always being an early riser. Thankfully Miss Pinchbeck was also absent.

Lady Rothay looked red-eyed and pale and Phoebe knew that the weight of suspicion hanging over her eldest son must be wearing on her. She tried to smile as Phoebe came in but it was a shadow of her normal vivacious beauty.

"Good morning, Phoebe dear," she said, picking half-heartedly at a bread roll.

"Lady Rothay," Phoebe replied, smiling as she sat down beside her.

"Oh do call me Lucilla, dear." She clasped her hand over Phoebe's and squeezed her fingers, her eyes full of such worry. "After all, if things were different ..." She pressed a handkerchief to her mouth and took a breath. "I think you should know I ... I should have dearly liked you for a daughter."

With that astonishing remark she gave a muffled sob and ran from the room leaving Phoebe and Lizzie alone.

"Oh," Phoebe gasped, quite taken aback at such an endorsement from Benedict's mother.

"The poor dear," Lizzie said, with a despairing look in her eyes. "She's so terribly worried about Benedict. Mr Formby has told him that if no other evidence is forthcoming, he'll be arrested Friday morning."

Phoebe cried out in shock. "No! No, he can't."

"Oh, Phoebe," she said, shaking her head and looking sickened. "He can and he will. Whatever can we do? Miss Pinchbeck has been ranting at him all morning, but I have to say I don't think that's the correct approach to take."

"No indeed," Phoebe said, her determination growing. "I must speak to Benedict at once."

"He's down by the river," Lizzie said with a soft smile. "He made certain that I should tell you that. Follow the path that leads down past the chapel and when you get to the river, turn left. You'll find him."

Phoebe let out a little sigh of relief. "Thank you, Lizzie."

Lizzie inclined her head with a smile. "He didn't eat any breakfast by the way."

Phoebe got to her feet, deciding she was not really hungry. "You know I have the sudden urge for a picnic," she replied, casting Lizzie a grateful expression before heading to the kitchen.

She made her way down the back stairs to the lower floor and the servant's domain. It was cool and dark down here and she paused outside the kitchen door as she heard a raised voice.

One of the footmen was being reprimanded for something and Phoebe stilled as she recognised the rather annoyed voice that was chastising them. Taking a breath she gave a brief knock and entered.

Mr Keane looked up as she entered and gave her a warm smile. "Miss Skeffington-Fox," he said, dismissing the unfortunate footman with a curt wave of his hand. "And to what do we owe the honour of this visit?"

"Hello, Keane," she replied closing the door behind her. "I was wondering if a picnic could be prepared. For two people please?"

"Why certainly, miss, and a lovely day for a picnic it is too."

"Yes," she replied nodding and looking at him carefully. "Is ... is everything alright?"

For just a moment Keane's eyes looked a little troubled and he frowned at her.

"I ... I heard a disagreement," she said, gesturing to the door she'd just come through. "Is someone in trouble?"

"Oh," Keane grinned at her, his face clearing. "No, miss. Just one of the wretched footmen, forgot to black Lord Rutland's boots."

"Oh dear," she replied with sympathy. "In a devilish temper was he?"

Keane gave her a reproachful look and cleared his throat. "I couldn't possibly say, miss," he replied with a twinkle of amusement in his eyes. "The picnic will be waiting for you in half an hour, if that suits you?"

"Perfect, Keane, thank you so much."

A little over a half hour later and carefully dressed in her favourite yellow muslin gown and Phoebe followed the path that Lizzie had explained to her.

It was, as Keane had so rightly observed, the perfect day for a picnic. Ox-Eye daisies bobbed their jolly heads as a soft breeze stirred the grasses in the meadows and the sun was warm on her face as she carried the little picnic basket along the dusty pathway. Finding herself facing the river she stood for just a moment and admired the scenery. The water burbled with a merry chuckling sound as it slid and tumbled over smooth green rocks, and dragon flies darted with quick, sharp movements, back and forth across the surface of the water.

Turning left as she'd been told, Phoebe hastened her step, more than anxious to find Benedict.

She found him in his shirt sleeves, fishing rod in hand and felt her heart leap in her chest as she took in the wonderful image before her. He was not dressed in the carefully pristine manner he normally would be and she found herself delighted by it. His hair was ruffled, as though he'd been running his hands through it as he often did when he was under pressure and his cravat had been abandoned, showing his throat and the strong line of his jaw. Phoebe gave a sigh of longing before closing the distance between them.

Benedict looked up as she drew closer and she was more than relieved to see the way his face lit up as he saw her approach.

"You came!" he said, smiling at her as she dropped the hamper and ran into his arms.

"Well, of course, you idiotish creature, as if you doubted it for a moment!" she added, laughing at him.

He gave a heavy sigh, his face growing darker. "You wouldn't if you had any sense at all," he replied.

"Well you must by now have realised I don't have the slightest amount of sense."

"I do," he said, his tone heavy though there was a warm look in his eyes. "And so I ought to be sensible for both of us, only ..."

"Only?" she whispered, seeing the expression on his face fill with longing.

He put his hand to her hair, stroking the thick curls and allowing them to wind around his fingers. "Only I had to see you. I can't bear it, love. I want to be with you so badly."

Phoebe silenced any further words and gave her own reply by reaching up to hold the back of his neck, tugging his head down until his lips met hers. It was still new and wonderful, this feeling of his mouth on hers, at once warm and tender and fierce. Possessive in a way that made her heart beat fast and her skin ache for more.

He pulled away, his breathing harsh as he gave her a smile and stepped away from her. "Don't encourage me, Phoebe, for heaven's sake. You're hard enough to resist."

"Then don't," she said, with perfect sincerity.

Benedict gave her a fierce look of warning before taking a deep breath. "Is that a picnic I see?" he asked, and she frowned, annoyed that he was changing the subject.

He went to fetch it and spread out the blanket he had brought on the bank of the river. Once they were comfortably arranged, Phoebe began to unpack the food, handing Benedict a dripping, cold bottle of beer.

"Benedict," she said, feeling a chill all over again as she remembered last night's conversation and this morning's revelation. "I have things to tell you."

"Oh?" he paused with the bottle half way to his lips and his eyes narrowed with obvious concern. "What the devil have you been up to now?"

Chapter 17

Love, all alike, no season knows, nor clime,
Nor hours, days, months, which are the rags of time. - John Donne

"Nothing!" Phoebe exclaimed, unwrapping a parcel to find several chicken drumsticks and thrusting one towards Benedict. "Two things have happened and I didn't go looking for them. For example, I was on my way to the kitchens to fetch this picnic when I overheard a man speaking, he was obviously angry and I realised I recognised the voice that Lord Rutland had been speaking to, the man he was blackmailing."

Benedict choked on his beer and stared at her. "Who?" he demanded.

"The butler, Keane!"

"Keane?" he repeated, frowning. "Good Lord, whatever can John have on the man, and what on earth was he expecting to get in return. I can't believe he has anything vast in the way of savings?"

"No, of course not, but don't you remember. John said *you have access to it.* It must be something in the house, something John wants him to steal."

Benedict continued to frown, staring at the river in silence. "Are you sure it was the same voice, Phoebe? We can't make a mistake in this."

"Yes of course I'm sure, I wouldn't say so if I had any doubt. It was Keane, I know it was. Why, don't you believe me?"

Benedict gave her a sudden smile and put down his beer to grasp her hand. "Of course I do, love. It's only ... Keane is a good man. One of the best in my opinion and I know he's loyal. Yet John said he'd already betrayed this family's trust badly. I ... just don't think it's possible. Keane is proud of his position with us and I'd swear he loves Sylvester."

Phoebe nodded. "I agree, Ben. I like Keane enormously but perhaps whatever it was only seems like a betrayal to John. You know what a stuck up prig he is. Nothing is more important to him than his wretched dogs and his own consequence."

Benedict laughed at her, amused by the heat with which she had summarised the man's character. "Well I don't disagree with you."

"I think we should speak to Keane, perhaps he'll confide in us?" Phoebe said, handing Benedict a plate filled with sandwiches before she tackled the wax paper parcel of pigeon pie.

"We shan't do anything of the kind," Benedict replied, his tone firm. "I do think it's a good idea that I speak to him, however."

Phoebe paused in unwrapping the wax paper to glare at him. "You've just said that Keane is a good and honest man, loyal to the family, which I agree with. So there is no danger in speaking to him. Furthermore, he's more likely to talk to me. He said only the other day that there is something about me that makes him say things he didn't ought to."

Benedict snorted at that. "Well he's got that right."

Phoebe stuck her tongue out at him which was childish but made him laugh. "We speak to him together, Benedict."

"Oh, ho, Benedict is it now?" he teased her, grinning. "Very well, I suppose I have to agree or we'll be back to *my Lord Rothay*."

"Indeed," she said, nodding her agreement and placing a generous slice of pigeon pie on his plate as he puffed out his cheeks at the way his plate was filling. "Well you did say you were hungry."

"And the second thing you discovered?" he asked, before taking a large bite from a chicken sandwich.

"Ah," she said, knowing this was going to be much harder. She took a moment to pour out a glass of lemonade and took a sip, finding it sharp and sweet and cold. "Well. I was on the terrace last night when Oliver came out to speak to me and ... Oh, Ben, I'm so sorry but he told me to be careful around you. He more or less told me you murdered Harold and I should stay out of your way."

Benedict's face clouded over and he nodded. "He's said some pretty damning things to Formby too," he said, his expression bleak. "I must say that I'm beyond hurt that he could believe such a thing of me."

"Oh, Ben!" Phoebe exclaimed in frustration, almost knocking her glass over as she threw her hands in the air. "Don't you see? It's him! It has to be. He's trying to deflect attention from himself."

Benedict scowled at that and hesitated, but a moment later he shook his head. "No, Phoebe. If he's wanting the title there is still John, myself and young Jessamy standing in his way. I can't believe his nefarious plan intends to have all of us bumped on the head."

"Well, before last night I wouldn't have believed it either," she admitted. "But you weren't there, Benedict, and I can only tell you that there was something about him that frightened me, and I don't frighten easily. There was something in his voice. I hate to say it but ... I wouldn't be the least surprised if he did mean you, John and even poor little Jessamy harm, and getting you out of the way by getting you convicted of his other murders would be a pretty neat way of removing you. Then an accident to finish John off on the hunting field shouldn't be so very hard to arrange. As for Jessamy, he's just a little boy ..." she said, her hand closing around her throat as real fear pricked at her eyes.

"Now, love, come along," Ben said, shaking his head. "You're getting yourself all het up." But nonetheless he stilled and became pensive as this information filtered through. "Just stay away from him," he said, looking up at her, his eyes intent. "I have to say I'm not convinced and I pray you're wrong, but ... if what you say is true he's ruthless and he'll stop at nothing."

Phoebe shuddered and nodded her agreement. "Oh, you don't need to tell me I assure you. At least he's away for a few days. Perhaps we could search his room while he's gone?"

"He's gone?" Benedict repeated.

"Yes," she replied, picking at a sandwich with little appetite. "Back to London it appears, but only for two or three days I think."

Benedict nodded, looking thoughtful. "Yes, I could check his room out, and *no,* you may not help me."

He laughed as she pouted at him and he lifted her hand to his lips, kissing her fingers. "Don't be cross, love. You have to let me have my own way now and then you know, it's only fair."

She laughed despite her annoyance. "Oh very well then," she said, trying to sound cross and failing.

They didn't talk any more about the murders by unspoken agreement and the rest of the picnic passed in a delightful manner, despite the glowering darkness on the horizon of their futures. For now Phoebe knew that both of them wanted to enjoy this moment, to hold these precious hours close, to remember if things did not work out the way they needed them to. But they would, she told herself, they had to. She couldn't allow anything else.

She looked up at Benedict as he tipped his head back to drain the last of the beer from the bottle before setting it aside. But what if she failed and never knew what it was to be loved by him? The idea was so appalling that she caught her breath.

Benedict looked around and must have seen the desperate look in her eyes for it was reflected in his own.

"Phoebe," he whispered, as helpless as she was to deny the feelings that were growing between them.

Before he could allow any nobler intentions to get in their way she leaned forward and kissed him, pulling at his neck as she lay down, forcing him to follow her.

He did as she wanted though he lay beside her, his lips still gentle and tentative and she knew he was determined to control himself. But that she didn't want.

Phoebe reached for the opening of his shirt and slid her hand under the fine linen, inhaling as her fingers smoothed over a tangle of wiry hair and the silky skin beneath. Ben's breathing hitched as her hand moved lower, gliding over the defined ridges of his abdomen.

"Your skin is so soft," she said, delighted at her discovery.

He gave a little huff of laughter and pulled her hand from his shirt. "Did you expect scales, love?"

"Don't be silly," she replied, indignant as she pulled his mouth back to her. Frustrated by the space between them she tugged at his hips but he remained stubbornly distant. Determined that she would not be thwarted she decided to make greater advance in her strategy. With that in mind she lowered her hand and, albeit a little nervously, allowed it to slide over the fall of his trousers.

Ben sucked in a breath and cursed, low and with some force as he reached to take her hand away.

"No," she replied, her voice adamant as her hand slid back and forth over the hard length that was only too obvious beneath the material of his trousers. "Let me, please."

Ben may have been the first man she'd ever kissed but she was in no way ignorant of what men liked in this situation. Growing up around an army she had overheard and seen many things that any other lady of her birth would never have been exposed to. So although the technical aspects of what she was attempting might be guesswork, she knew what she was doing and was not about to be deflected.

"Phoebe, stop, for the love of God," Ben groaned, covering his face with his hands. "You don't know what you're doing to me."

Phoebe gave a devilish chuckle, sitting up and gazing upon his prone figure with approval. "Oh, I have a fair idea," she murmured, hoping he wouldn't notice as she undid the buttons that kept his skin from her touch.

But Ben was too lost to notice and it wasn't until her hand breached the coverings of trousers and small clothes that he realised what she'd done.

"Dear God in heaven," he cried, as she wrapped her fingers around him. "You mustn't ... you ..." Words seemed to desert him at this point, for which Phoebe was relieved because she wanted to concentrate on the job at hand.

If she'd thought the skin over his stomach smooth, then this was a revelation. Her hand slid over warm silk as she explored the mysteries of the male form. Benedict made a despairing sound as she ran a fingertip over the blunt head, feeling moisture beneath her touch. She trailed her hand back down again, eager to discover more and finding the soft vulnerability of the skin beneath his shaft. She cupped the rounded forms within her palm before returning to stroke the rigid length that seemed to leap under her touch.

To her chagrin her investigations were halted as Ben moved and forced her onto her back, holding her hands captive above her head.

"Stop," he said, desperation in his tone and such desire in his eyes that her breath caught in her throat. The green was almost entirely swamped by black pupil and he was breathing hard. "You don't understand what you're doing," he rasped and she blinked up at him in annoyance.

"Don't be foolish, Ben, of course I do. My father is a rake and I was practically raised by the army. You must understand that even if papa had tried to shield me from such things he could never have managed it. So he took the more sensible approach and made sure I knew what was what, so I would never find myself in a situation I couldn't handle. I had a very nice lady explain everything to me very clearly."

Benedict looked shocked to his bones as he gaped at her. "Good God," he exclaimed. "What lady?"

Phoebe pouted and looked up at him, wondering how exactly to explain Madame Dede. "Well," she said, rather hesitant. "I think perhaps you'd call her a *bit of muslin?*" she queried. "Or perhaps a Cytherean?"

"Oh, dear Lord, save me," he muttered.

"What?" she demanded. "I'm sorry if I'm not the sweet little innocent you had hoped," she said to him, feeling rather hurt now and a little more unsure of herself. "But I can't change who I have become."

"Phoebe!" he cried, sounding horrified. "Heaven help me, as if I'd want you to change, you infuriating wretch!"

She glanced up at him and found him looking terribly frustrated for more than one reason. His face softened as he took in the anxious look that must have been visible in her eyes. He let go of one of her hands and smoothed his palm against her cheek.

"No matter what you think you may know, love, you are still very much an innocent and I'm supposed to protect you from the perils of this world. But you're not making it very easy."

She made a disparaging noise. "No, I should think not," she said with some heat. He shook his head in despair and she sighed. "Oh, Ben, I know you're trying to be noble but we can't pretend that things aren't desperate, can we?"

"No, love," he said, his voice heavy. "We can't."

"Well then, I have no intention of seeing you go to the scaffold, and if it comes to it, I'll hit you over the head and have Sylvester help me smuggle you to France! But either way I'm not giving you up and I refuse to let you hold yourself at a distance because of your damned honour!"

"And what if all your plans come to naught and I am hanged and you left with my bastard to care for?" he snapped, and she knew it was the fear in his eyes making his anger sharper and brighter.

She reached up her free hand and touched his mouth, praying he could see the sincerity in her eyes. "Then I should find the only joy that could possibly be left to me in seeing your child grow into someone as special as their father had been."

Benedict closed his eyes, but she had seen the pain there clearly enough. He rolled onto his back and lay with his arm across his eyes. Phoebe lay beside him, her head on his shoulder, knowing he would speak when he was ready.

"I'll not make love to you out here where anyone could trip over us, Phoebe."

"Alright, Ben," she whispered, only hearing that he wouldn't love her *here*. "But you *will?"*

He turned back to her and gathered her in his arms, his eyes full of love for her, though his smile was rueful. "I can't resist you, Phoebe. I want you so much and you're determined to rob me of what is left of my sanity. But not here, love, not now."

She sighed and smiled up at him. "I can wait," she said, though in truth she didn't want to wait at all, but she had won her victory, so he must be allowed to dictate the terms at least.

They spent the afternoon together, wrapped in each other's arms, talking and dreaming of what life might be like in the future, if they had a future at all. For even if they managed to acquit Ben of murder, there was still his fiancée to deal with. With a deal of wickedness Phoebe had to suppress the hope that the murderer might take exception to the woman and had to pray for forgiveness for such unchristian thoughts. She prayed harder that Ben would clear his name, however, as the sun began to sink lower.

"Goodness, it's getting late," Phoebe cried, aware that they'd been so wrapped up in each other they had not thought to check the time. "We'll be late for dinner if we don't hurry."

"You'd best go first love, I'll follow on in a bit," Benedict replied, looking just as regretful as she that the day was over. He pulled her close and kissed her again. A slow, soft kiss that spoke of everything that was in his heart. "I'll see you at dinner," he whispered, smiling at her.

Phoebe sighed and nodded, and picking up the now empty basket, ran back along the path.

Chapter 18

Strange is it that the godless, who have sprung
From evil-doers, should fare prosperously,
While good men, born of noble stock, should be
By adverse fortune vexed. - Sophocles.

Benedict sat down at the table and wondered how he was going to endure the coming ordeal. Try as he might he could not stop his eyes from returning to Phoebe. Dressed all in a vibrant blue silk gown trimmed with heavy white lace she looked so beautiful he could have cried with frustration. His mind wandered inevitably to the golden afternoon they had just shared and to how it had felt to have her hands upon him.

Snatching up his wine glass he downed the lot and gestured to one of the footmen to refill it.

"Benedict!" Miss Pinchbeck said in shock as he raised the second glass to his lips.

"I'm sorry, Theodora," Benedict replied, quite unable to keep the scorn from his voice despite his best effort. "Having a noose waved in one's face gives one a thirst you see."

"My Lord!" she exclaimed, looking at him aghast. "It is all just a terrible mistake and will be sorted out I promise you. You'll see." She unfolded her napkin with prim fingers and laid it carefully in her lap. "There is no need for us to lower our standards in the meantime."

Benedict snorted but was startled by a sob from the other end of the table. Horrified, he discovered that his mother was weeping.

"Lulu!" he exclaimed, the childish nickname falling from his lips quite unconsciously. He got to his feet and ran to his mother, pulling her into a rough embrace. "Forgive me," he pleaded, feeling horribly guilty for causing her pain. "I'm not done yet, love. I'll come about, you'll see."

Lady Rothay gave a last, desperate sob and then took a deep breath, the effort to compose herself quite obvious. "Yes," she said, nodding and giving him a tremulous smile. "Yes, you will. I know you will. You must!" she added, clinging to his hand, her lovely eyes full of fear for him.

He leaned down and kissed her forehead and made his way back to his seat.

"Where's John?" he asked Lady Rutland, suddenly aware that there was another empty space at the table beside Oliver's.

Lady Rutland looked up from the intense concentration she was applying to the entrée and cast Phoebe a dark look. "I don't know," she said, still scowling. "He went out with his gun and a picnic this morning and I've not seen him since."

"Oh well," Lizzie said with a bright smile. "You know what John is like when he's out hunting. He's no doubt walked miles tracking some poor, unfortunate creature and realised it's too late to come home. He'll likely be tucked up snug in some inn or other by now."

"No doubt," Lady Rutland said in disgust as she reapplied her attention to the meal.

Benedict noted Lizzie look across at Phoebe and wink and Benedict felt a sigh of relief that his darling girl had an ally here.

"I was thinking, Phoebe," Lizzie added, putting her knife and fork down. "Why don't we go into Hastings tomorrow and do some shopping. Lady Rothay you will come too won't you? I think it would do us all good to get away from here and stop moping about for a few hours?"

"A splendid idea, Lizzie," Benedict replied, smiling at her with warmth. It pleased him enormously to know Phoebe had such a friend in his cousin. He had always liked Lizzie and thought the family greatly underrated her. She kept Grizedale Court running like clockwork though she got little thanks for it. Not that Sylvester was uncaring, it was just that he didn't notice such things. Though Benedict knew the old man cared for her deeply.

He looked at the head of the table now to where his uncle was sat. He hadn't spoken all evening and his face was ashen. Ben knew the last days had taken it out of the old man and prayed it wouldn't be too much for him. Guilt prickled at his conscience as he should have been with Sylvester this afternoon as they'd arranged the day before, but had cried off to go fishing, knowing that Phoebe would seek him out. The old man had seemed happy enough that he go, chuckling about young people in a way that made Benedict wonder if he knew how he felt for Phoebe.

He knew he was not being arrogant in thinking that Mr Formby had been right about one thing. Sylvester had always wished that Benedict would inherit the title as he was one of the few men in the family that the old man had any affection and respect for. But now, far from inheriting, Benedict might not even outlive him.

He swallowed down that uncomfortable thought and took a deep drink of his wine, holding Theodora's gaze and daring her to comment. There was disapproval in her eyes but her expression was placid as she looked away from him.

Benedict drew his attention back to find the women discussing tomorrow morning's proposed outing.

"Please don't trouble yourselves to invite me," Miss Pinchbeck said, giving everyone a tight smile. "I have things to do tomorrow."

Lizzie's smile faltered as she realised her faux pas.

"Oh, well if you're sure, Miss Pinchbeck, you are of course very welcome to accompany us."

"How very gracious of you," Miss Pinchbeck replied with such a cold tone that Lizzie blushed and turned her attention back to her meal.

Benedict stared at Theodora in wonder. How could she be surprised at people not wanting her company when she was so damned supercilious and unpleasant to everyone? She seemed totally detached from the people around her, without the slightest comprehension of their feelings or thoughts. Sighing heavily Ben gestured to the footman to fill his glass again. Although he regretted that he could spend no more time in Phoebe's company, Benedict had to admit to deep relief when the interminable evening ended.

***

The next morning Benedict waved Phoebe, Lizzie, his mother and the children off as they set out early for Hastings. Selfishly he wished he could have snatched some more time with Phoebe but they would be home by mid-afternoon so perhaps there would still be time. He had considered going with them but such brazen behaviour was not in his nature. He could not subject Miss Pinchbeck to such a slight no matter how much she had begun to pain him. After all it was not her who had changed, it was him.

He was reluctant to go back into the house at all as the arrival of Mr Formby some moments earlier had cast a pall of gloom over the place. Benedict had been relieved to discover he had missed the man's visit yesterday afternoon but knew he couldn't avoid him forever.

Wandering back into the bright entrance hall of the great house he was just bracing himself for his next confrontation with the keen-eyed runner when he was startled by a slamming door. The sight of the normally dignified butler running hell for leather across the hall was enough to shock him into silence.

“My Lord!” Keane cried, his face white with horror. “Thank God you're here!”

“Keane!” Benedict exclaimed. “Calm yourself, man, whatever is the matter?”

Both men looked around as Mr Formby emerged from the library as Keane fought to catch his breath. "What's to do?" Formby demanded, his beady eyes bright with curiosity.

"You must come, my Lord," Keane said, looking too shaken to speak. "You too, if you please, sir," he added to Mr Formby.

Keane was silent as he led them back through the house and through the gardens. There was a large wall that separated the lovely landscaping of Mr Brown's design from the kitchen gardens that supplied the great house. Keane opened a wrought iron door that led them inside the kitchen garden area and Benedict was flooded with memories.

He hadn't been in here for years but as a lad he had been a regular, and not always welcome, visitor. He remembered many happy hours spent stealing strawberries and soft fruit and popping peas from their tight little cases, sweet and still warm from the sun. His nostalgia was abruptly halted, however, as Keane stopped and pointed to the far end of the garden.

"Over there, my Lord," he said, his tone even. "I beg you will forgive me if I do not go with you. I have no wish to set eyes upon it again."

Benedict and Mr Formby shared a grim look before they both set out towards the corner of the garden where the herb beds lay.

Benedict paused, his heart beating in his throat as he recognised the heavy build of the figure stretched out across the path. "Oh, dear God, no!" he exclaimed and ran forward, only to retch and cover his mouth as he took in the sight.

Lord John Rutland's face was twisted in agony, his eyes wide and unseeing.

"Step aside please, my Lord," Mr Formby said, his tone gentle as he manoeuvred Benedict out of the way to investigate the scene.

"Poisoned, by the looks of things," he said, grimacing as the body was laid in full sun and John had been violently ill before he died. "What's all that green leaf around his mouth," he wondered aloud, squinting at the body from as safe a distance as he could manage.

"Basil," Benedict said, his voice tight as nausea swirled in his gut. "He ate some poisonous berries once as a child, nightshade I think. They grow quite freely on the estate you see. As I remember his nanny saved him by making him drink vast amounts of basil tea."

"So he recognised his symptoms then," Mr Formby mused, straightening himself up and turning back to Benedict with a grim expression. "I'm no expert but I've seen a deal of poisoning cases in my line of work and I'd say he's likely been here since yesterday, late afternoon if I had to guess it," he added and Benedict felt his stomach drop in despair as he realised where this was going.

"If I might favour to ask you, my Lord. Where was you yesterday afternoon?"

Benedict swallowed and looked the man in the eye. "I suspect you know the answer to that as you asked for me when you came to the house yesterday, but I was fishing, down by the river."

Mr Formby nodded, his bright eyes intent. "Anyone corroborate that can they?"

Ben shook his head knowing there was no power on earth that would make him reveal Phoebe had been with him. "No. No one. I was alone."

Mr Formby rocked back on his heels, his head tilted a little to one side and showing a quizzical expression. "You didn't see anyone who might vouch for you?"

"No," he replied, his tone firm, even knowing he was likely sealing his fate.

Mr Formby nodded, his lips pursed. "You didn't happen to come across Lord John, here neither, I take it?"

"I did not," Benedict replied his jaw tight with stress.

Giving a great sigh of dejection Mr Formby shook his head. "Well it grieves me to do it, sir, I promise you, but I can't put off my duty no longer. I'm afraid I'm going to have to arrest you."

Benedict nodded, too numb to form any words of protest. He had known this was inevitable after all.

"Now, you'll not cause me any bother, will you, my Lord?" Formby asked him, his face open and questioning. " 'Cause I really don't want to have to put shackles on you."

Benedict snorted and shook his head. "No need, Formby. I'll come along, don't worry."

Mr Formby sighed and nodded, taking off his hat and scratching his bald head. "I know it, sir. You're a gentleman to your bones, that much is obvious." He walked companionably back down the path with Benedict as if they were just out for a stroll. "T'aint right," he grumbled to himself as they walked. "But I have to do it, my Lord."

"Don't trouble yourself, Formby," Benedict replied, his voice dull. "I understand it's not personal. Though if you could redouble your efforts to find the real culprit I'd be much obliged."

Mr Formby looked a little affronted by this. "Well now, sir. I've worked a deal of hours on this wretched case, so I have. I've done my best and so I always shall, so there's not the least bit of good reproaching me."

Benedict laughed, though it was a bitter sound. "No, I don't imagine there is."

Chapter 19

Pillow'd upon my fair love's ripening breast,
To feel for ever its soft fall and swell,
Awake for ever in a sweet unrest,
Still, still to hear her tender-taken breath,
And so live ever-or else swoon to death. - John Keats

Phoebe sat back the Barouche with Lady Rothay and Lizzie and felt impatient to be back at Grizedale. The children who were now hot and tired and rather irritable had been foisted on poor, good-natured Cecily and rode in the carriage behind them. In normal circumstances Phoebe would have thoroughly enjoyed their little jaunt to Hastings but she was far too aware that their time was running out. If they didn't figure out who was responsible for Harold and Lord Saltash's deaths then nothing would save Benedict unless he chose to run.

Phoebe had not been joking about smuggling him abroad either, unconscious if necessary. She felt sure Sylvester would help her with the arrangements if it came to it. She could only pray that it wouldn't.

"Whatever is going on?" Lizzie said, craning her neck as the great house came into view and the sight of Sylvester apparently laying into Mr Formby with his walking stick while Benedict tried to hold him off.

"Goodness gracious!" Phoebe exclaimed and urged the scandalised looking footman who was agog at seeing the duke in such a rage to stop gawping and let the steps down immediately.

"How dare you!" Sylvester raged, his face almost purple with fury, moustache bristling. "I'll be speaking to the Chief Magistrate about this. Infamy, that's what it is, infamy!"

Mr Formby was tugging at his already crooked cravat and looking awkward. "Now look here, your Grace. I don't say that I want to arrest him but he hasn't an alibi and the law is very clear."

"Damn the law!" Sylvester raged, stamping his stick on the ground in fury. "I'm the law around here, as was my father and his father before him going back to the ninth century confound it! You'll arrest my nephew over my dead body!"

"Whatever is going on!" Phoebe exclaimed, hurrying to Sylvester's side and taking his arm. She looked at Benedict in horror as the realisation that Mr Formby had been trying to arrest him filtered through to her.

"I'm afraid John's dead," Benedict said, his face grave and far too pale. "Poisoned. And Mr Formby here wants to arrest me for all three murders."

"Oh my!" Lady Rothay murmured and promptly fainted.

Thankfully Keane moved fast enough to catch her and lifted her up.

"Take her through to the drawing room please, Arnold," Lizzie said, smiling at him with gratitude. "Don't worry, Benedict, I'll see she's alright," she said patting his arm. "You sort this out with grandfather."

"Nothing to sort out," Sylvester shouted, enraged all over again. "Get off my land!" he shouted at Mr Formby. "Before I set my dogs on you!"

"Now then, your Grace," Mr Formby said, a warning note in his voice. "I'll go this time and no problem but attacking a runner is a crime that is, so have a care. But I'm afraid I'll be back again and then Lord Rothay will have to come along, like it or not."

They watched as the runner walked back around to the stables to seek his horse and everyone fell quiet.

"Man's a blasted fool," Sylvester cursed in fury.

Phoebe patted his hand as Ben took his other arm.

"He's no fool," he said, his voice grim. "I actually think he's on my side but the circumstantial evidence is pretty damning and the motive clear enough."

"Balderdash," Sylvester grumbled, stumbling a little as he walked up the steps and Phoebe could tell he was exhausted by his outburst.

"Now then, Sylvester," she said, infusing her voice with admiration but keeping the words firm. "You've defended Benedict magnificently today, I couldn't be more proud of you, but you must go and rest now if you are to be able to do so again."

Sylvester huffed and grumbled some more but agreed that a nap before dinner might not be such a bad idea. They helped him to his room and into the tender care of his valet until the two of them were left alone.

"You know just how to handle him," Benedict said, smiling at her. "No one else would have got him to rest without setting up his bristles."

She gave him a wan smile but was too terrified to be diverted. "Oh, Ben, whatever shall we do?"

"I don't know, love," he said, and she was horrified to hear him sound so defeated.

"Well first we must talk to Keane," she said, her voice firm. She wouldn't allow him to sink into depression and give up hope. "Though I have an idea, I know what John was blackmailing him about."

"Oh?" Benedict said in surprise. "What?"

"Let's go and talk to him," she said, ignoring his question and taking his arm. "If I'm right you'll find out soon enough, and if I'm wrong, it's better that I have suggested it and not you." They walked back down the stairs once more and Phoebe paused at the bottom to look up at him. "Where is Miss Pinchbeck?" she asked. "Surely she would have had something to say about Mr Formby trying to arrest you?"

Benedict shrugged. "I have no idea," he said. "I've not seen her all day so I don't suppose she knows anything about it."

They carried onto the drawing room to find Lizzie sitting with Benedict's mother while Keane poured her a glass of sherry.

"Poor Lulu," Benedict said with a sad smile, crossing the floor to give his mother an embrace. "What a fright you had. I'm so sorry, dearest."

"Oh, Ben," Lady Rothay said, her big eyes red from crying. "I can't bear it. That dreadful man. He mustn't take you. We must get you to France. I shall talk to Sylvester about it tonight," she said, accepting the sherry from Keane and downing it on one neat swallow.

"Hush now, mother," Ben said, his voice soothing. "I'm not convicted yet. There'll still need to be a trial and I have powerful friends, let us not predict my demise just yet, eh, love?"

"Oh." Lady Rothay buried her face against his shoulder and sobbed.

"I think perhaps mother would benefit from a lie down, Lizzie. Would you be an angel?" Ben asked her.

"Oh yes," Lizzie exclaimed, smiling at Benedict. "Of course I shall. Come now, Lucilla dear. Let us go to your room."

Once Lizzie and Lady Rothay had left the room Keane looked at Benedict with an enquiring expression.

"If there is nothing else then, my Lord?"

"Actually, Keane, we wanted to speak to you," Ben began, though he was unsurprised when Phoebe interrupted him.

"Yes, we do I'm afraid, about something I overheard the other day."

Phoebe made sure to keep her tone light and hoped her expression was sympathetic enough that he would confide in her.

"I got caught out the other night you see," she said, smiling at him. "You know I'm always in trouble for something," she added, trying to put him at his ease though there was a troubled look in the butler's eyes. "Well I couldn't sleep and so I came to get a glass of brandy. I know, shocking." She laughed throwing up her hands. "But of all the devilish luck I heard voices and I didn't want to be caught down here in my dressing gown. Happily though, Ben had shown me the priest's hole over there so I was able to hide. But ... well I overheard John blackmailing you."

Keane's face went a remarkable shade of white and his jaw was stiff with tension.

"I didn't kill him, Miss," he said, his voice rough but his eyes shining with sincerity. "If that's what you're thinking, you're off by a mile. I'll admit it, whoever rid the world of him did me a great service but I didn't kill him. I'll swear on the bible if you ask me to."

Phoebe crossed the room to him and laid her hand on his arm in a reassuring manner. "Oh, Keane, I never thought it. Truly I did not. But he was blackmailing you about Lizzie, wasn't he?"

Keane gaped at her, incredulous, and where he had been white before now two livid red spots appeared on his cheeks. "I ... I ..." he began to bluster.

"Oh come now, Keane. Surely you know you can trust myself and Benedict?" she said and tried to ignore the fact that Ben was also gaping at her in astonishment. "And it's no wonder if she does love you. You're a good and kind man and she has no one else here to take care of her or keep her spirits up in this big old house. I'm only grateful that she has you."

Keane let out a breath and sat down as though his legs had given out. "Well I'm blowed," he said, shaking his head and looking at

Phoebe with a rueful expression. "And we've been so careful. What did we do?"

Phoebe smiled and shrugged. "Honestly until this morning it was just a feeling I had when the two of you are together, but when Lady Rothay fainted, in the commotion Lizzie called you Arnold."

Sighing, Keane shook his head again. "Dear Lizzie. I knew she'd slip up one of these days. She finds it so hard to treat me as she ought now."

Ben cleared his throat and gave Keane a hard look. "Am I to take it that you and my cousin Elizabeth are ... are ..."

"Lovers," Phoebe supplied for him, giving him a stern look of her own and praying he heeded her warning. "Yes, Ben, dear. Isn't that romantic?"

Ben gaped at her for a moment and then let out a bark of laughter. "Very romantic."

Phoebe beamed at him before turning back to Mr Keane. "So John was blackmailing you and threatening to tell Sylvester about you and Lizzie."

Keane nodded. "Lizzie has a set of diamonds given to her by the late duchess. Worth a fortune I should think. Anyway he wanted me to take them from her but I refused. I figured if Sylvester wanted to throw me out after all these years ... Well," he said, shaking his head with such a dejected air that Phoebe's heart went out to him.

"He won't!" she said with such a decisive tone that Keane and Benedict just stared at her in alarm. "He wouldn't be so heartless, and if he considers it ... well, he'll have me to deal with." She ended her statement with a nod as if that matter was entirely settled and Keane gazed at her with undisguised admiration. His eyes flickered to Benedict and back again.

"Whoever marries you will be a lucky man," he said, grinning at her. "And a brave one I reckon," he added nodding at Benedict.

Benedict cleared his throat. "Yes, well. Now that is all cleared up," he said obviously trying to change the subject. He was helped in this as Lizzie came back into the room.

"Your mother is sleeping now," she said to Benedict with a reassuring smile and then paused as she noticed the way everyone was looking at her. "What? What did I miss?" she demanded, looking anxious.

"They know, Lizzie," Keane said to her, holding out his hand to her.

Lizzie swung around, her eyes blazing. "It wasn't his fault, y-you mustn't blame him!"

"Oh, Lizzie!" Phoebe cried. "We're not blaming anyone, I promise you. I'm so happy for you. We both are. Aren't we, Ben?" she added, with a slightly forceful note to her voice.

Ben rubbed the back of his neck and glowered a bit but nodded. "Yes, yes of course. Very happy."

Lizzie gave a little gasp of surprise and ran to Phoebe, pulling her into an embrace. "Oh, Phoebe!" she cried. "I can't tell you how glad I am that you're here, and I'm so happy you know and ... and you don't disapprove."

"Well, how could I?" Phoebe laughed, shaking her head. "I can see just why you fell for him," she added with a mischievous smile that made Keane snort with amusement.

"There see, Lizzie, my love. And didn't I say it was impossible to keep a secret from this foxy miss, eh?" he chuckled.

Lizzie blushed and gave him a shy smile but took his hand this time, leaning into his side and looking up at him with such adoration that Phoebe gave a happy sigh to see it.

"Well then," Keane said, slipping his arm around Lizzie's waist with a proprietary air. "That's all well and good. But it don't help his lordship here, does it?"

Phoebe sighed again, but this time it was a far less contented sound. "No," she replied sitting down as she suddenly felt very tired. "No it doesn't."

"And I was sure Lord John had done for Harold too," Keane said, frowning.

"Well maybe he did?" Lizzie said with an air of enquiry.

"Well then who killed John?" Phoebe demanded.

Lizzie shrugged and held up her hands. "I don't know! Maybe someone who knew he'd done it and wanted revenge?"

"Then why not tell Formby?" Benedict asked going to help himself to a glass of brandy and hesitating a moment before offering one to Keane too.

"Oh," Keane said, looking astonished at the gesture. "Well that's mighty kind of you, my Lord. But not while I'm working, perhaps."

"Oh go on, man," Ben said, sounding a little impatient. "I know I need one and I don't doubt you do too."

Keane accepted the drink without further demur. "Perhaps whoever it was didn't have any evidence for Formby," he offered before taking a large swallow of brandy. "Or perhaps the evidence would have incriminated him too?"

Benedict nodded, agreeing that was a possibility but Phoebe frowned. There had been something bothering her ever since she'd heard about John's death.

"Wait a minute," she said, holding up her hand for their attention. "Why are you all so certain the killer is a man? Women are just as capable of murder I can assure you."

Benedict gave her a slightly wide-eyed look of alarm. "A comforting thought," he murmured.

"Well it's true," she added. "And he was poisoned, and that's a woman's weapon." She shrugged as the three of them stared at her.

"Well it is," she said with a huff. "Women don't have the physical strength to overpower a large man perhaps, but they can feed him poison easily enough."

"Remind me not to get on the bad side of you," Benedict said with a frown.

Phoebe snorted. "You've lived this long haven't you?" she said with some asperity.

"Well I don't disagree, miss," Keane said with a thoughtful expression. "But Lord Saltash's curricle being tampered with? And Harold stabbed? I don't reckon a woman would have had the opportunity or the strength for that. Unless she took Harold by surprise, maybe?"

Phoebe gave a huff of frustration. "Oh!" she exclaimed. "This is getting us nowhere. Benedict, for heaven's sake get me a drink too!"

Chapter 20

"O fie, Miss, you must not kiss and tell." - *William Congreve*

Phoebe retraced her steps back to the house. Benedict was supposed to meet her by the river after breakfast but he hadn't shown up. Realising that something must have detained him she headed back towards the house. The lovely summer weather had turned sultry and heavy and the weighty feel of a thunder storm hung in the air like an unspoken threat.

Phoebe had always loved the feeling of calm before a storm hit, enjoying the warm, damp touch of the air, still and gentle and lulling you into believing nothing bad could happen with its lying caress.

She had just passed the chapel and gone through the wrought iron door in the big stone wall that edged this part of the garden when she heard a voice calling to her.

"Hey, cuz!"

She looked around and saw Oliver striding towards her.

"Oh, hello, Oliver," she said, smiling at him but still feeling rather anxious. It was true he was supposed to have been in London when John was murdered, but she was getting so suspicious of everyone that she wouldn't have been the least bit surprised to discover she'd done it herself. "Where did you get to? Have you just arrived?"

"Yes," he nodded. "Had a few things to do in London. Oh, I met a friend of yours I do believe," he said, giving her a wink.

"Really?" she said, looking at him in surprise.

"Oh, yes." He gave her a knowing smile. "A dashing, military type. Went by the name of Captain Dreyton."

"Oh." Phoebe knew she was blushing but she was well aware of what the good Captain might have had to say.

Oliver laughed. "And well you might blush, my girl," he said, shaking his head at her. "He's a broken man. You should have seen his eyes light up when I told him I was going to be seeing you."

"Oh, Oliver!" she exclaimed in horror, staring at him with wide eyes. "Tell me you didn't? You never invited him?"

Oliver just grinned at her for a moment before putting her out of her misery. "No! Of course not. What do you take me for?" he replied tutting at her. "Besides, that's all I need, *more* competition for your affections!"

"Oh do be serious," she said glowering at him. "I never gave Captain Dreyton the least encouragement and I can assure you he needed none. He's a very nice and kind man but ... but ..."

"Dull as ditch water?" Oliver suggested helpfully.

"Yes!" she said with relief. "Oh you do agree then?"

"Absolutely," he said, taking her hand and pulling it through his arm as they walked back to the house. "I bumped into him at Grillon's where I was staying. The place is devilish flat at this time of year. No you're well off without the handsome Captain if you ask me."

Phoebe paused and stared up at him. "Did you say you'd just arrived back?"

"Yes." He nodded at her, his face curious. "I was just walking back from the stables when I saw you coming up past the chapel."

"Oh my." Her stomach did a little flip as she realised he likely hadn't heard about John yet. "Then you don't know?"

She watched carefully as he frowned at her. "Know? Know what?"

Phoebe hesitated. If Oliver had met Captain Dreyton in London that was as solid an alibi as he could wish for; he simply couldn't have killed him. But she watched his reaction closely all the same. "John's been murdered."

The shock in his eyes was only too visible. "Good God," he said. He took a breath and ran a hand that shook a little through his hair. He turned back to her and then took both of her hands, his eyes serious. "You must stay away from Ben, love," he said, his voice urgent. "I know!" he said with considerable heat when she would have spoken. "I know you don't want to hear it but what else are we to think? Don't you see? He's marquess now, when Sylvester dies it will all be his!"

Phoebe bit her lip against the angry retort that came to mind at that but took a breath to moderate her response. She didn't want to give herself away. "I will not believe that Benedict did this, Oliver."

There was a flash of hurt in his expression for a moment but then he sighed. "How is it that people were quite happy to cast me as a murderer but dearest Ben is whiter than white no matter the evidence stacking against him?"

"I assure you that isn't the case," Phoebe replied, her tone cold. "Mr Formby tried to arrest him yesterday and only Sylvester kicking up merry hell was able to see him off. He's said he'll be back though."

A soft and far off rumble of thunder rolled over the landscape, a small threat of trouble to come as the skies darkened and the evening drew in early. They had reached the front of the Court by now and as they entered the front doors it became clear that Mr Formby had indeed returned as raised voices came from the drawing room.

Phoebe saw Miss Pinchbeck opening the door to the room and crossed the hall as fast as she could with Oliver in her wake.

"Look, my Lord," Mr Formby was saying, standing in front of the fireplace with his arms crossed. "I've told you twice now. The only way I can defer arresting you any longer is if you can give me an alibi for the time when Lord Rutland was murdered."

Phoebe blanched as she saw the mutinous look in Benedict's face and the uncompromising set of his jaw. With a sinking feeling she realised it had been when they had been together down by the river. Benedict would never be so unchivalrous as to besmirch her name by allowing people to know they had been alone together all afternoon even if he was to hang for it. Feeling her heart swell at the idea he would implicate himself in a murder before he damaged her reputation, she stepped forward to put Mr Formby straight and give him his alibi.

To her surprise she was stopped in this endeavour by Miss Pinchbeck.

"Mr Formby," she said, her tone cold and imperious as she looked down her nose at the runner. "If you must have it, Lord Rothay was with me. He would never tell you as he seeks to protect my reputation but as we are engaged to be married and the situation is so serious I feel you must know the truth. We went fishing together and didn't return until shortly before dinner. He did not leave my sight all afternoon."

Phoebe knew that both she and Benedict were staring at Miss Pinchbeck in astonishment. It did, however, seem as though Mr Formby was satisfied.

"Well then," he said, a glimmer of curiosity twinkling in his eyes. "That's more like it. Though why we should have had all that go around the houses I don't know." He stared at Miss Pinchbeck, a considering expression on his face and Phoebe wondered if perhaps he wasn't really as convinced as he made out. "Very well then, Lord Rothay, it seems as though you may be in the clear, for this last one at least. Don't go thinking you're off the hook for the first two mind," he said, with a jovial air.

Benedict looked at him with a weary expression. "I wouldn't dream of it," he muttered.

"Very well then." Mr Formby said, picking up his habitual notepad and taking his hat in hand. "I've some more questions for the garden staff so I'll be off and bid you good day, ladies, my Lords."

They watched as he closed the door behind him and Phoebe stared in confusion at Miss Pinchbeck, wondering what on earth she was up to.

"Well, well, Miss Pinchbeck," Oliver said, his tone mocking. "You are full of surprises now aren't you."

Benedict gave Oliver a hard look but did not look back at Phoebe.

"If you would both excuse us," he said, his voice rather cool. "I would like a word with Theodora in private."

"Why of course, old boy," Oliver said, looking back at him with curiosity shining in his eyes. "We quite understand. Come along, Phoebe, let us leave the two love birds to coo alone."

Phoebe gritted her teeth at that but managed to nod and leave the room when Oliver opened the door for her.

Once alone in the hall again, Oliver turned to her, a rather smug look in his eyes. "She's covering for him," he said, sounding triumphant. "I don't doubt the mean-spirited old bird covets the idea of being duchess as much as he does being duke!"

"Oliver!" Phoebe cried in disgust. Though she experienced a prickle of alarm as she realised there was part of that statement she didn't disagree with.

"Oh come now, Phoebe. You can't possibly believe that guff about her being alone with him all afternoon. She barely uses his given name. I doubt she's so much as kissed him on the mouth let alone given him any other liberties! It's too much to believe. She's lying through her teeth, it was clear as the day is long," he added, and then frowned. "Beats me why that Formby fellow didn't see through her though," he added. "I'd thought he was a pretty sharp character."

"Yes," Phoebe replied, realising she'd thought the same. "He did seem to accept it rather easily, but then I don't think he's ever believed Benedict is guilty."

Oliver snorted. "Why doesn't that surprise me?" he said, glowering rather.

"Oh, Oliver," Phoebe exclaimed. "You must see that Benedict is the most honourable of men. Is it any wonder no one can believe it of him?"

"Well that's because they've all forgotten the rakehell he was before his father died!" he retorted. "But I assure you I haven't. Good God there was none wilder than him. Made me look like a milk sop in comparison."

"Benedict?" Phoebe stared at him in surprise. She'd long known that his father's death had changed him but she'd believed he had always been rather a sober kind of man.

"Good Lord, Phoebe. The things he got up to would curl your hair," he said in frustration as the thunder outside became ever more present. "His father's doing of course, egging him on. Almost seemed to take a pride in the devilish larks he'd kick up, not to mention the petticoats he took up with."

"I think that will be quite enough reminiscing," she said, her tone cold and rather prim. "I don't think this is a suitable topic of conversation." Not that she was the least bit concerned by Benedict's past. Her step father had educated her fully enough on all the folly a man could get himself into. But that he was trying yet again to discredit Ben in her eyes did not make her think well of him.

"Now if you will excuse me I am rather tired. I think I shall have a lie down before dinner." With that she left him, fully intending to talk everything through with her maid, Sarah. Because there was too much that simply didn't add up.

***

Benedict stood by the fireplace, his expression serious and his mood dark indeed. No matter that he was grateful to Theodora for stepping in and giving him an alibi, he couldn't help but wish she hadn't. He would never have implicated Phoebe of course and he'd been horribly afraid Phoebe was about to do that herself when Theodora spoke up. Now, however, he was in her debt and any thoughts he may have had about extricating himself from their marriage seemed even less possible than they ever had. So either he would be accused of murder and hang for it, or he'd face a life sentence married to Theodora.

Either way he looked at it he was well and truly trapped.

"What is it, Benedict?" Miss Pinchbeck demanded, sounding cross and irritable. "I have a headache and I would like to rest before dinner."

He looked at her in surprise. Although she was cold and joyless she had never before spoken to him with anything less than perfect politeness.

"I'm grateful to you for what you did, Theodora," he said, wondering just how he should approach this. "Though I wish you had not. There was no need."

"Of course there was a need, you fool," she snapped at him. "That little slut you did spend your afternoon with was about to open her mouth. And if you think I'm going to let people tattle about your sordid affair before we are even married you are quite far and wide of the mark."

Benedict stared at her in shock. Not only at the fact that she knew, but at both the vitriol behind her words and the fact that she had still stood by him, even knowing he'd been with Phoebe.

"How did you know?" he asked.

She snorted, her expression one of disgust. "I went to look for you. Keane said you'd taken a fishing rod with you so it wasn't hard to narrow down where to look for you. I saw both of you lying on the ground together like two common peasants."

He scowled at that but he had to allow her to be angry after all. He had been unfaithful and broken their vow before they'd even wed. It was no wonder she was angry. "Theodora," he said, wondering how to proceed but thinking that maybe this was a blessing in disguise. Time to make a clean breast of things. "I'm very sorry to have hurt you and ... and gone behind your back. You don't need to tell me it was a despicable thing to have done, I know it was. But we should never have got engaged. You must see we are not well suited and ... the truth is that I'm in love with Phoebe. I don't understand how or why as she seems to delight in infuriating me but it's true. I think it would be best for both of us if we parted. I would only make you unhappy, for I will never live up to your high expectations."

He looked back at her, waiting for her reaction. Expecting fury, tears, recriminations ... anything. But her face was perfectly composed and as cool as the marble beauty he had once compared her to.

"No," she said, as the room lit with lighting as the storm drew ever closer. She smiled at him, though it was not in any way a pleasant expression. "I don't care what you get up to with that whore or any other. I have no interest in it. Men are feeble creatures, always at the beck and call of their baser instincts and I expected nothing else from you. If, however, you think I am going to walk away from our marriage now, you are very much mistaken. We will marry, my Lord. For if you do not I will sue you for breach of promise, and you may be very sure that I will be vocal about your dear Phoebe's part in the breaking of our contract."

Benedict stared at her in horror, a cold, clammy feeling prickling over his skin.

"Now, then. I don't have any more time to waste on such foolishness, so I will see you at dinner." And with an imperious sweep of her skirts she left the room and Benedict with a sense of growing doom.

Chapter 21

If thou wilt leave me, do not leave me last,
When other petty griefs have done their spite
But in the onset come; so shall I taste
At first the very worst of fortune's might,
And other strains of woe, which now seem woe,
Compared with loss of thee will not seem so. - Shakespeare

Phoebe sat staring at her reflection in the looking glass as Sarah brushed her hair. The storm was still rumbling around with a threatening air outside but as yet it hadn't come to anything more than a bit of noise and the odd flash of lightning. She wished now it would just hurry up and break as the air had become oppressive and she felt she couldn't draw a breath at all.

"Now, now, my lamb," Sarah chided, her tone gentle as her hand swept the brush with soothing strokes over Phoebe's thick blonde hair. "There's not the least bit of good you falling into the dismals and well you know it."

Sighing, Phoebe put her head in her hands. "I know, Sarah, but what am I to do? That wretched woman will never give him up now, you mark my words," she cried feeling despair creeping up on her. "She's on her way to being a duchess and she cared nothing for him in the first place."

Sarah leaned down and gave her a hug but her eyes were sad as she looked at Phoebe in the mirror. "I warned you no good would come of this, little Bee," she said, sounding as though her heart ached for Phoebe. "And now look, both of you breaking your hearts and neither of you any closer to being together. You should have let him be, love."

"No!" Phoebe objected, hot tears prickling behind her eyes. "If I had, he'd have spent his whole life ignoring the beauty to be found in the world, never seeing the love that his family have for him, the joy to be found in their company if he'd just stop disapproving of them for a moment. At least now he's remembered what it is to live and to love. That has to be worth something doesn't it?"

She looked up at Sarah with pleading in her eyes.

"Aye, my little Bee, but is it worth your heart?"

Phoebe shrugged. "I know what it feels like now, Sarah. I know that he's the only man I'll ever feel this way for. I can't regret it, no matter how it hurts." She took a deep breath and sat up straight, brushing away her tears with irritation. "But I'm not done yet," she added.

"Oh Lordy," Sarah muttered, putting the brush aside and screwing up the fischu Phoebe had just discarded in agitation. "Whatever are you thinking of now?"

Phoebe pursed her lips. "Probably best you don't know, Sarah dear," she said with a sympathetic smile. "But the thing that's worrying me most is that we still don't know who the murderer is."

"Well there's nothing changed there," Sarah said in disgust. The poor woman sat down on the bed with a sob of distress. "I'll say it again, love, you should leave and go back to London. I can't believe I got you through a war safe and sound and the moment we set foot back in England you're embroiled in a murder!"

"Well it's not like I planned it!" Phoebe replied with indignation, but on seeing Sarah's distress she relented and moved to sit beside her. "The thing is, Sarah, we know that Benedict is innocent, and that means that the real murderer is still out there and ... Ben is next in line now. So far three men have died and ... each one of them was the next in line to the dukedom."

Sarah's face paled as she realised what Phoebe was saying. "Oh, my Lord, you think he's next!"

Phoebe swallowed, her throat tight with worry. "I'm sure of it."

She watched as Sarah's eyes grew wide and round with fear as she realised something else. "Oh, gracious heavens, you think you're going to save him!"

Her maid's face settled into something harder, a look that Phoebe recognised as capable of reducing grown men to gibbering. "Something needs to be done, my girl," Sarah said, her tone dark and forbidding. "But not by you," she added, eyes flashing with determination. "You swear to me you'll stay out of it!"

It took Phoebe a full hour to calm Sarah and get her to go to bed with promises that she wouldn't do anything rash. Though they both knew she had no intention of keeping those promises.

She sat and read to while away the time until the house fell quiet and everyone was asleep but found herself rereading the same page over and again and still not taking it in. Finally, however, she thought it was safe enough for her to leave her room.

Taking a candle in hand she opened her door as quietly as she could manage and tiptoed out into the corridor. She had barely gone two steps when the storm finally decided it was time to make itself felt and a sharp crack of lightning lit the corridor as the skies split with white light. Phoebe paused, hardly daring to breathe as she waited for the thunder to follow but it was still a little way off yet, though it grew closer, louder.

Running on silent feet she flew down the corridor and found Benedict's door.

Taking the hair pin she had brought to unpick the lock - it was amazing the useful tricks the men of her father's regiment had taught her over the years - she bent to open it and frowned as she found it was already unlocked.

It was perhaps possible that Ben was still downstairs in the library she supposed, but she ought to check his room first. If he was here, she would scold him soundly. A murderer was on the loose and Ben the next target. Locking his damn door was the least he could do!

She opened it with care, thankful to Lizzie for keeping the staff on their toes and the hinges well-oiled as it opened without a murmur.

Stepping inside she closed it with equal stealth and was about to move forwards when another crack of lightening illuminated the room to show a figure approaching the bed, knife in hand.

"Ben!" she cried and dropped the candle in her haste to get to the bed. It snuffed out and the lightning was gone, plunging them into darkness. She heard the sound of a scuffle and a groan of pain as a fist connected with flesh and the next flash of lightening showed two figures grappling and stumbling towards the balcony. Stifling the urge to scream and panic, Phoebe groped about for a weapon and found the silver candle stick. She ran forward with it held aloft and prayed for another flash of lightening to be able to identify the intruder but none came. A crash sounded, the jolt of a heavy body falling and she stumbled over someone laying prone on the floor. Drawing a breath she went to scream but a hand covered her mouth.

"It's me," Ben hissed and her heart almost burst with relief. She watched his shadowy figure as he jumped to his feet and they both ran to look over the balcony but there was nothing to be seen. Whoever it had been had escaped. But now the rain had begun, lashing against the building whilst lightening crazed the angry skies.

"Ben!" Phoebe cried, throwing her arms around him. "Oh, Ben, are you hurt?"

"I'm fine, love, I'm fine, hush now," he said, pulling her inside and out of the rain. He forced the doors shut as the wind howled past and fought to smash them open again, and the next moment the great house was quiet apart from the storm that boiled around it.

"Did you see anything?" he demanded as he lit the candles by the bed. "Did you see who it was?"

"No," she replied, shaking her head and wrapping her arms about herself and beginning to tremble as fear and cold made themselves known. "A man, *I think* from the little I saw but ... I can't even be sure of that. You saw nothing?"

Benedict shook his head, his expression blank. "No. Nothing and I'd say it was a man, though they were more slippery than strong."

"You hit him?"

Ben nodded. "Yes, to the stomach, nothing that would show but I'll wager it hurt."

Phoebe stood shivering, the gauzy material of her dressing gown sodden and clinging to her like a second skin.

"You're freezing," Ben muttered, averting his eyes as he crossed back to the bed and went to pull the bedspread off to wrap around her.

By the time he turned around, however, Phoebe had discarded the gown and it lie around her feet in disarray.

***

Ben sucked in a breath as the candle light illuminated her perfect form in soft golden curves and valleys. He was in turmoil, his nerves shot and his senses all on alert, and now Phoebe stood in front of him like temptation incarnate.

"What ..." he began, but the words wouldn't seem to come. He was too stunned.

Someone had tried to kill him.

But more than that, *worse* than that ... he and Phoebe could never be. He remembered the disastrous conversation with Theodora earlier and knew that they could never be together. "Phoebe," he began again. "I hardly think this is the time ..."

Phoebe ran to him and wrapped her arms around his neck, her body at once warm and chilled by the rain. Her damp skin pressed against his bare chest as desire exploded to life beneath his flesh.

"You nearly died," she wept, clinging to him. "If I hadn't come, you could have died and I would have never known what it meant to be loved by you. It's exactly the right time, Ben. Don't you see? I don't care about what comes next. If you were to die, I wouldn't care what else there was to come for everything I love most in the world would be gone. What will be, will be," she said, the pleading in her expression only too visible. "For better or for worse, Ben. No matter if we have spoken the vows in church. I love you, you alone and forsaking all others. And I want you. Now. Tonight. Even if it is the only time we ever have."

"Phoebe," he whispered, his heart so full of love and misery that he hardly knew what he felt. "Love, she'll never let me go. She'd drag both of our names through the dirt before she gave me up."

"Then let her!" Phoebe cried and he watched in dismay as quick tears rolled down her lovely face, those big blue eyes filled with misery. "I don't care, Ben. Let them say what they like about us, we'll go away and be together and none of it will matter."

"And what about mother, and Cecily, and the twins and Jessamy? They'll all be tainted by the scandal, love. The girls will never find a decent man to take them and they'll have to live with the gossip and the whispers." He felt his heart break as she sobbed and laid her head against his chest. "I'd do anything for you, Phoebe. I don't care for myself but I can't destroy their lives along with my own. Not even for you."

Phoebe nodded, though she didn't look up at him. "I know," she mumbled, her voice unsteady. "I know you wouldn't. You're too good, too honourable. I'm sorry."

Ben sighed and wondered why life was so determined to break him. Wasn't his father's disaster enough for him to have dragged them all through? Why did the fates keep punishing him? What had he done to deserve such treatment?

"Don't be sorry," he replied, his voice rough as he tilted her head up to look at him. He realised too late that this was a mistake. There was such love and desire in her eyes, her lips a little parted to receive his kiss as she reached up on tiptoe for him. He was lost, too angry with the world, too miserable that he had made such a mess of everything to consider that this could surely only make things worse.

They didn't seem worse as his mouth met hers. For the first time in longer than he could remember everything seemed to make perfect sense. He loved this woman. He loved her to distraction, beyond sense and rationality and what he ought to do. There was only here and now and Phoebe in his arms. For now at least, everything else could go to the devil.

"Take me to bed, Ben," she murmured as he released her mouth to trail his lips down the elegant column of her neck. "You promised. You promised you would."

"Yes, love," he murmured. "Yes I did." Lifting her into his arms he moved to the bed and placed her gently on the mattress before divesting himself of the now sodden drawers he'd fallen into bed in. He'd drunk too much tonight. Too full of misery to sleep without the help of a fair amount of brandy, but now he felt none of it. He was sober and awake and he'd never felt more alive than he did in this moment.

He smiled as Phoebe's eyes roved over him with an appreciative air. His Phoebe, so brave and bold and fearless, more than he'd ever been. Though he was going to change that. He would find a way for them. A way to be together without hurting the people they cared for.

She lay back on the pillows, her blonde hair tangling into curls, the tresses damp and darker than usual, old gold in the light of the candles.

"You take my breath away," he whispered, reaching out to touch her face.

She smiled and turned towards his hand, raising her own to press his hand closer, her lips, warm and soft, touched his palm. He knelt over her, feeling her hands on his waist, moving to his back, pulling him closer as he dipped his head and kissed her again.

Her mouth was a revelation, sweeter than anything he'd ever tasted, silken and warm and so desperately inviting. He pulled back, reluctant to leave but eager to taste everything she offered him. Nuzzling her neck he moved lower as she sighed, her fingers tangling in his hair as he found her breast. She sighed deeper and arched towards him as his mouth closed over her, teasing the tight bud of her nipple as it grew taut beneath his tongue.

The sighs and the soft noises she made were a delight and a torment, driving him on, demanding he hurry and linger at one and the same time.

He moved farther down the bed, pausing for just a moment to return to her mouth and steal another kiss from lips that were rosy from kissing already.

If she was shocked by the path he was taking, she made no demur, her limbs pliant for him, her eyes full of curiosity and such trust that he thought his heart would break.

"I'm so in love with you," he whispered against her skin. The words came out harsh with fear and wonder as the feeling swept over him all over again. Such power that feeling brought, the force of it made him feel strong enough to conquer the world, and yet totally helpless against it. There was no denying it, no pretending it wasn't so ... He was hers, heart, body and soul till his days were done.

"Ben," she gasped, arching beneath him as his tongue found her most delicate skin, hidden beneath the sweet, blonde triangle of curls. He liked the sound of his name spoken like that. She sounded breathless and on edge and desperate for him. There could never be enough of that sound, he thought as he settled to pleasure her, determined to make her cry it out louder while the storm still raged around them.

She seemed quite happy to give him what he wanted, her cries increasingly breathless and ragged as he tormented the tiny peak of her sex until she was clutching at the bedclothes, her body taut with need as her own storm broke over her, his name as powerful as the thunder that shook the world as she came for him - shattering beneath him and lying boneless and sated, dark-eyed with reverence.

Chapter 22

Or scorn, or pity on me take,
I must the true relation make,
I'm undone to-night:
Love in a subtle dream disguised,
hath both my heart and me surprised, - Ben Johnson

Phoebe came back to herself and found she was laughing. She wasn't quite sure why, but it was perfectly wonderful. Ben stared down at her with amusement and such love in his eyes that it only made it more deliciously absurd and she pulled him to her, murmuring his name and wishing the night would never end.

The storm outside raged on with ever more fury, and yet it seemed a friendly thing to her now. The thunder that crashed outside and the lightning that split the skies so ferociously seemed to rage for them, to scream against the unfairness of it all while they were left with one, perfect night in a desperately imperfect world.

Ben pulled her into his arms and she relished the weight and warmth of his body as he settled over her. She gasped as his body slid against the slick skin between her legs and he captured her open mouth as his hands moved over her, both reverent and demanding. As he moved her legs further apart with his knees, she complied happily, needing what came next, wanting to join herself to him in any way possible.

This was their promise to each other, she knew that. He was too good, too honourable and he would never take her unless he was committed to their future, to finding a way past the madness and the unfairness of life to a place where love could win, and not only survive but prosper.

Perhaps they'd fail, perhaps Theodora would win in the end and she would take his name, but she would never have this. She would never have *him*, his heart, his soul. That was hers and hers alone and she would hold on to it with everything she had.

She drew in a breath as he pushed into her just a little, the feeling both incredible and overpowering.

"Hush," he murmured, growing still as his breath fluttered over her, hot against her skin. "Relax," he said as he stroked his hand over her thigh, up her side, "Oh, God, love," he groaned and he took his weight from her, raising himself on his arms. "You feel so good. I want to be inside you so much."

"Don't stop then", she muttered, smiling as he huffed out a breath of laughter.

"Trying to be gentle," he gasped as he eased into her a little more.

The sensation of fullness was incredible, almost too much as her skin began to protest a little and she experienced a tremor of doubt. But then he moved, harder and deeper and so fast that there was no time to do anything but exclaim and cling to him.

"Sorry," he whispered, kissing her shoulder. "I'm sorry."

But she wasn't sorry as he continued to move, joining them together with an intimacy so profound that she couldn't imagine how men threw this away on any woman who came their way. It was too precious for such careless behaviour.

Any further thoughts, profound or otherwise were lost to her after that. She'd become all instinct, a bundle of nerves and sensations that were lost to the pleasure of him as the feelings heightened and grew. There was nothing but this. They'd become deaf to the world outside, too lost to the gathering storm they were building themselves to pay any heed to lightening that lit the room like daylight, or thunder that shook the old building to its foundations.

Phoebe just held on as the feeling grew and pulled her further in, trusting her own instincts and the man who murmured endearments as his voice became ever more ragged. She gasped as he cried out, calling her name as they clung together and she followed him blindly into the pulsing heart of pleasure.

It took a little while for her to come back to herself, too pleased and lost in the sated, heavy-limbed languor of the afterglow to want to return to the real world. But Ben was there so she forced her eyes open, smiling with a sigh of deep contentment at the anxiety in his eyes.

"Lovely," she murmured, blinking up at him as he drew in a breath and then shook his head, laughing slightly. "What?" she asked, trying to focus and wondering what she'd said now.

"Nothing at all," he whispered, kissing her forehead. "Only that I can't be without you now, my dearest love. I can't bear the thought of it." He sighed and rested his head against hers. "Whatever shall we do? Oh God, Phoebe, I can't bear it."

Phoebe reached up and stroked his face, not knowing the answer any more than he did. "We'll find a way, Ben. We will because we must."

He nodded and turned her in his arms, pulling her back to his chest and wrapping his arms around her. "Sleep now, love," he whispered. "I'll wake you early enough to go to your room."

She felt the touch of his lips to her shoulder and was too warm and pleasantly tired for even such troubling thoughts to keep her from sleep. So she let herself drift, content to be here at last, in his arms, where she belonged.

***

Ben watched the first lightening of the skies behind the curtains, the stillness of the coming morning almost overwhelming after the fierce storms of the night.

Glancing down he watched the light illuminate the sleeping woman in his arms and felt his heart catch. Oh God, what had he done?

And yet he found it hard to regret any of it. He'd had lovers aplenty in his time, though they'd been guilt-ridden, speedy couplings in recent years. Once he had gloried in the decadent side of life, but after his father died, he only returned briefly to his old haunts as a matter of desperation. When the need to feel another's touch was too much to be fought any longer, he'd retrace the paths he had followed so gleefully in his youth. But now he always left feeling guilty and shamefaced.

He didn't feel that now. He couldn't. Being with Phoebe, with a woman he loved with his whole heart was a revelation so stunning that he didn't know how to process it. He only knew that if his actions should ever cause her harm he would despise himself.

Terror wound itself round his heart like a briar and it pulled tight as he realised she could even now be carrying his child, and there he was with his first foot on the scaffold. But surely now Formby would believe him? He would believe that someone had come to his room last night with the intention of murdering him? Though he would have to convince Phoebe to keep her mouth shut. He knew only too well she would allow her own character to be destroyed in order to save him.

It was both a horrifying and heart-warming thought.

She stirred in his arms and he smiled down at her, watching with an ache in his chest as she blinked up at him, still sleepy and hazy yet.

"Good morning," he murmured, kissing her nose and making her smile as she wound her arms around his neck. Oh, how he wanted this, wanted it to keep, forever.

She didn't answer but sighed and buried into his neck, clinging to him and making desire burn all over again. Knowing it was madness but knowing too he was powerless against this press of emotion filling his chest, he allowed her to pull him back to her.

They fitted together so flawlessly, the slide of his flesh against hers an exquisite creation, sublime in its perfection.

"Yes," she murmured, her hands gliding down his back. "Oh, yes please."

Even if time had been on their side, he'd have been hard-pressed to fight the tide of desire that swept over him. The pleasure of being inside her became too irresistible to deny as the climax pulled him down.

He muffled his cries, his face pressed into her hair as she gasped and clutched at him, too aware now of the precariousness of her being here.

Looking down at her as the ecstasy left her eyes darkened and lazy he wished they could stay here all morning, all day, forever. But none of those things were possible.

"It kills me to say it, love, but you have to go back to your room."

She nodded, her eyes growing sad now and he hated himself for it. "One day," she said, her voice firm and full of confidence as though she had heard his unspoken wish. "One day we will stay in bed all day and scandalise the staff. Perhaps we'll even send them away for a week and never get up at all," she added, grinning at him.

He laughed, admiring the spirit and determination that had once terrified him so badly. For he had known even then that she would set his world on its head. He hadn't realised, though, how desperately grateful he would be for it.

"We must speak to Mr Formby," she said as he forced himself to leave the comfort of her arms and get out of bed.

"We will do nothing of the kind," he replied, his voice brooking no argument, though he knew the idea that she would heed that was a forlorn hope indeed.

"Oh, Ben," she exclaimed, though she kept her voice low. "Do you really think my reputation matters when your life is in danger."

"Yes!" he replied, trying to tamp down on the fury that she could possibly believe otherwise. "I will see Formby and explain it all. But there is no need to say you were here."

"But of course there is!" she persisted, sliding out of bed and going to pick up her dressing gown from the damp pile she'd left it in last night. "How much more convincing if we both saw him ... or her!" The sight of her bare bottom as she reached down to pick it up from the floor was so distracting he almost forgot to remonstrate with her.

"W-what ...? *No!"* he said in a rush, pulling his shirt over his head and regretting the sight that met him as he emerged, her lovely figure disappearing beneath the delicate material of her dressing gown.

She shivered as the damp gauze covered her skin and then scowled at him. "Ben, for heaven's sake, don't be foolish," she said, sounding truly irritated. "I won't let your manly pride send you to the scaffold *or* get you murdered!" Frustrated on too many counts his temper was too near the surface for such a tone.

"Damn it, Phoebe! Just once will you do as you're told!" he exploded, glaring at her as she stalked towards him.

"You really haven't learnt much have you?" she said with a snort of disgust before kissing him on the mouth and heading for the door.

"Wait!" he hissed, fighting with one foot in his trousers to dress and follow her at the same time but he stumbled and ended up sitting heavily on the bed. Phoebe just paused in the doorway and grinned at him, blowing him a kiss.

"I love you," she whispered with a saucy wink, before slipping out through the door and away from any further argument.

Benedict cursed and then stifled a bark of laughter. “Well damn,” he muttered. God save him from independent, stubborn, infuriating, heart-stealing females.

Chapter 23

A thing of beauty is a joy for ever:
Its loveliness increases; it will never
Pass into nothingness; but still will keep
A bower quiet for us, and a sleep
Full of sweet dreams, and health, and quiet breathing. - Keats

By the time his valet reached him, Ben was already dressed and shaved and only needed the man's help to ease his perfectly cut coat over his shoulders. Ignoring murmurs of reproach from his employee that his help had not been required, Ben left the man to sulk in private and went downstairs.

He slipped past the breakfast parlour, resisting with great difficulty the urge to see if Phoebe was down yet. He had to see Mr Formby and fast before the wretched woman could go and shred her own reputation with such a gleeful want of care.

He waited, tapping his boot with frustration as his horse was saddled, and he set off for the village where he knew Mr Formby was installed at the local inn.

So it was with feelings of deep foreboding that he saw one of Sylvester's carriages waiting outside The King's Arms and felt the weight of the narrow-eyed scowl from Phoebe's maid as he walked past.

Damn and blast the woman!

He paused in the doorway to see Mr Formby laughing with obvious delight at something the wretched creature had said while she poured him a cup of tea.

"Ben!" she exclaimed, smiling at him with such pleasure he wanted to shake her. "There you see, Mr Formby, I told you he'd get here eventually," she added, casting Ben a look of pure devilry.

"Whatever she's said it's a damned lie," he raged, closing the door and stalking over to glower down at Mr Formby.

The man raised an eyebrow at him and Ben cursed, knowing it was impossible. He sat down at the table opposite her, scowling with fury.

"The devil take it, Phoebe!" he muttered, throwing his hat and gloves on the table with frustration. "You'll be the death of me long before any jury can convict me."

"There, there," she murmured with the tone of an adult soothing an overexcited child. "Drink your tea," she added, sliding a cup and saucer towards him. "You'll feel much more the thing after you've had that." She turned back to Mr Formby with a reassuring smile. "He's dreadfully grouchy if he doesn't get his breakfast you know," she added in a confiding undertone to the man, whose eyes glittered with amusement much to Benedict's irritation.

"What have you told him?" Benedict demanded, ignoring the tea and the plate of bread and butter that Phoebe put in front of him.

"Why everything, darling, as one should with an officer of the law," she replied, her big blue eyes wide and guileless.

Ben groaned.

"Come, come, my Lord," Mr Formby said, his eyes surprisingly warm and understanding. "I can well see you've got your hands full with this young woman and I would like nothing more than to wish you both very happy," he added, winking at Phoebe who beamed at him. He nodded and reached for the ubiquitous pencil and notepad as he spoke. "So why don't you just trust me and I promise I'll do everything I can to keep you out of trouble, young man," he said, his voice rather stern. "Though right at this moment it beats me how we're to do it, for of course you won't want this young lady's testimony to save you!"

"Indeed not!" Benedict replied in horror, feeling quite nauseated at the very idea of it.

"Well really," Phoebe exclaimed in annoyance, looking between the two men with a frown.

"Now then, you dreadful creature," Mr Formby said, grinning at her and wagging his pencil in her direction. "If it comes to a decision between his neck and your honour I swear you'll testify," he added, ignoring Ben's explosion of fury. "But let's concentrate on figuring out who the devil is causing this mess first, eh?"

"Very well," Phoebe replied, apparently mollified.

Benedict allowed his temper to cool, with some difficulty, and together they tried to collate the pieces of information to date.

"Are you sure there is no other reason for anyone to have a grudge against the family?" Mr Formby pressed and Benedict sighed, having heard this question too many times to count now.

"None," he replied in irritation.

"Oh, Ben!" Phoebe replied with a snort of disgust. "Don't be ridiculous, of course there is."

Benedict opened his mouth to reply but wasn't allowed the opportunity.

"There was a boundary dispute with a Lord Ormsley," she said, raising one finger as if to keep a count. "That got very heated and I believe there was a duel, oh ... must be over a hundred years ago now, but you know how these feuds keep running through the generations. Then there's a mad cousin of Sylvester's, despises him by all accounts and is always writing threatening letters predicting doom. Though he's been doing it for more than fifty years now so I can't believe he's suddenly decided to act upon it. Gracious, the fellow must be at least as old as Sylvester himself!" she exclaimed with a shake of her head that made her ringlets dance about her face in a rather enchanting fashion. She raised a third finger. "Then there was the husband of Lady Bradford, she had an affair with Sylvester you see," she said, lowering her voice a little further. "Well no one knew until after she died a couple of years ago ..."

Ben listened to a further litany of family iniquities, torn between chagrin and laughter as Phoebe ticked each one off on her fingers.

"And then of course, there is the nose," she added with a frown.

"What?" Mr Formby and Benedict said in unison.

"The nose," she replied, waving her hand at Benedict's visage as if this explained everything. "Well you must see how Sylvester and Ben have the same nose. John did too and I'm told Anthony as well though I never saw him."

"What the devil are you on about now, love?" Benedict demanded in frustration.

Phoebe blinked at him, looking annoyed at his apparent stupidity. "Well that's a very common nose in these parts," she replied with an expressive lift of one eyebrow.

"Oh," Mr Formby replied, giving Benedict a dark look.

"Well it's none of my doing!" Benedict retorted, looking horrified.

"Well, perhaps, dear," Phoebe said, looking a little sceptical. "But can you be certain? I mean, you *were* rather wild in your younger days I hear?"

If it hadn't been for the twinkle in her eyes, he might have walked away in fury. As it was he glared back at her and made himself the promise that she would pay dearly for that remark.

"Well, as interesting as this dissection of mine and my family's characters has been," Benedict replied with an acerbic tone. "I don't see that it's getting us anywhere."

"Well then," Mr Formby said, scratching at his chin. "After you I believe your youngest brother is in line for the title?"

Benedict nodded, feeling a stab of fear at the idea of anyone hurting his little brother.

"Then I think it wise if you are very vigilant for the foreseeable future," Formby replied, his expression grave. "Whoever is responsible for these killings will clearly stop at nothing to get what they want. I doubt if an eleven-year-old boy will stand in their way. Likely that would be rather easier than bumping you off for someone with no conscience."

He watched Phoebe shudder visibly and could only echo her revulsion. His stomach twisted at the idea that someone he knew, maybe even cared for, was responsible for all that had passed.

"Have you any further information to share with us?" Phoebe asked Mr Formby with a smile calculated to twist any man around her finger - the devil.

Formby, who by now had Phoebe's measure, just smiled at her. "Sadly I really don't. Lord Rutland was poisoned as we'd supposed but how or what exactly is not known. Though I am told it would have worked quickly after he ingested the poison."

"And what of Oliver?" she demanded. Benedict frowned. He knew something had happened to put Phoebe on her guard around Oliver though he wasn't entirely sorry for that. He was, however, sceptical that Oliver could be responsible for such reprehensible crimes. He'd known the man since they were born and they'd been childhood friends. He had never detected anything cruel or vindictive in his nature before. Indeed at one time they'd been as close as brothers. The idea that Oliver could seriously consider hurting him or Jessamy ... No. He refused to believe it.

Mr Formby shrugged. "I'm waiting for his alibi to be confirmed but it sounds water tight to me I have to say."

"Unless he had an accomplice," Phoebe added, one eyebrow raised. Well she was determined, Ben thought with an inward smile of pride. You had to give her that.

Formby, who was chewing the end of his pencil in a contemplative manner chuckled. “Sharp, ain’t she?” he asked Ben, his eyes twinkling.

“You have no idea,” Ben replied, casting her a wry look of amusement.

“It’s certainly an angle that needs considering,” Formby replied, sticking the abused pencil behind his ear for safekeeping.

“I did have another thought,” Ben offered and Formby gestured for him to carry on. “Well, I still don’t think Oliver is your man,” he replied, sighing as Phoebe rolled her eyes at him in annoyance. “And so, if not him you must start looking at the next branch of the family, yes?” He watched the runner nod and flick through the pages of his notebook. “Your cousin I believe? A Mr. Charles Grantham.”

Benedict nodded, leaning forward over the table. “Sylvester’s father and his aunt, his father’s sister, had a grave falling out and he never spoke to her again. Whatever the rift was it never healed and they refused to have anything to do with Sylvester even after his father died. It occurs to me there could well be resentment there. The last I heard the man had done well in the city but ...”

“But that’s not the same as having a dukedom is it, my Lord?” Formby replied, a sardonic lift to his mouth.

Ben snorted but shook his head. “I imagine not.”

“Well I have a colleague tracking down Grantham as we speak so we’ll see where that line of enquiry leads us,” Formby said, tucking his notebook away and signalling the end of the interview. He shook Benedict’s hand, his expression grave.

“Now you do as you’re bid and have a care, my Lord. I’d be sorry to see you laid out as the next victim or marching up the steps at Tyburn so don’t go doing anything rash and stay where everyone can see you at all times.”

Wondering how exactly he was supposed to achieve that Ben kept his own council but thanked Formby for his concern before the man left them alone.

"Well then, you wretch," he said to Phoebe with a sigh of frustration. "If you think you've meddled enough for one day, we'd best get back for lunch."

"Yes, Ben," Phoebe said, her tone meek and blinking at him with a guileless expression.

Now having a rather deeper understanding of the lady's character ... it didn't fool him for a moment.

***

"Glad to see you, my boy," Sylvester said, smiling at him as entered the old man's room. He'd not been down today and Benedict could see he was tired. All the stress and upset was taking its toll on him. Benedict felt a sudden rush of fury for whoever was hurting his elderly uncle. He should be enjoying this time, having the family here around him and someone was spoiling what may well be one of the old fellow's last summers.

"Good to see you too, Sir," Ben said, giving his proffered hand a warm squeeze.

"That Formby fellow not been bothering you again has he?" Sylvester demanded, a forbidding look that boded ill glinting in his deep green eyes.

"No," Benedict rushed to assure him. "No. The fellow's been mighty decent in fact. He believes I'm innocent at all events, even if he can't prove it."

"Prove it?" Sylvester barked, slapping the arm of his chair and sounding utterly incredulous. "I say it's so! My word should be enough. Don't know what things are coming to," he grumbled, shaking his head. "Times are changing, and not for the better," he added, waving a finger at Benedict. "When the time comes for you to take my mantle there'll be precious little good in having it. Nothing but a damned lot of work and bother," he said with a huff.

"Well then," Benedict said, trying to keep his laughter in check. "If it's all the same to you, you'd best keep it as long as possible."

Sylvester snorted and looked at Ben with affection. "Don't sweat, lad," he said, chuckling at the idea. "I'm not about to fall off my twig yet, no matter what anyone else thinks. I'll keep you waiting a while yet." He fell silent for a moment, apparently contemplating something and then he favoured Benedict with one of those steely, green-eyed looks that reminded Ben that his uncle could be a ruthless man.

"I oughtn't say it I know, but I'm damned glad you'll inherit, Ben. Never could stand my own lads. No honour among 'em," he said with clear annoyance. "Always trying to get one over on the other or blame their own troubles on each other. Their sons were no better. Lizzie's the only one worth a damn. Good girl she is," he said in approval. "But my boys." He sighed, shaking his head, his arthritic fingers plucking at the velvet covering of the chair with a distracted air.

"My fault of course. Never spent enough time with them when they were boys, always too busy, too concerned with my own affairs. Regret it now ... still," he added, sounding rather melancholy. "Water under the bridge now." He looked up at Ben, affection in his expression. "Don't make the same mistake, lad. Marry that Phoebe, not that Pinchpenny creature for starters. Not an ounce of good in that fiancée of yours I tell you straight. Phoebe, she's the one. You marry her, my lad. She'll give you many a sleepless night I don't doubt but she's fierce and loyal to my mind ... and she'll give you fine sons I reckon," he added with a wink. "And you make sure you get to know them. Give them your time while you can. Turn out anything like you and you'll be proud I know."

Benedict took a breath and smiled. He was more than touched by his uncle's words and he only wished it was as simple as Sylvester seemed to think.

"I want to marry Phoebe, Sylvester. I'd do anything to be able to, but Theodora ... she's made it quite plain she's unwilling to give up on our betrothal. She'll drag our names through the mud before I'm free of her."

"So she says!" Sylvester barked, turning purple with rage. "I don't believe a word of it. For all the mud she could sling you could give it back ..." he frowned at Benedict and then sighed. "Though I suppose you wouldn't," he grumbled. "Well let her anyway. You'll be a duke soon enough, dammit. God knows everyone in the damned line has had a scandal somewhere along the way. One thing about the title, people's memories tend to be a bit hazier when there's the power of a dukedom to be remembered. It's not like anyone would dare shun you is it, nor any of your close kin. Tell her to do her worst, lad. Call her bluff."

"But Cecily, the twins ..."

An outrageous noise of ridicule followed this half spoken fear. "By God, you think the kind of dowry you could bequeath them with now will not be enough to dangle for a decent husband, let alone their own charms. Fine looking girl that Cecily, like her mother," he said with clear approval. "And the twins are showing fair too, they'll have no problems finding a match."

Benedict frowned at the old man as hope flickered to life. "But you wouldn't care? The scandal, the gossip?"

Sylvester made a noise of disgust. "Don't be so hen-hearted, Ben. You want Phoebe, you've got to take the chances to get her. What does she say about it?"

"The exact same as you," Benedict said with a rueful sigh.

"There you are then," Sylvester nodded, as though it was all settled.

"But her reputation," Benedict objected, thinking about how bad it could get. "The things people will say about her!"

"She can stay here with me until it all blows over. Be sooner than you think I reckon, and once she's a duchess, no one would dare breathe a word. If she's brave enough to face it, you should be brave enough to stand by her."

Benedict spluttered with outrage. "You surely can't believe that I lack the courage," he exclaimed, hurt by the implication. "I'm trying to protect her!"

"Oh yes," Sylvester said, his tone dry. "By making her your mistress? Or by waiting until Miss Pinchbeck turns up her toes so you can marry her when you're both in your dotage. I'm sure that will make her very happy."

Benedict fell silent, struck by the force of his uncle's argument.

"That's right, my boy." Sylvester grinned at him and reached out to pat his hand. "Took a while, but we got there in the end, eh?"

Benedict snorted and shook his head. "Yes, uncle."

Chapter 24

We are the clouds that veil the midnight moon;
How restlessly they speed, and gleam, and quiver,
Streaking the darkness radiantly!–yet soon
Night closes round, and they are lost forever - Shelley

Phoebe had just come in from walking the gardens with Lady Rothay when she met Oliver exiting the drawing room. His face was ashen and he looked rather unwell.

"Phoebe," he said, his face relaxing a little. "A friendly face," he added with a sigh of relief.

"Why do you say that?" she asked, taking off her bonnet and giving him a curious look.

Oliver jerked his head in the direction of the drawing room and grimaced. "Mr Formby," he said, his voice tight with anxiety. "Seems to be of the opinion I have an accomplice!"

"Oh," Phoebe exclaimed and tried to infuse her expression with one of complete innocence and sympathy. She assumed she succeeded as he took a step closer.

"Come into the library and have a drink with me before dinner," he asked, his tone rather pleading. "I'm dashed tired and I can't face the mob without a snifter to keep my spirits up."

Phoebe squashed a tremor of alarm. Whether or not he was guilty of any crime she didn't trust Oliver as far as she could throw him, not now. But she didn't believe he meant her any harm. Miss Pinchbeck's disapproving expression floated to mind and made up her own.

"Lead on then," she said with a merry smile. "If you slip me a brandy in a sherry glass I shan't complain you know."

Oliver laughed, delighted. "That's the spirit! I say but you do chase the clouds away, Phoebe. Never fail but to cheer me up."

She smiled at him in thanks for the compliment and followed him into the library. He was quiet while he fixed them both drinks and she thought he seemed nervous all of a sudden. This was borne out when he next spoke.

"Actually, I ... I've been wanting to speak to you alone," he said, his blue eyes giving her a warm if slightly anxious look.

"Oh?" Phoebe replied with a sinking feeling and sipping her brandy as alarm bells began to ring.

"Yes," he said, downing his drink and pouring another one. "The truth is I'm sick of this place," he said with some heat. "I'm sick of all the same faces, all the same places ... I keep thinking things will change but ... they never will."

Phoebe watched him, seeing the emotions chase across his face and wondering where he was going with this.

"I'm going to America," he announced. He laughed at the shock in her eyes. "Didn't expect that did you?"

"I ... no!" she admitted, shaking her head. "No, I didn't. You've surprised me."

He moved suddenly and put down his empty glass, coming to sit beside her. "Come with me!" he said, his voice urgent as he took her hand in his. He gave her a crooked smile as she gasped in shock. "No you didn't expect that either I suppose," he added.

He was quiet for a moment while Phoebe tried to gather her wits and decide what to say to him. "I know I'm not Benedict," he said, his voice quiet. "I've often wished I was," he admitted. "At least until his father died perhaps," he added with a grin. "But ... I'm not so bad, Phoebe. We could be happy you and I. My word, a woman like you in America! Think of it, Phoebe! They're not half so stuffy over there. Think of all the things we could do if you married me, the places we could see. We'd paint the town red, I dare swear."

He looked back at her with expectation in his eyes but try as she might she couldn't find a word to say to him.

"Don't answer me now," he said, his voice soft again now and his expression full of hope. "But promise me you'll think about it, won't you? Please?"

Phoebe nodded. She hadn't the least intention of accepting him but her thoughts were all up in the air and she didn't know what to think or what to say for the best.

"Good girl," he replied, apparently satisfied anyway. "At least if I leave it might convince that bloody runner I don't give a damn about the dukedom," he said with a bitter tone. "I don't know what else I must do to convince the blasted fellow." He sighed and got up. "Ah well, I'd better dash, I'm going to be frightfully late for dinner. See you anon," he said, sounding far more cheerful than he had just moments earlier.

***

Benedict strolled along the path that led out of the vast grounds of Grizedale with his thoughts full of the conversation with Sylvester. He had no intention of walking as far as the pretty village that lay at the end of this track but his footsteps had begun along the familiar pathway and he'd just kept going as his mind turned over the same dilemma over and again.

The thought of subjecting Phoebe to all the scandal and gossip that such an undertaking would inevitably surround her with if Theodora made good on her promise made him feel physically ill. But he knew that Sylvester was right in his estimation of Phoebe. She was the bravest, most single-minded person he'd ever met, and he knew she wouldn't give a damn for what anyone said about her.

The trouble was that he did.

Well just let them say anything in his hearing that was all ... It could well be he'd give Formby a real reason to march him to the scaffold, he thought with a wave of fury.

Hearing footsteps behind him on the path he turned and grimaced inwardly as he saw Theodora walking the same path with a covered basket over her arm.

"Good afternoon," he said, keeping his tone bland as she approached.

"Good afternoon, my Lord," she replied, a tight smile at her lips. "Keeping an assignation?" she demanded with the lift of one imperious eyebrow.

"No, Theodora, just walking," he replied, his tone as icy as his affection for her had become, if indeed it had ever existed in the first place.

"Oh, yes, that's right. I saw Miss Skeffington-Fox back at the house, going into the drawing room alone with Oliver," she added with a sneer. "She doesn't care a hoot for her reputation, I'll give her that."

Benedict glared at her noting that she was very pale, her eyes heavy with shadows. "Be very careful, Theodora," he warned her. "I will only allow you to push me so far."

She snorted at him, disgust in her expression as she stood taller and then winced.

His eyes narrowed at her. "Are you unwell?"

Giving a tight shake of her head she turned away. "A persistent headache," she said with accusation in her tone, as if it was his fault. "A walk in the fresh air will see to it I'm sure. I'll bid you good day, my Lord. I have letters to post in the village. No doubt I will see you at dinner."

Benedict merely nodded to her, which was as far as his manners would allow him to go, but he felt sure his expression must hold all the animosity he now felt for the woman and watched her walk out of sight. Damn her, why couldn't she just let it go. Why wouldn't she let *him* go? Though he knew the answer well enough. Not only was the title of duchess one she would relish, it was well known the estate was a vastly wealthy one. It appeared money and power was more than enough reason to marry a man you despised even if he more than returned the feeling. For a considerable time he just stood staring out at the landscape that comprised a small fraction of the wealth and power of Grizedale Court. This was what his fiancée wanted, not him. But if this was to be his home, then he would share it with Phoebe and no one else.

Theodora was in for a shock.

With a determined set to his shoulders Benedict turned and began to retrace his steps when a shot rang out.

Feeling a sharp pinch to his left arm, for a moment he was too surprised to think what might have happened. When his fingers came away bloody and the wound began to throb, however, he knew well enough and flung himself off the path and into the woodland. Not a moment too late as another shot rang out, the sound echoing across the estate and the thud of the bullet piercing the tree he stood behind.

With sweat prickling down the back of his neck he took a breath to calm himself. The shot had come from higher ground, most likely in the upper part of the south wood which ran along the path. There was plenty of cover for his assailant up there or he'd have seen anyone else out in the grounds. Which meant they were a fair way off at least.

Heart thundering in his chest he headed deeper into the woodland and took the long route back to the house. At any moment he expected his pursuer to appear from behind a tree or leap out from a bush, but by the time he arrived back at the house he knew he was safe, for the moment at least.

Not wanting to terrify his mother or Phoebe any further, he went straight to his valet to get the wound dressed. Benedict then sent word to Formby, letting him know what had happened and requesting him to call at the house, that evening if possible.

Once this was done, he dressed for dinner and went downstairs as if nothing had happened. If whoever was doing this hoped to frighten him, he was damned if he would let it show. Rattled he may be, but he wasn't about to cower in his room. Deciding that his previous decision was more important than ever, he realised that he needed to marry Phoebe with all haste. At least then if something did happen ... well she would be well provided for.

With that rather bleak idea giving him a melancholy feeling, he went to search out the one woman who could always chase his sorrows far from his mind. The thought of seeing her was enough to cheer him, and despite his recent fright he found himself chuckling with amusement at how she was likely to react to his decision about their future.

***

Phoebe had waited until Oliver left the room and let out a sigh of relief. She'd known Oliver enjoyed flirting with her, but she'd never once expected a proposal of marriage! Whatever would Benedict say about it? Setting out to find him and discover the answer she'd searched most of the house before she stumbled upon Keane. The butler smiled at her in an informal manner and told her Lord Rothay had gone for a walk but was expected back shortly. With frustration she went back to the library and picked up a book which failed to hold her attention as she sat there with impatience until the door finally opened.

"There you are!" she said in relief as Benedict's large frame entered the room. It never ceased to amaze her how much room the man took up.

"Hello," he said, a rather animated twinkle in his eyes at seeing her.

She beamed at him, feeling her heart give an uncharacteristic flutter in her chest. Good Lord, if this kept up she'd have to start reading dreadful love poetry or some such nonsense.

"Hello yourself," she replied as he ducked his head and stole a kiss. He lingered a moment, their mouths almost but not quite touching. "You're being very daring," she teased.

"Well," he said, his voice low. "If we're going to let Theodora sue me for breach of promise, I suppose I'll have to get used to gossip and scandal."

She just stared at him for a moment, not entirely sure she was understanding his meaning but in the end it sank in. "Benedict!" she cried, leaping to her feet so quickly he only just moved before their heads cracked together.

"Have a care, love," he said, laughing at her as she flung her arms around his neck and peppered his face with kisses. "I haven't even proposed yet," he added with a scolding tone which she completely ignored, just as she was supposed to.

"I don't care!" she crowed, practically bouncing on the spot with delight. "Oh, I'm so happy."

"Yes," he said, his expression wry. "I can quite imagine how you'll enjoy Theodora's fury. You'll be the only one," he added with a grimace. "However I've been told not to be so damned hen-hearted."

"Sylvester!" she exclaimed, clapping her hands together with glee.

He nodded, amusement glittering in his eyes. "Apparently, it's *de rigueur* for a duke to have at least one scandal under his belt so I may as well get my hand in," he muttered with a grin.

"Oh, Ben!" she laughed, shaking her head. "How funny you are. But what a dear old fellow Sylvester is. I must find a special way to thank him."

Benedict gave a huff of amusement and went to fix himself a drink. His powerful frame was lit up by the sunshine glittering through the window behind him and she felt a rush of happiness that she would finally be able to call him her own. "You might look a bit more anxious about the fact your reputation is about to go to hell, young lady," he scolded. "Once your father finds out, I have every expectation of being hunted down like a dog."

"Oh, no," Phoebe replied with perfect equanimity. "I wrote to papa days ago to tell him everything. He'll understand perfectly I assure you."

Benedict froze, glass in hand and turned a quite startling shade of white as dust motes danced in the sunbeams illuminating his still figure. "You ... you told him ... *everything?"*

Phoebe pursed her lips and gave him a teasing look. "Well almost."

"Good Lord," he said with a groan, downing his drink in one large swallow. "You'll be the death of me yet, woman."

"Oh don't say it!" Phoebe cried, a stab of fear piercing her heart. "Don't even joke about it." Her heart squeezed in her chest as she remembered the dreadful glimpse of a figure bending over his bed, knife in hand and tears prickled behind her eyes.

"There now, love," Benedict murmured, his voice soft as he set the glass down and pulled her to him once more. "Don't go getting yourself all in a fluster. I'm fine, and I'm not so very easy to kill you know. Have a little faith, eh?"

Phoebe sniffed and nodded, telling herself off for being so emotional. The last thing the poor man needed was her going to pieces and weeping on his sleeve. She clung to him hard though and he held her tight in return. Looking up she saw him wince as if he was in pain.

"What is it?" she asked in alarm. "Are you hurt?"

He seemed to hesitate for a moment before smiling at her and shaking his head. "No, love," he said with a chuckle. "You just don't know your own strength."

She huffed at him, knowing he was teasing but still a little unsure if he was telling the truth. But she had news of her own which she needed to tell him and so she let it pass.

"Oh, Ben, I must tell you," she said, clutching at his hand as he released her. "Oliver came to see me and ... well you'll never guess!" she exclaimed, looking at him and feeling shocked all over again.

"What?" Benedict demanded, his green eyes darkening with suspicion.

"He's going to America!"

"Really?" he said, frowning and looking sceptical.

"Yes! But that's the least of it," she added, wondering just how he would react to the next piece of news. "Ben, he proposed to me! He wants me to go with him."

"He did what!" Ben exploded, looking utterly furious. "Do you mean to say he's been in here, trying to make love to you and seduce you into running away with him?"

"Oh, Ben," Phoebe said, quite unable to keep her laughter in check. "There's really no need to fly into the boughs. It's not as if I accepted him."

"By God I should think not!" he raged, his fists clenched.

"No of course not," she added, her contrary nature finding his fury quite irresistible. "I told him I'd think about it." Somehow she managed to keep her face perfectly placid whilst she watched the incredulous play of emotions across his face.

"You did what!"

Unable to contain herself any longer Phoebe went off into peals of laughter. "Oh, I'm sorry, darling but your face is a picture. No, don't eat me!" she begged, holding out her hand as he looked ever more indignant. "I only said it to buy time. I simply didn't know what to say to him. There's me spending half the morning trying to convince Formby he's our man, and the next minute he's wanting to run away with me and leave it all behind. I swear I didn't know where to put myself, let alone how to answer him."

"Well, I take it you have your answer now?" Benedict demanded, not sounding the least bit mollified.

"Yes, darling," she whispered, standing on tip toes to give him a kiss. "Of course I do."

"Hmph," was all the reply she was granted but he kissed her again so she assumed she'd been forgiven. He pulled back as the dinner gong sounded.

"Oh well," he said, gloomily. "Another family ordeal to get through. At least mother had the sense to send Cecily and the twins to escape to cousin Edith's for a while until after the funeral. Pity she wouldn't have Jessamy too. What a summer the poor children have had." He gave a heavy sigh and looked at her with longing. "I wish we could run away from it all too."

"Oh it's not so bad now, surely?" Phoebe asked smiling at him. "With the funeral tomorrow Lady Rutland will go home after, and she never comes down in any case. So there's only Miss Pinchbeck to upset you, oh and Oliver now, I guess," she added with a smirk. "Well alright, but if we could get rid of those two it would be a perfectly cosy evening."

"True," Benedict replied with a snort of amusement. "But for God's sake don't let old Formby hear you say so or he'll have you clapped in irons before you can say Jack Robinson."

She laughed at that but then she remembered the other niggling suspicion that had been eating away at her peace of mind.

"Ben," she said, her voice hesitant, wondering if he'd just think she was being vindictive. "You know I said how poison is a woman's weapon?"

Benedict narrowed his eyes at her. "Yes, love, I remember. Why?"

"You don't think ... Miss Pinchbeck?"

To her surprise he didn't immediately shrug the idea off. "A few days ago I'd have said you were way off the mark," he admitted, his face troubled. "But now ... I simply don't know. I think she really does want that title," he added and then sighed, shaking his head. "But stabbing Harold, disabling Tony's curricle? No," he said, his voice decisive. "I could believe her guilty of all manner of things now, but not either of those crimes. They involve getting your hands dirty and Theodora would never sully herself."

Phoebe shrugged, acknowledging the truth of his argument but he still looked grave.

"Phoebe," he said, concern in his green eyes. "How long ago was Oliver here?"

"Oh," she said, trying to remember how long she'd been looking for Ben. "I've really no idea. At least an hour, perhaps more? Why?"

He smiled at her, a bit too suddenly perhaps and the serious look fell away. "No reason love," he said, and followed her out of the room to dinner.

Chapter 25

To see a world in a grain of sand
And a heaven in a wild flower,
Hold infinity in the palm of your hand
And eternity in an hour. - William Blake

Benedict thought he survived the ordeal of another family meal with remarkable fortitude. Though he did drink rather more wine than was usual. He told himself it was for medicinal purposes as his arm was throbbing like the devil.

His valet, who had a little skill in wounds, had seen to arranging a discreet visit from the doctor for later that night. But he spent much of the evening casting dark looks in Oliver's direction when the man wasn't looking. Benedict thought he seemed quiet tonight and not quite himself.

Ben declined dessert, reaching for his glass instead. Summer pudding was the one dessert he particularly disliked. The blackberry seeds always got stuck in your teeth.

Lizzie looked up in surprise as Sylvester also refused. "No dessert?" she exclaimed as he too sat back with a glass of wine.

"No," he grumbled, smoothing one hand over his belly. "That beef was devilish good but I think I overindulged," he said with a rueful smile.

Lizzie laughed at him and Benedict saw her share a fond look with Keane over the table. She should have a care to be more subtle. He wondered just how Sylvester would take that news when it was finally revealed - and revealed it would be. No secret could be kept forever and somehow he doubted Keane was a man who would put up with this cloak and dagger way of life for too much longer. He had too much pride.

Benedict saw Theodora cast Sylvester a look of disgust before taking a dainty bite of her own dessert. Miserable old ... He stopped himself from calling her names - even in his head, he wasn't a child after all. To his amusement he saw a silent communication go on between Jessamy and Phoebe. Phoebe had taken to asking for a particularly large dessert which she would eat half of. She'd then quietly swap plates with Jessamy who insisted on sitting beside her at all mealtimes. It of course fooled no one but at least it was less obvious than him running around the table and swiping her bowl with glee.

Once again, he looked back to Theodora to see if she was giving them looks of disgust too but her eyes were focused on her own bowl.

They talked for a little after dessert, polite nonsense that bored Benedict to tears and he looked to Phoebe, expecting to be given a sympathetic smile. Instead she looked flushed, her lovely blue eyes dark and the pupils dilated.

"Phoebe?" he questioned her, noticing her breathing was fast and shallow. Before he could say another word, however, Jessamy had given a cry of pain and collapsed clutching at his stomach and falling from his chair.

"Jessamy!" his mother cried, leaping to her feet and running to her son.

"Oh, Ben," Phoebe said, her eyes suddenly wide with panic. "I think ..."

But she didn't get to finish the sentence as her eyes rolled up in her head.

"Phoebe!" Benedict cried, catching her as she tumbled from her chair. He patted her face in alarm, trying to revive her but she just moaned, her lovely skin damp with sweat. "I sent for a doctor earlier!" he shouted at the nearest footman. "See if he's arrived yet." The man ran from the room to do his bidding as Benedict gathered Phoebe up in his arms and turned to ask for help, only to discover that Theodora was clinging to her chair, clutching at her stomach with the same fevered look to her skin as Phoebe and Jessamy. Oliver was sitting with his hands at his throat, gasping for breath, his eyes wide with terror.

"What's happening?" Sylvester demanded, getting to his feet and looking around him in horror. "What is it?"

"They've been poisoned," Benedict said, seeing with relief that his mother hadn't changed the habit of a lifetime and eaten any dessert. He tried not to panic with his little brother convulsing on the floor while his mother wept and screamed for help and Phoebe laboured to breathe in his arms. He issued instructions to the remaining staff to get everyone to their rooms and bring whatever medical supplies were at hand. He hoped to God someone had some knowledge of treating poisoning as basil hadn't helped John in the least and he doubted there was enough on the estate to save them all in any case.

He watched one of the footmen lift his little brother and felt his heart constrict with fear as two of the people he loved most in the world looked to be in mortal danger. God help them if Benedict ever found who was responsible for this. Death would not be good enough.

Half an hour later and Benedict had never been more grateful for the calm good sense of a woman like Sarah Huckington. After an initial cry of distress, Phoebe's maid had been all efficiency, thrusting Benedict out of the way while she applied cold compresses and stripped Phoebe of her stays to ease her breathing. To her annoyance the doctor bustled in just as she had Phoebe laid comfortably against the pillows.

"We'll need to bleed them all," the doctor said, shaking his head and tutting over the rapidity of her heart beat.

"That you will not!" Sarah exploded, with such fury that even Benedict was startled. "The poor lamb's been poisoned," she raged. "Any damn fool can see that." She stood in front of Phoebe just like a lioness guarding her young. “This woman is in my care and you’ll not touch her, you blasted quack! She needs charcoal to absorb the poison from her stomach and blood.”

“Preposterous!” the doctor exploded, looking more than affronted. “I never heard such fustian. Old wives tales and superstition.” He turned to Benedict and held his hand out to the woman with disdain. “I suggest you remove this creature from the room forthwith if you’d like the young lady to survive the night, my Lord,” he said, his voice icy.

Sarah glared at the doctor but then pushed past him to Benedict, grasping his hand with pleading in her eyes. “Trust me, my Lord. *Please.* I can save her. I saw this with the soldiers. There was a bad time in Spain, food ran short and the men ate wild berries as there was nought else. Belladonna the locals called it that’s what makes their eyes go wide and black like that. The men from the city couldn’t tell a blackberry from nightshade and they looked just like this after they’d eaten it. There was a Spanish lady, a wise woman I guess, and I saw her make them drink water and ground charcoal and they all lived. Every one of them.”

Benedict felt fear clench his stomach. There was sincerity and terror in Sarah’s eyes, determination too. The doctor merely looked furious. “Do it,” he said to Sarah. “Do whatever you think best but for the love of God hurry.”

Sarah didn’t wait to reply but ran to prepare what she needed. The doctor stepped towards him with a look of disgust. “You have just condemned your family to die,” he said, his eyes cold with rage. “I hope you will be satisfied with the outcome.”

“Get out!” Benedict raged, terror making his temper snap as he bodily forced the man from the room and slammed the door on him. Praying that the doctor was wrong and he hadn’t just made a horrific error in judgement, he ran to sit beside the bed. Taking Phoebe’s hand he was appalled and frightened by the ragged sound of her breathing. She had begun to murmur in her sleep, clutching at the bed covers and shouting at some unknown presence, angry incoherent words. Benedict took her hand, holding on tight as she began to thrash about in feverish rage.

"Please, love, please," he said over and over, and prayed for deliverance. "Be strong, Phoebe. I know you are, sweet girl and you must be, my love. Please fight this ... for me."

***

The night that followed was the longest of Benedict's life. He spent most of it outside Phoebe's door, only tearing himself away at times to check on Jessamy. Sarah had banned him point blank from remaining after she'd begun feeding Phoebe the disgusting charcoal mix. She said the effects were unpleasant and Phoebe would never forgive her if she allowed him to see her in such a state. She swore to him that it would work though and promised to call him in the moment there was any change.

With nothing more that he could do he went to see Jessamy, holding his breath as the child fought for his life. Seeing his little brother's slight form looking so very fragile, his slim chest struggling to breathe and sweating freely was more than he could bear. The charcoal mix was making him vomit profusely and he was hallucinating, screaming in terror at monsters looming over his bed. Benedict's heart went out to him and his poor mother who wept ceaselessly at his bedside.

The same treatment was given to everyone who had been taken ill. This comprised Phoebe, Jessamy, Oliver and to a lesser extent Theodora and Lizzie who had both eaten very little of the dessert, which had to have been the cause of the poisoning.

Formby, whom Benedict had asked to visit earlier in the day had come up to offer such words of comfort as he had and now just clasped Ben's hand in a warm manner. With a troubled look in his eyes, the runner turned to walk away from him.

"Formby," Benedict said, making him pause. "Sarah Huckington, Phoebe's maid. She said it looked like nightshade poisoning. There was summer pudding for dessert and everyone fell ill quickly after." Formby nodded, his expression dark with understanding before turning and hurrying off to investigate.

Benedict knew that the fact both he and Sylvester had refused dessert would be damning, for both of them. His mother was famous for watching her figure and not touching sweet things but he wondered if she too could now fall under suspicion, though what they could believe she would gain from it he couldn't fathom, though *poison was a woman's weapon.* He shuddered at the idea. Anyone who believed she would risk her precious youngest son's life for any reason would be out of their damned minds.

He spent the rest of the night either pacing and raging against the world or sitting on the floor with his head in his hands, praying and begging God to help the woman in the next room. Without her nothing else in his life would ever matter again. And Jessamy, poor, dear Jessamy who he had allowed to become so distant from him. If he never got the chance to make up for becoming the cold, disciplinarian that Phoebe had discovered him to be, he would never forgive himself.

***

It was late the following morning before Sarah came out of the room and leaned against the wall, her usually plump face drawn and taut with the stresses of the night. Benedict shot to his feet, watching her exhausted eyes lift to his and certain that his heart had stopped beating as he waited for her to speak. He had heard several hours ago that Jessamy had pulled through and Oliver, Theodora and Lizzie would all be fine, but Phoebe had been taken the worst of all of them.

"She's going to be alright," she said, and then put her hand to her mouth and began to sob. Big, heart-wrenching sobs that the woman had clearly been holding back all night whilst she tended to the young lady who she so obviously loved like her own daughter.

"Thank God," Benedict cried before damning propriety and hauling the woman into his arms. "Thank God for you, Sarah

Huckington," he said, weeping and laughing too as the woman looked up at him in shock. "I swear nothing will ever be too good for you. You're a damned miracle worker." To her obvious astonishment he put his hands to her face and kissed her.

Sarah sniffed and wiped her eyes, apparently not knowing whether to laugh or cry herself. "You just make sure you marry her!" she scolded, wagging her finger at him. "I don't need aught else but to know she's happy, and she won't never be happy without you, as you well know," she said with a huff.

Benedict took her hand and stared at her, perfectly solemn now. "You have my word, Sarah, if it is the last thing I do. Phoebe will be my wife."

She nodded at that and gave a final sniff. "Well then. If you'll excuse me, my little Bee will be wanting to tidy herself up before she sees you."

"Oh damn that!" he exploded, frustrated beyond sanity. "I want to see her now!"

Sarah gave him a remarkably fierce look. "If you know what's good for you," she said with a dangerous note in her voice. "You'll stay right there until I bid you enter." And with that she shut the door in his face.

***

Phoebe lay in bed, propped up on a mountain of pillows as Sarah put a glass of water to her parched lips.

"I'm so thirsty," Phoebe complained once she had drained the glass.

"Aye, love, that's the nightshade," she replied nodding and then muttering for the tenth time in as many minutes. "By everything that's holy, if I ever get my hands on the wicked creature as did this," she raged. "And that poor little lad too. My Lord, if I hadn't been here!" She smothered her face with a large handkerchief for a moment before taking a breath and righting herself again.

Phoebe held out her hand to her. "Dearest, darling, Sarah," she said, looking at the woman who had been the closest thing to a mother she had ever had. "You must never ever leave me!" she said laughing, though there were tears in her eyes. "You saved my life and I won't ever have a doctor near me again," she added, after hearing how the fool man who'd come to see her had acted and been treated in return. "So you'd better brush up on your midwifery skills," she added with a saucy wink. "For I hated being an only child and I intend to have a huge family."

"Phoebe!" Sarah replied, quite obviously torn between looking scandalised and enraptured at the idea of having babies to look after.

Phoebe laughed unrepentantly and then regretted it as exhaustion rolled over her.

"Now, do send poor Ben in, Sarah," she whispered. "I must see him before I fall asleep again."

Sarah nodded and patted her hand and she closed her eyes for a moment as exhaustion pulled at her eyelids. She opened them a moment later as a large, warm palm covered her hand and she blinked sleepily.

"Ben!" she sighed happily, feeling her heart clench with sorrow at the fear she could see in his eyes. "I'm quite alright now," she said, trying and failing to force some energy into her voice. "Be right as ninepence tomorrow, you'll see."

She looked up to find Ben holding her hand to his mouth, his face ashen. "By God, love," he said, his voice rough and somewhat unsteady. "You frightened me so."

"Frightened myself," she whispered with a weary smile.

She could see now, the weight of emotion in his eyes and the rigid set of his shoulders and squeezed his hand, too exhausted to speak any further. His eyes glittered, over bright before he closed them, pressing her hand to his face with a stifled sob. Phoebe sighed, happy and secure now with him near, before closing her eyes and hearing *I love you* murmur through her mind, before allowing sleep to take her away.

Chapter 26

I was angry with my friend:
I told my wrath, my wrath did end.
I was angry with my foe:
I told it not, my wrath did grow. - *William Blake*

It was two more days before Phoebe was strong enough to get out of bed. A fact which she resented profoundly, and she didn't hesitate to make her feelings known. Benedict bore it all with delight, too amused by her bad temper and too damn relieved that she was with him to be the slightest bit impatient with her. The fact that he couldn't be riled merely seemed to infuriate her all the more though. Neither did he give a damn if the whole household was scandalised by the time he spent in her room. Everyone was by now well aware of his feelings for her. That bridge had long since been crossed as far as he was concerned.

So it was with great relief on all sides that he went to her room the next morning to find her dressed and waiting for him when he called after breakfast.

"Darling," he said, with a smile. Noting that the colour was returning to her cheeks and a little of the sparkle was back in her eyes he felt the last claws of anxiety retract and release their grip on his heart. "Well aren't you a sight for sore eyes."

She beamed at him and did a little twirl, showing off a pretty yellow muslin dress. "Do you like it?" she asked with a coquettish grin. "It's one of my favourites and I needed cheering up."

"You look exquisite as always, love," he said, beaming at her with appreciation. "Are you up to a stroll around the garden then?"

"Try and stop me!"

A little later, once Sarah had forced Phoebe to wrap a pretty shawl around her shoulders, they sat on a bench in the sun with Phoebe leaning her head against him. She seemed rather abstracted and he realised she was thinking hard about something. Looking down he found her smooth brow furrowed with consternation.

"What does Formby say?" she asked him, looking up. For a moment he didn't answer, too caught by those wide blue eyes to think of anything but the fact she had nearly been taken from him. He leaned down and pressed a kiss to her mouth, not giving a damn if there was anyone nearby to see it. He knew what was important now.

"They found nightshade berries in the dessert," he said, putting his arm around her waist. "The gardeners swear they only brought black and red currants, blackberries and the usual soft fruits which the cook confirmed. But the nightshade berries could easily have been slipped in with the black currants and no one any the wiser. Both Sylvester and I are now chief suspects," he added with a grimace. "Formby ..." he hesitated, knowing that this would upset her and not wanting to spoil the day, but the coming trial was going to be inescapable. "Formby says that more men are being sent down to investigate, including his superior. He won't be able to protect me any longer. Unless he can convince the man that I'm not working in collusion with Sylvester ..." He paused and looked away, not wanting to say it out loud.

"You'll both be arrested," she finished for him.

He nodded, unable to look in her eyes and see the fear he knew was there. He could feel it quite strongly enough himself.

"No!" she said, her voice full of fury. "No. I won't let them."

To his alarm she leapt to her feet and stormed back towards the house. "Phoebe!" he exclaimed, striding to catch up with her. "What are you doing?"

"Going to speak with your blasted fiancée!" she shouted, her rage only too apparent.

"Phoebe, don't be foolish!" he said, fearing that she would over exert herself and become ill again. "You'll only have a dreadful row, and what good will that serve?"

"It will make me feel a great deal better for one!" she returned with asperity as she swept through the doors of the great house and up the stairs. "And that woman knows something," she added, pausing on the steps with such fury glinting in her eyes that he was quite taken aback. "She's a part of this, Ben, I'd swear to it."

Before he could get her to see that confronting Theodora in this manner was a bad idea, she was pounding on the woman's bedroom door.

"Come out, Miss Pinchbeck," she shouted through the door, her slim frame practically quivering with anger. "I know you've had a hand in this!" she yelled, as no answer was forthcoming. She raised her hand to bang on the door again and then paused as a moan of pain was heard. "Ben!" she said in alarm. "Did you hear that?"

The sound came again and Benedict banged on the door. "Theodora? Theodora, are you alright? Answer me?"

But there was no answer.

Benedict rattled the handle but the door was locked. "Dammit," he cursed. "Stand back."

Unable to use his injured shoulder, Benedict resorted to kicking the door down.

They ran into the room to find Theodora gasping and thrashing around on the floor. Ben ran to kneel beside her, lifting her up and finding himself horrified by the dilated wildness in her eyes. They drifted to Phoebe and the hatred he saw there quite stole his breath.

"Should be dead," Theodora hissed, her body beginning to convulse. "She should be dead, Oliver too ... all of them." Her breath caught and held and Ben regarded her with revulsion as she became too still and too quiet. Her eyes stared at the ceiling, wide and glassy now, and he noticed the dark berries that lay scattered over the floor, her lips stained by them. Surely she had just been ranting as the poison took hold? Surely she couldn't be responsible for so much death? Phoebe screamed behind him, a strange, muffled sound that took his attention. He looked back at the doorway expecting to see horror in her eyes at Theodora's demise, but Oliver had her in fierce a grip, his arm holding her close, and a gun in his other hand.

"You!" Ben exclaimed, his blood turning to ice in his veins as he saw the hold the man had on Phoebe. His heart raced as his mind tried to devise a way to get her safe. Good God, hadn't they endured enough? "Oliver, let Phoebe go. You've got me. I'm not going anywhere."

"No, Ben, you're not," Oliver said, his expression apologetic. "And I'm truly sorry about that but there's no other choice now. Pity I didn't spend more time practising with this little beauty eh?" he added, waving the gun in the air. "A clean shot the other night would have made life much simpler." Phoebe squealed in alarm and tried to elbow him but he just tightened his hold on her. "Now, now, love," he said, his voice soothing. "We're going on a little trip you and I."

"Why Theodora?" Benedict demanded, forcing Oliver's attention back to him and praying he could delay him enough for the runners to arrive or someone to discover them.

Oliver snorted with amusement and Benedict was horrified to see the glittering look in his eyes. The man was insane, he had to be. "Well she saw me in the woods the other night for one," he said, shaking his head with a frustrated expression. "Careless of me but I'd been so damn close. How is the arm by the way?" he added with a solicitous air.

"Fine," Ben gritted out. "If that's true, why didn't she tell anyone it was you that tried to kill me?"

"Oh because Theodora had rather more permanent plans that would rid her of two rather large problems."

Benedict stared at him aghast as he realised that Phoebe had been right all along.

"You knew I couldn't have killed John, you fool!" Oliver sneered in disgust. "Though I would have got around to it in the end I was planning on giving him another year yet, let the fuss die down a little. But when I came back and found the fellow dead, I couldn't have been more surprised. Pleased too ... at first anyway."

Phoebe wriggled in his grasp and he pressed the barrel of the gun to her temple. "Hush, Phoebe, there's a good girl."

Ben felt his heart clench as Phoebe's eyes widened with horror.

"Don't hurt her, Oliver," he begged.

"Oh, I won't if I can help it," Oliver replied, his tone conversational. "She's going to marry me you see."

"Why weren't you pleased in the end?" Benedict demanded in desperation, ignoring the madman's rantings and trying to hold his attention a little longer. Please, God, let someone come and find them.

Oliver frowned, trying to recall the thread of the conversation.

"Oh!" he said, waving the gun as it came back to him. "That's right, because she suspected it was me and she knew you were next. Well Theodora did so want to be a duchess, Ben," Oliver said with a reproving tone. "So she poisoned the dessert." He looked back at Phoebe with a rueful grin. "The perils of a sweet tooth, love. Neither of us can ever refuse dessert, can we? The bitch had obviously noticed." He shrugged. "She ate just enough herself to be convincing of course. I might even have forgiven her for that if she'd done the job with young Jessamy too; mighty convenient that would have been," he said with a nasty grin that made Benedict's skin prickle with fear for Phoebe.

"But she tried to kill me *and* Phoebe. Poor Phoebe," he crooned, pressing his face to hers as Phoebe flinched away in horror.

"Don't worry, my love, I made sure she knew I was doing it for you when I forced those berries down her throat."

Phoebe made a noise of sheer terror and Benedict glanced around the room, desperate for anything that he could use as a weapon, any help he could give her. But Oliver had her tightly held and that gun now pressed against the side of her head.

"No foolish heroics now, Benedict," Oliver said with a remarkably placid smile. "I shan't kill you if you don't force the issue. You never know, you might come about again," he added with an encouraging wink. "No, not if I'm going to arrange it so that the runners find you here with dear Theodora. I wrote to Formby's boss you see, all about your infatuation with Phoebe and how she was afraid of you. I went to Eton with his son, did you know that? Yes, an awful commoner really but a useful connection. He'd love his son to be well in with a duke too, I'm sure. No end of good I could do him."

"Well you've thought of everything I see," Benedict said, trying to infuse his voice with admiration. "You always were thorough. I suppose I killed Theodora to free myself of her so I can force Phoebe into marriage."

Oliver laughed, a dark sound that made chills shiver down Ben's back. "Well, something like that," Oliver admitted. "I'm sure the Bow street boys will tidy the ends up as they see fit. I expect they can be an imaginative lot when the mood takes them," he added with a grin.

"No doubt." Ben stared at him, wondering how he could have been so deceived for so many years as boyhood memories of the two of them camping and fishing and sleeping out under the stars flooded his mind. "Why, Oliver?"

The man gave a snort of derision, staring at Ben with hatred. "Because you always got everything in the end. I thought you were ruined when your father died but no, you came about again, and with such a damned smug air about you. The whole damned family, all of them, all looking down their noses at me. I hated them all!"

"But that's not true, Oliver," Benedict protested. "You were loved, we all loved you. You were always welcomed and feted, far more than I ever was!"

"Rubbish," Oliver snapped, his eyes blazing with fury. "Perhaps after you'd decided to act the martyr to keep the family's morality intact. But I was only ever light entertainment, always trailing in your wake. Someone to give you all a laugh, never to be taken seriously."

"You were my friend, Oliver, my brother."

The look Oliver returned at that was startling in the depth of loathing he saw there but the man said nothing, just turned back to Phoebe with an unpleasant smile.

"Well then, we can't stand around here chatting, can we love?" he asked Phoebe, that unsettling glittering look returning to his eyes.

"Where are you taking her?" Ben demanded.

"Don't be tedious, Ben," Oliver said, his face changing once more with shocking suddenness, cold-eyed and furious again now. "Turn around like a good fellow and perhaps you and Phoebe will get out of this alive."

Benedict hesitated for just a moment before lunging forward and trying to grab Oliver's arm. But he'd been too far away and the man was fast. The next thing he knew, blinding pain exploded behind his eyes and the world went dark.

Chapter 27

For I had rather owner be,
Of thee one hour, than all else ever - John Donne

Phoebe broke free with a scream as Oliver lashed out with the gun and she ran to where Benedict had fallen. There was a massive lump on his head and he was out cold but she was overjoyed to hear his heart thudding strong and even beneath her ear.

She turned, intending to tell him exactly what she thought of him when she saw his hand swipe towards her and knew she was too late ...

Phoebe awoke to a sickening pain in her head which was not helped in the slightest by the jolting of the carriage she was being conveyed in. They were clearly moving at breakneck speed and she cursed inwardly as she was jolted again and her head throbbed so hard she wanted to vomit. This however was not an option as she was gagged and bound and the windows of the carriage obscured so she had no notion of where she was going to. She could however take a guess.

Oliver would no doubt want to remove himself from England until he was certain that Benedict had been convicted for his crimes. That would leave only poor little Jessamy to stand between him and everything he wanted. He would go to America, just as he had obviously been planning to do from the start.

She shivered as she remembered the maniacal look in his eyes. She had been right that evening on the terrace. Cursing herself she wished she'd tried harder to convince Benedict of how she'd felt that night. But she'd even found it hard to convince herself in the times she'd met him since then. He could be so perfectly charming, so sincere, and yet underneath it all he truly was a monster.

Real fear prickled under her skin and she felt her heart pick up, panic clawing at her throat. She fought against the gag, needing more air and feeling as though she would pass out. That she couldn't afford.

It took a great effort of will to calm herself but if Phoebe was known for anything, it was being stubborn as a mule. Well she was damned if she would allow Oliver to ruin her and Ben's lives. She was sickened by what had happened to Miss Pinchbeck but the truth was the woman had tried to kill her. That being the case, she felt little guilt in realising her death had freed Benedict. They could marry now with no impediment. At least, they could once the small hindrances of her escaping a madman and Ben escaping the hangman's noose had been dealt with.

A welcome burst of rage flooded her veins and fear receded as she fed her anger. Oliver had killed two men and a woman, another man had died as a result of his actions, and she and Jessamy had almost lost their lives. If Oliver's plan worked, Ben and Jessamy would surely follow and sooner or later her too. For only a madman could believe she would marry him and say nothing of what had happened. Well maybe he truly was insane but there were bursts enough of sanity when he would realise that she was a liability. She had little doubt what her end would be, the only variant would be how and when she reached it. Looking at it that way she knew she had nothing to lose. And everything to gain.

***

Benedict groaned as rough hands shook him, one slapping his face none too gently as an urgent voice demanded he wake up.

He forced his eyes open, wincing as the too bright daylight worsened the pain.

"Formby," he croaked, recognising at last the concerned face that was bending over him.

"Get up, get up, man," Formby urged him, putting his arm under Ben's and forcing him to his feet.

"Christ, my head," Benedict groaned as he fought to remember what the devil had happened.

"Lad, you need to get out of here and fast," Formby said, sounding more serious than Benedict had ever heard him. He looked around as a terrible feeling grew in his chest and his eyes fell upon Theodora's lifeless body.

"Oh God," he whispered. "Phoebe!" He clutched at Formby's arm as earlier events came back to him in all their stark clarity. "It's Oliver!" he explained, heading for the door. "Oliver killed them all, except for John and the poisoning the other night, that was Theodora so he killed her too and now he has Phoebe! We must get her back."

Formby stilled him, his hand clutching his arm with purposeful force. "Alright, but I tell you now there are three more runners searching this house with a warrant for your arrest. My superior is among them and he don't care too much for details, my Lord. He finds you here and a dead body and you'll swing 'cause it's nice and tidy. Less paperwork you see."

Ben swallowed and gave a taut nod. "Very well, what then?"

Formby gave a nod towards the window. "Any good at climbing?"

"I'll manage," he replied, striding to the window with a grim set to his jaw.

"Good man." Formby replied with a humourless smile. They both stilled as a shout was heard along the corridor but the sound faded away as footsteps retreated. "Where will this Oliver chap run to then?" Formby asked, his voice low as Ben slid the window open and looked out.

"He was talking about going to America," Ben said, fury and terror in his heart as he imagined Phoebe in that man's hands. By God he'd kill him. "He proposed to Phoebe and asked her to go with him. Now she's being taken by force."

"America!" the man exclaimed. "Well we can't be having that. Where would he sail from?"

"Dover," Ben replied, certain that this must be where Oliver was headed. "It's a good three-hour trip and he'll have had to put Phoebe in a carriage. I don't know how long I've been out but on horseback I may have a chance to catch up with him. In any case he'll need to hang tight until the boat is ready to sail. We must search everywhere in and around the docks but failing that you can get him as he boards."

"If we have evidence to hold him," Formby replied. To Ben's relief the man didn't spell out the fact that if Phoebe wasn't around to testify, it would be Ben's word against Oliver's. "Right you are then." Formby said, his expression decisive. "You get out and round to the stables. I'll hold on here and make sure no one looks your way. Once you're clear, I'll try to get them to see what's really going on and we'll be right behind you."

"Thank you, Formby," Benedict said, with real gratitude. "I'll not forget this."

"You'd best not, damn you," Formby replied with a crooked smile. "This could cost me my job. Now be away with you."

Benedict didn't need telling twice and swung himself out of the window.

As an adventurous boy, Benedict had climbed out of many of the windows of Grizedale and shimmied down drainpipes. The fact that many of these adventures had been shared with Oliver wasn't lost on him. The man he was now, however, was a great deal bigger, heavier and more cumbersome than the lithe little boy he'd once been.

He experienced a moment of sheer panic as a wrought-iron railing of a Juliet balcony bent and buckled with a shriek of tortured metal and threatened to throw him the considerable distance to the ground. But it held long enough for him to move on and it was with a vast amount of relief he hit the ground. With terra firma once more beneath his feet he cast a furtive glance around and ran for the stables.

***

By the time the carriage came to a halt Phoebe had been jolted black and blue and her head was throbbing with dull insistence. She felt nauseous and exhausted, her recent illness having robbed her of any reserves of energy. So it was little effort to pretend that she was still unconscious as her captor walked outside, presumably to remove her from the carriage.

In the last hour of her interminable journey she had noticed the noise around her increasing and she knew Oliver must have brought her to the busy sea port of Dover as she imagined he would have. The raucous cries of sea gulls shrieked overhead, stabbing at her tender brain and adding to the general cacophony of noise and chaos that attended any port in the world.

She heard men's voices talking low and urgent outside the carriage and strained to try to hear what they were saying.

"All you have to do is help me get her aboard, dammit. I've paid you well enough for a simple task, don't you dare back out now."

"No, my Lord, indeed not," said an anxious voice. "Only I thought you said she was your fiancée. I didn't know this was an abduction, did I? I mean that's another matter ain't it," the man said, his voice reasonable. "Tis against the law, my Lord and I'm risking a deal more than just getting an unmarried lady put in your cabin."

"Very well," Oliver replied, his voice increasingly impatient. "I'll double your price but that will include a place to keep her quiet until we're ready to board."

"Done," the man said, sounding pleased with the arrangement. "I've got a little place, just around the corner. A bit out o' the way but still close to the docks an' that suits you nice I reckon."

Oliver nodded. "Show me the way."

The carriage rocked as the two men climbed aboard and they were once again in motion, albeit a lot slower this time as the carriage negotiated the busy, cobbled streets behind the docks.

Phoebe strained her ears, trying to find anything that could help to orientate her but she felt too ill and too tired by now and nothing obvious, like church bells, could be discerned.

A short time later the carriage stopped once more and this time the carriage door did open. Phoebe laid still and limp though it was hard to disguise her disgust as Oliver hauled her into his arms and out of the carriage. It seemed very bright after the darkness of the closed conveyance but she cracked her eyelids a little to try to get some idea of her surroundings.

They seemed to be at the end of a wide road and surrounded by warehouses, but here, at the very end of the road stood a small, single storey brick building, all by itself with the larger buildings looming about it with a menacing air. It had the look of a disused office with one tiny window.

Everywhere lining the filthy street there were empty crates and rubbish, debris from the docks, all piled about in a careless manner.

Oliver carried her into the building and she closed her eyes again, fighting not to retch as the smell overpowered her. It reeked of cats and dirt and unwashed man and it was all she could do not to flinch as she was set down on a lumpy surface. The smell of an uncivilised male was stronger here and she guessed this was Oliver's companion's bed.

Oliver made a disgusted noise of contempt as he took in the hovel.

"Tain't much perhaps," his companion said, sounding rather defensive.

"It's revolting and beyond comprehension you should live in such filth," Oliver said with fury. "Good God man, can't you even sweep a damn floor. The place is obviously infested. If rats attack my fiancée here during her stay I promise to deduct every injury from your price, believe me."

Phoebe felt terror and nausea roil in her belly and forced herself not to react.

"Well, that's easy dealt with," the man said, sounding cheerful and not the least bit affronted. "I'll go fetch a cat to keep her company."

"You do that," Oliver said, his tone dark.

Phoebe heard a door open and shut and her pulse sped as she heard Oliver approach the squalid cot she'd been laid upon.

"Now then, sweet Phoebe," he said, his voice full of amusement. "You can stop pretending. I know you're awake."

Phoebe opened her eyes as there was obviously no value in continuing the charade.

"Good girl," Oliver said with approval, beaming at her. "Now then, the ship doesn't sail until the morning tide at half-past eleven. So I'm afraid you will have an uncomfortable night of it. I'm sorry for it, love. But if you behave like the sensible girl I know you are I'll make it up to you. And if all goes to plan, by this time next year you should find yourself married to a duke."

Phoebe cursed him from behind the gag and struggled against her bindings but Oliver just gave a jovial laugh. "Yes, love, I know. It's not what you're used to but it's not for long. Now I must go and arrange my own lodgings for the night. I don't expect I'll see you again until the morning when my rather uncouth companion will bring you to me. But don't worry, I've made it very clear you are not to be harmed in any way. Good night, Phoebe."

And with that Oliver left her alone. She heard the sounds of locks being turned and found she was too exhausted to do anything else but slip into a troubled sleep.

Chapter 28

There is no greater hell than to be a prisoner of fear - Ben Johnson

As Benedict rode into the large port of Dover, he realised with a sinking heart just what a challenge lay ahead of him. Finding one woman among the morass of humanity before him would be nigh on impossible. The place was seething, teeming with little back streets and dark allies and with cavernous warehouses closer to the docks themselves. Trying to simply search for her would be impossible.

So he would have to start by finding which ship was sailing for the Americas next and when it would leave. Giving his exhausted horse a pat of encouragement he moved towards the dockyards where he hoped to find someone to send him in the right direction.

After a fruitless hour being directed from pillar to post he was finally sent to the booking office for the Isabella, due to depart tomorrow morning at eleven thirty.

It was a tiny office, though neat and clean, the one window shining brightly and a small, efficient looking clerk sitting behind the desk with a large ledger spread before him.

"Name," the clerk intoned without looking up.

"Benedict Rutland, the Marquess of Saltash," Benedict replied. His shiny new title had the desired effect as the clerk peered up at him with wide eyes and leapt to his feet.

"Good afternoon, my Lord," the man said, staring rather myopically through a thick pair of glasses. "May I be of service?"

"I hope so," Benedict replied, his tone rather terse by now as his patience was all used up. Phoebe was alone somewhere with a bloody madman and it seemed there was damn all he could do about it. "My fiancée, a Miss Skeffington-Fox has been kidnapped and a man posing as my cousin Lord Oliver Bradshaw is booked upon the Isabella. He is, in fact a common criminal and highly dangerous, I believe armed. He is going to try to take her aboard against her will and remove her to America."

"Good God," the man exclaimed, pushing his spectacles further up his narrow nose. "I ... I ..."

"You'll be wanting to speak to the captain of the vessel I imagine to appraise him of the facts," Benedict replied for him, not in the mood to dealing with stammering incompetence. The clerk nodded with vigour and went to leave the room. "You should also be informed that there are Bow street runners coming this way with the intention of apprehending this man. You will also request that the captain immediately provide me with a list of names - and addresses where possible, of all of his crew, down to the lowliest cabin boy. The man won't get Miss Skeffington-Fox aboard willingly. She'll scream blue murder to be frank so there must be someone among the crew who has been paid to help him. I want that man."

"Yes, my Lord," the man replied looking rather dazed, before running from the room.

Benedict sat in the tiny office and put his head in his hands. His skull still throbbed like fury and a breakneck ride that had pushed both him and his horse to the limits had not helped. He was tired and dirty and terrified. His only hope was that Oliver had some affection for Phoebe somewhere in his twisted mind and really did intend that they should marry as absurd as that was. He could only pray that Phoebe was sensible enough to play along until such time as they could hope to rescue her.

He wondered how far behind him Formby was if indeed he had managed to persuade them that Oliver was the real culprit. For if not they could well be breathing down his neck any minute now. He prayed at least that his assertion that Oliver was not in fact Lord Bradford but an imposter might slow things down as he would be forced to prove his identity.

He knew well enough, however, that if he was cornered, Phoebe's life was in grave danger. If she didn't live, there was plenty of evidence to imply that Benedict was the murderer, not Oliver if a few salient facts were swept under carpets and ignored. If Oliver was to be believed the man in charge of this investigation would only be too happy to listen to his side of the story so Ben needed proof. Though in truth, if Phoebe didn't make it through this dreadful ordeal they could march him to the scaffold with his blessing, he wouldn't give a damn.

***

Phoebe woke to darkness and the sound of bolts sliding. With a jolt her heart leapt with fear as she was plunged back into the reality of her situation. She had to keep calm though her pulse was speeding and she felt sick. She hadn't eaten since breakfast time and combined with her lack of strength after her illness she felt light-headed and quite ill-equipped to deal with such drama. But there was little choice and she was determined that Oliver should not win this game. Sheer pig-headedness had saved her skin before now during the war and if Napoleon hadn't done for her she was damned if some mad Englishman would manage the job.

The door creaked open, bringing with it a blast of fresh air into the mouldering stench of her prison. Lamp light illuminated the outline of Oliver's companion and she pushed back a wave of terror at the idea of being alone and bound and at the man's mercy. Oliver had assured her she would not be harmed, yet at least. She had to pray he was paying the man enough to make that true.

"Evening, Miss," the man said, sounding rather awkward as well he might. She wondered what the etiquette was for greeting a woman who'd been abducted and bound. "I've brought you a bite to eat," he said, waving a small parcel at her.

Phoebe raised one eloquent eyebrow. Seeing as she was bound and gagged, eating presented something of a challenge.

"Alright, I'll take the gag out, but you scream and it'll be the back of my hand you'll be feelin'. Do you understand me?"

Phoebe nodded her agreement and held herself very still while the man moved closer and fumbled with the binding around her mouth.

"There now," he said, as though he'd done her some great service. "Better ain't it?"

"Much," Phoebe said, deciding that she must try to befriend this great oaf. Maybe if she could get him on side, he'd help her. "Thank you, Sir."

She looked up at him with big eyes and as innocent an expression as she could muster. His face was obscured by darkness but he rubbed the back of his neck in a gesture telling of discomfort.

"What time is it?" she asked, trying to gauge how long she'd been there.

"Bout half nine," he replied, his voice low and his presence a big looming shape in the darkness.

"Please, may I have something to drink," she whispered, keeping her voice meek and frightened, which was rather easier than she might have hoped.

The man said nothing but reached for his inside pocket and a small silver flask. For a moment Phoebe considered demurring and implying she would never touch strong liquor, but the idea of a nip of brandy to give her courage was too great and she allowed him to put the flask to her lips. As it was the liquor was raw and fierce, nothing like the quality she was used to and she coughed and spluttered, gasping for breath as it burned its way down her throat.

The fellow chuckled, shaking his head. "Tain't water, Miss. Suppose I should ha' thought of that. I'll bring you some presently."

"Thank you," she gasped as the liquor pooled into a little puddle of warmth in her stomach. "Did you say there was food," she asked, looking up at him again. She needed to try to get back some of her strength if she was to survive this ordeal. “I’m most terribly hungry. Oliver hasn’t given me anything at all, I’m so famished I think I may swoon.”

This had the desired effect as the fellow looked horrified by the notion and went to a rickety table he’d set the lamp on to retrieve the parcel he’d brought. She could see him a little better in the lamplight. He was a fairly large man, more broad than tall with thick dark hair and a beard that matched.

“Just some bread and cheese but it’ll fill a hole. Guess it won’t be what you’re used to but you’ll have to make do.”

“Bread and cheese would be wonderful, thank you.”

The man grunted as he undid the parcel and she wondered if her efforts were being cast upon stony ground.

“You didn’t bring a cat then?” she asked, trying to keep her tone conversational. He turned, eyeing her with a frown and then shrugged.

“Couldn’t catch one,” he replied with a snort, adding only, “Rats won’t bite you, I ain’t never been bitten. Keep still and don’t wriggle, they’ll not bother you none, they just scurry around is all.” With this reassuring advice he brought the parcel over to her and then paused as he realised she would be unable to eat unless he fed her or untied her bindings.

“I think it’s unlikely I could overpower a big man like you,” Phoebe said with a wry smile. This was greeted with a grunt of assent and she held her hands out so he could untie the ropes.

She made a great show of rubbing her slender wrists - which were indeed bruised and sore and weeping a little in the hopes of moving him to pity.

“I’m sorry,” she said, wiping her eyes on her sleeve. “Oliver has treated me so roughly and ... and it’s not at all what I’m used to.”

A snort of amusement followed. “I don’t doubt it.”

“He seemed like such a nice young man too,” she added with a forlorn sigh. “I was never more deceived in anyone.”

“That’s men for ye,” the fellow said, to her surprise shaking his head and handing her a rough hunk of bread and a thick slice of cheese. She looked up at him with curiosity as she took a bite of bread and chewed, grateful for anything to fill the clawing hunger in her belly.

“Yes,” she said after she’d swallowed the first bite. “I believed he loved me too, but it seems he just wants my money.” She forced herself not to look at him and bit into the cheese which was tart and creamy at the same time and so good she almost sighed. “Papa is very wealthy,” she added as an afterthought. “Though not as wealthy as my fiancé of course.” She gave a heavy sigh. “He’ll be a duke any day now you know. The old duke is on his last legs. “She affected another sigh. “I should have liked to have been a duchess.” She didn’t wait to see what effect this information was having but shook her head in a defeated manner. “Still, I suppose I shall have to get used to being penniless now.”

“Penniless?” the man retorted with a snort. “The young lord didn’t look like he was short o’ a bob or two.”

“Oh all to pieces,” Phoebe replied, shaking her head as the man grew still. “That’s why he’s running for America, *and* why papa wouldn’t let me marry him. I would have, you see. I’d have even given up the duke for him but papa said he was only a step away from the Marshalsea prison. There're runners after him,” she added with a sudden burst of inspiration.

“Is there now?” the man said, his voice dark and unhappy.

“Oh yes,” Phoebe confirmed before taking another bite of bread. She chewed for a little, allowing the man to digest everything she’d said. “But of course he won’t get a penny now, neither of us will,” she said, sniffing and sounding heartbroken. “Papa will abandon me to my fate and I’ll not get a penny of his money. Papa always liked my sisters better than me. So now I’m worthless if I’m not to marry a duke and ... and Oliver never loved me at all, only ... only my money." Phoebe gave an agonised sob and hid her face in her hands. "And once he realises there will be no money ... oh ... oh ..." she wailed, growing ever more hysterical.

"'Ere, stop that caterwauling," the man said, his voice terse. "This is a pretty kettle o' fish an' no mistake."

"Oh dear." Phoebe looked up at him, her eyes wide and round with pity. "You don't mean to say he hasn't paid you yet?"

"A little bit, but nought like I been promised," the man groused. "An' I had expenses," he added with growing indignation. "That rope don't come cheap you know, nor he didn't give me nought for your supper."

Phoebe bit back the angry retort that flew to her lips and took another bite of cheese instead, chewing with quiet fury. "Well, that's just like Oliver, I'm afraid," she said. "Leaves debts wherever he goes. Not like dear Benedict."

"Benedict?" the man demanded, his eyes lighting up. "Who's he then?"

"Oh, that's the Marquess of Saltash, my fiancé, he'll be the Duke of Denholm shortly."

"Denholm, eh?" the man mused, and she could hear the scratching of his fingers rasping against his stubbly chin. "Fond of you is he?"

"Oh the darling man," Phoebe cried, giving a theatrical sob. "He's so in love with me. I imagine he'll hunt Oliver down for this, no expense spared," she added. "He'll be devastated, the poor lamb."

She said nothing more, judging that the seeds of doubt and discontent had found fertile enough ground as her captor began to pace. Instead she applied herself to the bread and cheese and found herself a little more hopeful than she had been.

"Reckon he'd be glad to get you back, this duke of yourn?" the man demanded at length as Phoebe brushed the bread crumbs from her skirts.

"Glad!" she exclaimed in astonishment. "Goodness, he'd likely pay a king's ransom for me," she said, praying Benedict would forgive her if this plan went awry.

"Aye," the fellow said, his voice dark. "I reckon he may at that."

"But you'd have to take care to get to him before morning. If Oliver found out ..." She shuddered and trailed off.

Sitting back on the rancid bunk she wrapped her arms about herself. The filthy shack was chilly though it was a warm night. Her shawl had been lost somewhere and the little puff sleeves of her muslin gown were not made for warmth.

"Where do you reckon I might find this duke then?" the man demanded, his eyes glinting with avarice in the darkness.

"Well," Phoebe said, applying her mind to the problem as Ben must have done himself. "He's not duke just yet you understand, or at least he may be," she added, praying Sylvester was in good health and would forgive her. "But anyway he won't have any idea of where Oliver has hidden me of course, so I imagine he'll have to track down the boat first. He knows Oliver was intending to go to America," she said, thinking out loud now. "So I'm certain Dover will be the first place he will look. So he'll be searching out the next boat due to leave, so I imagine if you were to go to the booking office and ask for the Marquess of Saltash ..."

Chapter 29

What is our life? A play of passion,
Our mirth the music of division,
Our mother's wombs the tiring-houses be,
Where we are dressed for this short comedy.
Heaven the judicious sharp spectator is,
That sits and marks still who doth act amiss.
Our graves that hide us from the setting sun
Are like drawn curtains when the play is done.
Thus march we, playing, to our latest rest,
Only we die in earnest, that's no jest. - Raleigh

Benedict paced the confines of the gaol cell with impotent fury whilst he awaited the dubious pleasure of meeting Formby's superior officer.

Mr Gillerthwaite, the constable in charge of this case, had issued a warrant for Benedict's immediate arrest, and neither Formby's admonitions, Benedict's ranting nor the threat of the present duke's fury would sway him.

So despite Formby's dire predictions that they were committing a grave error the two runners had hauled him off to gaol where he now awaited interview with Gillerthwaite. He'd been there the whole damned night, wasting precious time when he could be looking for Phoebe. Benedict wondered if they were thinking of restraining him for the event because if they didn't he was going to wring the blasted man's neck with his bare hands.

His only hope now rested in Formby. The man had promised to stake out the booking office and to take Oliver down the moment he saw him.

Benedict looked up as the rattle of keys was heard and the local officer of the law came towards his cell.

"Mr Gillerthwaite will see you now, my Lord," he said, opening up the cell.

"Oh will he?" Benedict snapped, storming through the opening. "How very gracious of him."

He followed in the man's wake until he was led back upstairs and into a dingy office. It was perhaps a little after eight am and a lamp was still burning, shedding a feeble light as the morning crept with more hope than expectation behind the filthy glass of the tiny window panes.

Gillerthwaite was a tall, sparse man with thick white hair and a vast opinion of his own consequence.

"God, is this the best Dover has to offer," the man said in disgust, looking around the shabby room. "You," he said, pointing to one of the men who had arrested Benedict. "Get me some coffee at once."

Benedict didn't notice the loathing in the man's eyes as he left the room, and no wonder. If Gillerthwaite couldn't be bothered to learn his own men's names, he was unlikely to breed loyalty.

"Well, my Lord," he said, looking Benedict over with contempt. "We have run you to ground at last. After weeks of incompetence by that fool Formby."

"The only fool here is you, Sir," Benedict said, stepping forward. Gillerthwaite may be a tall man but he was thin and the wrong side of fifty and Ben had no compunction about using his own bulk to intimidate the man. "Formby knows damn well Lord Bradshaw is the villain here, as he is the one who has abducted Miss Skeffington-Fox!"

"Ah, well you would say that, though wouldn't you, Sir," he replied with a thin smile. "I don't doubt we'll turn up the poor young lady's body sooner or later, once we discover what you've done with her."

"What I've done with her!" Benedict raged, lunging for the man and finding himself held back as three men threw themselves at him. "You blithering idiot! If she dies, you'd better hope you get me to the gallows fast for I'll kill you the first chance I get!"

"Yes, well it is certainly clear you are a violent man," Gillerthwaite said, looking rather shaken as one of the men handcuffed him to the chair. "Just as Lord Bradshaw said you would be."

"You have no idea," Benedict replied, his voice dark. He was damned now either way but he had to make the man see that Phoebe was still out there. "I tell you now, you cretinous imbecile, if you don't make this charge stick, anything that Oliver has offered you will be as nothing compared to the damage which I and my uncle will do to you. And if you believe any lies Oliver has given you that the present duke is about to breathe his last you're far and wide of the mark. There's many a good fight left in my uncle and he will destroy you if I don't live to do it myself."

He paused for breath as Gillerthwaite blanched a little. "I might remind you that Lord Bradshaw is a long way from the dukedom yet, if that's what he's implied is awaiting him. For once I am gone my young brother is next in line though I doubt the murder of a little boy will weigh on your conscience any will it? For once I'm gone there will be no one left to protect him from the man who is *still out there!"* he shouted, with such rage that the men who had restrained him stepped forward again, despite the fact he was now chained. "And that man has Miss Skeffington-Fox," he added, his voice fierce with emotion. "And if anything happens to her ... by God, I'll make you pay and happily swing for it."

Before Gillerthwaite could begin to reply there was a frantic knock at the door and Formby burst in.

“Mr Formby!” Gillerthwaite, expostulated in fury. “A little decorum please.”

“No time, Sir,” Formby replied, giving the man a look of contempt. “I’ve just made contact with a man who says he has Miss Skeffington-Fox in his keeping. He wants to make a deal with the marquess here. Says he’ll give him over to him instead of Oliver for a price.”

“Any price, man,” Benedict cried, hope leaping to life as he struggled to get up and the cuffs restrained him.

“I told him you’d bite, lad, don’t fret!” Formby said, his tone soothing. “But we ain’t got long. He’s meeting Bradshaw at half nine so we need to get moving.” He turned to one of his comrades. “Undo his restraints, you bloody imbeciles, how much more proof do you want that his lordship is innocent?”

“These men are not under your command, Formby,” Gillerthwaite raged, slamming his hand down on the desk in fury.

“No, Sir,” Formby said, his tone frank. “Nor they ain’t, but if I have my way they won’t be yours neither, not after this balls up.”

“You’ll have my full support, Formby” Benedict said with loathing, springing to his feet. “I’ve not finished with you,” he added with a snarl of such ferocity to Gillerthwaite that he took a step back. But there was no time for the pleasure of wringing the man’s neck now- all that mattered was getting to Phoebe. “Where is he?” Benedict demanded as he, Formby and the other two runners thundered down the stairs and out into the road.

“We’re to meet him opposite The White Horse and it’ll be quicker on foot,” Formby yelled over his shoulder as he hit the street running and Benedict sprinted after him.

It took them a good five minutes to reach The White Horse and Formby waved him back, making him stand out of sight before they turned the corner. “Fred,” he said, speaking to one of the two runners. “You go round the back, make sure we don’t miss him if he gets spooked, right? Bill, you stay here out a sight an’ tail us, in case we get in any bother." The two men nodded and Formby turned to Benedict. "Right, my Lord. I need you to keep your temper in line and hold your nerve. No heroics and no silly buggers, and maybe you, me and your young lady will all come out o' this smellin' of roses."

"Whatever happens, Formby, I shan't forget this," Benedict replied, knowing how much the man had risked by not simply following orders.

"Well, I shan't complain then," Formby said, grinning at him.

As one they stepped around the corner and Formby nudged him as he gestured towards a furtive looking man, lurking in the mouth of the alley beside the pub.

Benedict felt his emotions spiral out of control at the idea of his lovely Phoebe in the hands of this dirty looking, brute. He was broad and swarthy with a thick dark beard and fists like hams. By God if he'd laid a hand on Phoebe he'd kill him. Taking a breath he put his feelings aside for a moment and did a mental tally of anything of worth he had on him. He had maybe twenty guineas, a fob watch that must be worth at least a thousand and a heavy gold signet ring. He would happily hand them over as a guarantee until he had time to get hold of more funds. He only hoped the man was reasonable enough to understand he couldn't just lay his hands on a large sum of money with no warning.

"Here you are now, Sir," Formby said as they approached the man who was looking increasingly wary. "This is the marquess and he's most anxious to get his young lady back."

"Is she hurt?" Benedict demanded, his voice harsh and more than relieved to see an affronted look in the man's eyes.

"No, my Lord. I ain't never hit a woman and I don't figure to start now. Though that Bradshaw tied her up too tight, so she's a bruise or two but none of 'em was my doin' an' she'll tell you so. She's been fed and watered too, though 'e gave me no money for such things."

“Take me to her,” Benedict demanded, wanting to strangle the man for any bruise whether he’d made it or not.

“Now then, my Lord,” the man replied, his eyes alight with avarice. “She’s worth a pretty penny to you, I reckon.”

Benedict nodded, his desire to kill the man so great he had to clench his fists to stop himself from giving into the desire to do so. “How much?”

“Well,” Formby said before the man could speak. “You think a bit afore you reply, my man. There’s runners all about lookin’ for Bradshaw and the girl, so you won’t be headin’ for no bank. What you need is a fast getaway before any’s the wiser or you’ll not get a chance to spend a farthing afore you’re finding yourself at the end of a short rope an’ a long drop.”

This reasoning seemed to hit home and Benedict sent Formby a look of gratitude as the bearded fellow looked at him, considering. Benedict slipped his grandfather’s gold ring from his hand. “Solid gold,” he said to the fellow as he took off his watch and chain. “This is too,” he added. “And set with diamonds as you can see.”

The lure of gold and diamonds seemed to do the trick. “Right you are then,” he said, sliding the valuables into his pockets. “Follow me.”

***

Phoebe wriggled on the bed, trying to ease the bindings off her wrists to no avail. She prayed that Davy, which was apparently the name of her would-be kidnapper, had managed to track Ben down with no problem and was even now on his way back to her. But she could not rely on that fact and she was only too aware that time was ticking. The boat sailed on the next tide at eleven thirty and it had been daylight for some hours now. Oliver would need time to get her aboard unnoticed, she assumed hidden in some kind of crate or barrel, as she’d certainly not go willingly. So he would likely be coming back for her at any time now.

Davy had obliged her by not tying her up as tightly as Oliver had in deference to her bruised wrists, but sadly he wasn't fool enough to leave her free. There was a small amount of movement to be gained but not enough to get loose a hand. Phoebe cursed with frustration and wondered how she might manage to get them off. At least her captor was not so very cruel as he might have been and had lit the fire that morning. She had been shivering hard after a whole night in the place and her teeth had chattered so loudly he'd said it was giving him an earache. The little hut was well hidden from sunlight in the shadow of the larger buildings beside it and no warmth seemed to creep into its gloomy confines. Now it was no longer cold but the room was stuffy and airless. Looking up at the blue sky visible through the truly filthy glass of the one little window she had a sudden inspiration.

Thankfully Davy had judged that leaving her hands tied in front of her and her mouth gagged was restraint enough. They were certainly nowhere where anyone would come running if they heard a thud or crash and the door was well secured. As it was Phoebe was able to get to her feet and look about for something she could use. With a muffled exclamation of delight she bent down and grasped the poker leaning beside the glowing embers of the little hearth and turned back to the window. The glass shattered with a satisfying crash, as shards showered down on her, but to Phoebe's relief some pieces remained, stuck in the putty around the sides. Looking back around she used her foot to hook under a chair and drag it closer so she could reach the window more easily. It took two attempts to stand on the wretched thing with her skirts getting in the way but she managed it and began to saw away at the bindings that held her captive.

It was not as easy as it appeared to be and Phoebe had to force herself not to rush and risk cutting her own wrists. Little by little she worked the thick rope over the broken glass until it was cut clean through and she was free. It took a moment more to remove the gag which was tightly bound and it was with a huge sigh of relief that her aching jaw returned to its usual place. Reaching for the poker once more, Phoebe knocked all of the remaining glass free of the window frame and was about to climb out when she looked back at the fire and decided on one last touch before she left.

Chapter 30

Escape me?
Never—
Beloved!
While I am I, and you are you,
So long as the world contains us both,
Me the loving and you the loth,
While the one eludes, must the other pursue. - Robert Browning.

"Hurry, man, for the love of God!" Benedict shouted at the man who led them towards where his poor lovely girl had been stashed a long and lonely night. "Bradshaw will get there before us if you don't make haste.

"Alright!" the fellow exclaimed, breaking into a run. "Though we said nine thirty for the meeting and it ain't nine yet."

"He won't be late," Benedict replied with surety. "So if you want to get clear you'd best move yourself."

Accordingly the man picked up his pace and they ran the filthy maze of back streets like starving rats as workmen, sailors and washerwomen leapt out of their way. People shouted encouragement or abuse depending on what they believed they were about but soon the people disappeared as they ran into a truly desperate part of town.

Suddenly their guide stopped and pointed towards a tiny ramshackle shed huddled in the shadow of the much larger buildings surrounding it.

"Here's as far as I go," the man said, stepping away from them. "Your girl's in the hut down there. I'm away before Bradshaw or the runners catch me. Nice doin' business with you gents." With that he tipped his filthy hat and began to run away.

"Oi!" Formby yelled, but Benedict didn't much care for the fellow at the moment; nothing mattered but seeing Phoebe was safe and well.

"Come on," he cursed, seeing Formby give a signal to the runner who had been tailing them to keep after the man.

Not waiting to see if Formby was with him or not, Benedict turned and ran towards the hut. As he approached, he realised he could smell smoke and the sunrise glinted in the glass of the window. Except as he drew closer he realised sunrise was well passed and what he was seeing was flames. "Phoebe!" he cried as he reached the building.

He battered against the door, kicking it and not feeling the pain in his injured shoulder as he barged the door open and stumbled inside. The tiny space was all alight, flames licking up the walls and the room filled with thick, acrid smoke. But one thing was clear enough. Phoebe wasn't here. Had it all been a trick?

Benedict stumbled outside gagging and choking and gasping for air as Formby caught up with him.

"She's not there," he cried, terror and anger raging for dominance. By God, where was she? *Where was she?* "We're either too late or we've been duped," he said, his voice full of misery.

"No, lad, don't reckon we have," Formby said, growing very still beside him, his voice quiet.

He looked up as a shabby hackney carriage stopped not far from them and the disreputable-looking driver jumped down and opened the door. Benedict watched as Oliver stepped out and then paused before his foot hit the ground. Their eyes met across the cobbled courtyard and Benedict felt a burst of rage so fierce he thought he might combust from the sheer heat of it.

Oliver froze, his eyes darting to the building which was now fully alight and sending plumes of black smoke and sparks spiralling up into the cloudless summer skies.

"Where is she?" Benedict raged, storming towards Oliver and then forcing himself to stop as the man drew out a pistol.

"Not where I left her, clearly," Oliver replied looking more amused than annoyed. "How like a woman to over set all my plans." He stepped to the floor and gestured to the driver. "Turn around and come back for me," he instructed before casting his eyes around the place. "I can only assume that she did a clever little number on Hubert, the damned fool. I should have known not to leave anything to chance. She's too clever a girl to think she wouldn't try to escape." He sounded rather admiring but Benedict just wanted to kill him for everything he had put her through. "I suppose she convinced him you were a better bet for a ripe plucking," he replied with a laugh. "True enough I suppose as I had planned to kill him." His head quirked to one side a little as he grinned. "Perhaps he wasn't as stupid as he looked. The devil of it is I'll have to catch her again now."

He held the gun trained on Benedict but began to look about at the abandoned warehouses that surrounded them. "Well now, Ben. Do you remember when we were boys, we used to play at hide and seek?" he asked walking backwards away from him but not dropping the gun. "I think Phoebe wants us to play," he said, with a nasty expression. "Finders keepers," he called in a sing song voice before running into one of the buildings.

"Phoebe!" Benedict cried, his voice echoing around the empty buildings. "Phoebe! Oliver is here, he's armed love. Hide yourself and stay put."

With his heart beating in a sickening fashion, Benedict prayed for her safety and ran into the building after Oliver. Formby had disappeared, but he hoped the fellow was up to something, and that he was armed.

***

Phoebe shifted in her hiding spot and then froze as Benedict's voice rang out across the morning. Despite the warning in his words she could have cried with relief. He'd come! Not that she'd had any doubt of his intentions, but so many things could have gone wrong. She held her breath as footsteps rang out downstairs. They weren't out of the woods yet.

Moving forwards she crawled on hands and knees over the dusty floor and peered down between some broken floorboards. She caught a brief glimpse of Oliver making towards the stairs before he was lost from sight. He was coming up.

Scurrying backwards she returned to her hiding place with her heart thudding in her chest and looked about for a weapon. There were broken and empty crates and barrels all around her and lying on the floor about ten feet away lay an iron crow bar. Damn. Why hadn't she seen it earlier? Now all she could do was duck down out of sight.

"Phoebe," Oliver called, his tone light hearted. "Come out, love," he said. "We'll miss our boat if you don't hurry. Remember what fun we'll have in America. There'll be so many less-judgemental fools over there forever droning on about propriety and manners. You'll be so much freer. We both shall!"

Good Lord, he was mad. He simply had to be to believe she would ever willingly go with him. Or perhaps he was just playing with her, and as soon as she was discovered he'd put that pistol to good use. Either way, she knew his intentions were dark. Hardly daring to breathe she kept perfectly still as he walked past the barrels she was sheltering behind and on into the next room. As he went out of sight she heard footsteps downstairs and her heart leapt with fear as she realised Ben had followed him into the building. If he came up now and Oliver heard him he'd be a sitting duck.

With her mind racing Phoebe tried to make some sort of plan. There was a large empty crate just a few feet away, large enough for someone to hide in. As quickly and quietly as she could she tore a strip off the now ragged muslin dress she wore and ran to the crate. She lifted the lid and left the strip dangling over the edge, praying that Oliver would see it and take the bait as she ran back to her hiding place, picking up the crowbar as she went.

She found her place not a second too soon as Oliver returned from his fruitless search of the other room.

His footsteps paused and she prayed that he had seen the tattered yellow fabric. Daring to peer out from her hiding place she saw that he had indeed taken the bait. To her surprise and delight he put the pistol down on top of one of the barrels beside the crate before stepping closer and with deft, quiet moves, reaching to lift the lid of the crate.

The stairs creaked behind her and she knew Benedict was on his way up. She didn't hesitate. Deciding a gun was more threatening than relying on having enough strength to knock him out with the crowbar she lunged forward, snatching up the gun.

If she had hoped Oliver to stand docile with his hands up, she was sorely disappointed. Rage lit his eyes and he struck out at her. Phoebe squeezed the trigger and the gun fired but he had skewed her aim as he pushed her. He roared in pain as the bullet grazed his side but it was neither a fatal wound nor one that seemed to slow him down as he forced her to the floor.

His weight falling upon her on the hard floor knocked the air from her lungs and for a moment she was dazed and breathless as Oliver seemed to lift magically from her ... until she saw Benedict's towering form hauling him away. He hit Oliver, a terrific blow that made her gasp in shock at the force with which it hit home. Oliver flew backwards but did not appear to be about to give in. He knew it was the gallows for him now if he didn't get away and his eyes glittered with rage and madness. He leapt back to his feet, circling Benedict as he took off the elegant jacket that was hindering his movements. He hissed as he pulled it away from the gunshot wound, offering Phoebe a nasty smile. "You'll pay for that, love," he said, before snatching up the crowbar that Phoebe had so foolishly discarded.

He gave a roar of rage as he threw himself upon Benedict, and she watched in horror as Ben caught his arm before the heavy iron bar smashed into his skull. The two men fought, pushing and shoving, each of them trying to get in a blow.

Phoebe looked around, hoping against hope that there was a weapon to hand and her eyes fell upon the spent gun. If only the bloody thing was loaded, but she had no shot nor powder. With a burst of hope she saw Oliver's discarded jacket and grabbed for it, praying for an inside pocket. To her joy she found a small brass powder flask and a drawstring bag of shot and proceeded to load the pistol. She glanced up, almost scattering the shot across the floor as a crash sounded across the room and saw with alarm the two man fall heavily to the floor. Oliver was still wielding the iron bar and she returned her attention to the pistol, thanking her papa heartily for having shown her the skill. A life among the army was a dangerous one for a pretty young girl and it was only since she'd returned to England that she stopped carrying her own gun.

With deft, sure moves she loaded and primed the pistol and scrambled to her feet just as the iron bar flew from Oliver's hand and skidded across the room. Her relief was short lived, however, as Oliver reached down into his boot and she saw the glint of a blade. The two men were still fighting close, inches between them as Oliver slashed out with the blade and caught Benedict across the arm before thrusting closer. Benedict caught hold of Oliver's wrist as the knife angled down at his neck. Whatever madness had Oliver in his grip it gave him strength and she saw the murderous rage in his eyes; he would not stop until Ben was dead.

Terror seizing her heart, she raised the gun and knew she could not miss but the two men were moving and the slightest miscalculation could be fatal. But Oliver caught Ben's foot and he stumbled, his hold on Oliver's wrist slipping from his grasp, and the knife descended. There was no time for thought, no time to consider if this was the best option. She fired.

The report in the cavernous space was thunderous, echoing and repeating around the room as the two men froze in shock. Time hung suspended and her heart filled with fear as neither moved and then ... Oliver dropped like a stone.

Ben stood, staring down at him in numb disbelief, his chest heaving with effort as he turned to stare at Phoebe, the smoking pistol still in her hand.

"Ben!" she cried, dropping the gun and running to him.

He caught her in his arms, his hands running over her, looking for signs of injury. "I'm all right!" she exclaimed, hearing the tremor in her voice as the reality of the past moments caught up with her. "I'm fine," she repeated, laughing with a touch of hysteria as the fear continued to shine in his eyes and he pulled her to him. He was silent but his arms held her so tight she could barely breathe and she could hear the thundering of his heart clear enough.

"Oh," she exclaimed, seeing blood seeping through the arm of his jacket. "You're hurt."

"It's nothing," he said, sounding just as unsteady as she had though he managed a crooked smile. "Could have been a lot worse. That was quite a shot, love," he added, not hiding the astonishment in his eyes.

She swallowed and nodded. "Thank my father," she said, her voice quiet. "He made me practise daily. Soldiers aren't to be trusted you see ..." she added with a shrug and by way of explanation.

There were heavy footsteps on the stairs and Formby appeared at the top, he was bloody and dazed and he took one look at them and Oliver's body close by and fell to his knees, gasping for breath. "Thank God," he rasped, pulling at his dishevelled cravat to try to get some air.

"Where the devil were you?" Benedict demanded in fury though Phoebe thought it plain enough the man had found his own fight to content with.

"The carriage driver," Formby rasped, wiping his brow with his cravat. "Nasty piece of work. I was right behind you but he jumped me. Knew I recognised him - hung his brother last week. Fellow wanted revenge."

"You alright?" Ben asked, as they moved towards him. Formby nodded. "Need a holiday," he said with a wry grin. "Do me a favour, my Lord?" he added looking up at Ben with a beseeching expression.

"Anything," Ben replied, with real sincerity in his voice.

"try to keep your family alive for the foreseeable, eh?" he said, raising one eyebrow. "Least ways until I've got me breath back."

Epilogue

And on that cheek, and o'er that brow,
So soft, so calm, yet eloquent,
The smiles that win, the tints that glow,
But tell of days in goodness spent,
A mind at peace with all below,
A heart whose love is innocent! - Byron

Six weeks later and Benedict found himself handing his wife down from the carriage outside the towering grandeur of Grizedale Court.

The twins squealed as they ran for him and he swept them both up, one in each arm as they pressed kisses to his cheek. Watching with a feeling of such happiness he thought his poor heart would struggle to contain it, he saw his mother embrace Phoebe, her eyes shining with delight at her new daughter-in-law. Jessamy hugged her in turn once his mother let her go, beaming with delight at his wonderful new sister-in-law, and Cecily could not have looked more delighted. In fact the only one whose felicity seemed to outshine everyone's by a mile or more was Sylvester's. He was beaming from ear to bewhiskered ear and looking like he'd arranged everything to his own complete satisfaction. This impression was only clarified further as Phoebe hugged him and kissed his bristly cheek.

"Ha!" the old duke barked with satisfaction, waving his stick in Ben's direction. "Lucky for you I'm not a younger man, Ben!" he exclaimed. "I'd have fought you tooth and nail for her."

Ben laughed and walked up the steps to shake his uncle's hand with a warm smile. "And won too, no doubt, you old reprobate," he replied, grinning with a deep affection for the old man.

They walked into the bright white entrance hall and out of the heat of the late afternoon sun. The summer was burnishing the countryside with a last defiant show of heat before the autumn crept in to take up its mantle. As the familiar surroundings of Grizedale wrapped around him, Ben felt for the first time like he had truly come home.

Sylvester had demanded that he and Phoebe, and the rest of the family consider Grizedale as their home now. It would all be Ben's soon enough in any case, he said, though privately Ben thought - and hoped - that the old man would go on for a good while yet. But Sylvester insisted that he get to know the estate and everything he was taking on while he himself was still on hand to advise him. Phoebe had been enchanted by the idea and though they must return to London for Cecily's first season, he knew they would be happy here.

They made their way to the drawing room where tea and cakes had been provided after their ten days honeymoon in Scotland. Benedict had offered Phoebe a trip to Paris but she said she'd had quite enough of France and Spain thank you very much. In fact all either of them truly wanted was to establish themselves in their new life at Grizedale, and with this accord they had decided against a lengthy stay away. There would be time enough to travel and see the world if they so chose. For now they were content to be among their family in the place they belonged.

Benedict's butler, Combes, escorted them through and oversaw the tea things with all the solemnity of a man who has recently found himself serving a duke and a marquess, rather than a mere earl.

Keane, however, was at this moment honeymooning in the Lake District with Lizzie. When Lizzie had finally confessed her love for the man with a combination of blushing defiance, Sylvester had just given a bark of laughter. "Do you think I don't have eyes in my head, girl?" he'd demanded, waving her off. "Go marry him if it will make you happy. You've spent time enough running at my beck and call and you know your own mind. If you're ready to face the difficulties in marrying beneath you, I'll not be the one to put a spoke in your wheel."

Lizzie had been beyond herself, in a daze of happiness that Ben and Phoebe could well comprehend. Sylvester had gifted them a lovely house on the estate with a hundred acres and promised to help Keane with his ambition to start a stud farm with the fine bloodline of Sylvester's own stable. He'd apparently been in league with the head groom for some time and plans were well advanced.

They looked up now as Combes reappeared and gave a polite cough. "A Mr Formby for you, my Lord," he said with dignity.

Benedict nodded and a moment later Formby strode into the room and Ben got to his feet to greet him. "Formby," he said, his smile warm and welcoming. "Devilish glad to see you, man, how are you?"

"Well, my Lord," Formby replied shaking his hand with enthusiasm. "And no more glad than I. After the trial things were in such a stir I never got the chance to congratulate you and Lady Saltash," he said, smiling at Phoebe who beamed at him in return. He held out a lovely bunch of white roses to Phoebe looking a touch bashful. "It's not much but I wanted to felicitate you on your nuptials. They're from my garden," he added, gesturing to the beautiful blooms

"Oh, Mr Formby!" Phoebe exclaimed, quite obviously delighted and touched by the gesture. "What a dear you are!" She took the roses from him and kissed his cheek, making him blush profusely. "They're perfectly lovely."

"You got your watch and things back then," Formby grinned as Benedict looked down at his grandfather's gold ring.

"I did, not that I cared for these until Phoebe was safe," he said, looking at his wife with adoration. "But I should have been sorry to lose them, so I thank you for that too."

Formby shrugged. "A pleasure to do so, my Lord."

"I hear you've been promoted," Benedict said, grinning at him as he saw the man stand a little straighter.

"That I have," he said, a look of deep appreciation in his eyes. "And no small thanks to you and his Grace," he added, nodding to Sylvester who waved away his thanks. "And even better that fool Gillerthwaite has been given the heave ho," he added with a dark chuckle.

"There is nothing to thank me for, that's for certain," Benedict said, shaking his head. "If not for you ..." He turned and took Phoebe's hand and she squeezed it, knowing just how badly things could have gone. "Well, we will forever be in your debt, Mr Formby. I pray you don't forget it."

Mr Formby rubbed the back of his neck and shuffled about a bit looking awkward.

"Well, perhaps you'd do me the kindness of calling me Robert," he said, with a grin. "I'd be pleased enough with that."

"Robert it is," Phoebe replied. "In which case you must call his Lordship, Ben," she added with a mischievous smile.

Ben looked at her with amusement as Robert looked horrified. "Oh I couldn't," he exclaimed

"You could and you shall," Ben said nodding. "And we have been wondering if you and your wife and family would care to stay on the estate for a holiday. There is a lovely cottage down by the river. It's yours for as many weeks as you care to take it every year, and for as long as you wish to use it."

Robert gaped at him in astonishment. "There's trout in that river," he said, sounding a little overwhelmed.

"So there is." Ben nodded. "And we'll try for them together the first time you're here."

Once Mr Formby had gone, beaming with delight at his good fortune, Ben and Phoebe escaped the house and the family and wandered down to the river themselves.

They strolled along the bank, watching dragonflies dart around the rushes as the water tumbled with a merry burble over smooth rocks and stones. Benedict looked down at the angelic blonde beside him and felt an impossible swell of happiness. Such a short time ago he'd been completely unaware of the joylessness of his own life, let alone the unhappiness he had unwittingly inflicted on those he loved most. Then Phoebe arrived and they'd been plunged into such a series of events that he had at times despaired that there would be any escape for him.

Now, in this moment, to find himself here, married to the woman who both infuriated and delighted him beyond anything he had thought possible, he found his good fortune hard to believe.

"Happy, love?" he asked, stopping so that she turned to look up at him.

"How can you even ask?" she replied, smiling at him, her cheeks dimpling as her eyes lit with that mischievous look that both enchanted and terrified him. "I never thought to be so completely content." She leaned her head against his chest and sighed. "Although," she added as her hand slid down his chest. Her hand continued to slide lower and he sucked in a breath.

"Although, you never did make love to me beside the river and I really think you ought to."

"I ought to?" he replied, snorting with amusement and then growing very still as her clever fingers dealt with the fall on his trousers and slid beneath.

"Oh yes," she replied, with perfect sincerity. "You see, when we first met, I made myself a promise."

"What promise?" he murmured, feeling any grasp on sanity or decorum flying far from his grasp as her hands moved upon him.

"I promised myself I would teach you to be brave."

Benedict laughed and shook his head, lifting her into his arms and laying her down on the bank. "Brave is it?" he demanded, covering her body with his own. “You don’t mean brave, you mean reckless, wanton and abandoned to all good sense!”

Her brow furrowed, her expression serious as he looked down at his lovely wife with amusement.

“Yes,” she replied. “That too!”

With a laugh filled with love and the joy of the moment Benedict nodded. “Have no fear, I’m every one of those things where you are concerned, my love,” he replied before ducking his head and proceeding to prove it to her very thoroughly indeed.

***

If you enjoyed this book, please support this indie author by leaving a review. Thank you!

For a sneak peek of the next exciting book in The Regency Romance Series, keep reading.

A Dog in A Doublet

The Regency Romance Mysteries Book 2

Harry Browning was a motherless guttersnipe, and the morning he came across the elderly Lord Preston clinging to a sheer rock face he didn't believe in fate. But the fates have plans for Harry whether he believes or not, and he's not entirely sure he likes them.

As a reward for his bravery, and in an unusual moment of charity, miserly Lord Preston takes him on. He is taught to read, to manage the vast and crumbling estate, and to behave like a gentleman, but Harry knows that is something he will never truly be.

Already running from a dark past, his future is becoming increasingly complex as he finds himself caught in a tangled web of jealousy and revenge.

Temptation, in the form of the lovely Lady Clarinda Bow, is a constant threat to his peace of mind, enticing him to be something he isn't. But when the old man dies his will makes a surprising demand,

and the fates might just give Harry the chance to have everything he ever desired, including Clara, if only he dares.

And as those close to the Preston family begin to die, Harry may not have any choice.

Available to read on Kindle Unlimited

A Dog in a Doublet

A Dog in a Doublet

Prologue

Harry watched with trepidation as his aunt's husband lumbered about the room. Young as he was, Harry knew that getting in his Uncle Joe's way after a night drinking was a bad idea. Clasping his skinny knees tight to his chest, Harry tried to make himself as small and inconspicuous as possible in the dim hope that he could escape a beating.

He never knew why he'd been beaten, and never really even questioned it. His mother was dead, his father gone before he was born, and so he'd ended up with his mother's sister. He had never been anything, but a blessed nuisance to his Aunt Nelly, who was ready enough to belt him if he was too noisy or got under her feet, which was most of the time. But Joe was far bigger and stronger, and the last time had hurt so bad that Harry trembled at the idea of repeating it. He was eight now and was used to spending most of his time in the streets to escape either Nelly's or Joe's attentions. But it was a bitter cold night, and so he'd crept home, hoping Joe would stay out. But luck wasn't with him tonight.

Harry gasped as a big hand reached beneath the table and hauled him out by the ear. The shouting started, just as he'd known it would. He should never have come back. Why Joe hated him quite so ferociously, Harry couldn't fathom, but he knew as Joe pulled the glowing poker from the fire that if he survived ...

He'd never be coming back home again.

Chapter 1

A Dog in a Doublet - A daring, resolute fellow
- The 1811 Dictionary of the Vulgar Tongue, by Francis Grose.

November 1807

Eleven years later ...

"Ah, come on, Harry," Ivor said, failing to keep the impatience from his sly blue eyes though his tone was wheeling. "It'll be easy. The latch is broke an' we know they'll be out."

Harry hunched his shoulders, keeping his eyes on the bottom of his glass which was depressingly close to being empty. "No," he replied, wishing Ivor would damn well change his tune, as he'd been singing the same sorry song for the past two days.

"But why?" Ivor insisted, sounding more angry than impatient now. "We need a bit o' muscle in case there's any bother. I never believed you'd let me down."

Harry snorted and looked up at his onetime crony.

"Thought you said it was easy and there'd be no bother?" he said, his tone dry. "And I ain't lettin' no one down. I ain't no cracksman and well you know it. I may 'a lifted a wallet or two in my time, but house-breakin' ... that's not my line an' never has been."

"But this is a fat pigeon, Harry, ripe for pluckin'!" Ivor hissed, leaning across the table towards him.

Harry flinched as Ivor's foul breath rolled across the table to him. "All the more for you, then, Ivor," Harry replied, tired of the same old argument. He'd had a close shave with the law six months earlier and narrowly avoided deportation. Now he'd found himself honest work labouring at the docks and a little self-respect, even if the pay was barely enough to feed a mangy dog, let alone a man of his size. Still, the idea of crossing the oceans to some foreign hellhole had put the fear of God in him, and he'd resolved to stay out of trouble from now on and keep his temper, no matter what. So Ivor could nag and whine and berate him all he liked - and he had, but it would change nothing. He reached for his hat and stood as Ivor's hand reached out and grabbed at his wrist.

"You'll regret it," Ivor snarled, any pretence of friendship chased out by the glittering anger in his eyes.

"Maybe," Harry said with a shrug. "Maybe not." He looked long and hard at the filthy fist grasping at his sleeve and gave Ivor a pointed look. The man dropped his hand, looking sulky as hell, but thankfully not stupid enough to do anything about it. For good or for bad, Harry had a reputation with his fists, and no one angered him unnecessarily or they tended to regret it for a good long while after.

Leaving Ivor to nurse his disappointment, Harry headed outside. The stench outside was just as foul as that in the tavern, just a damn sight colder. As he pulled his thin coat closer to him, Harry shuddered and decided to head over to The Lamb and Flag. Moll might be in a generous mood and give him a bowl of soup. His guts were clamouring as he'd eaten nothing since the night before; but as he'd not a farthing to his name until pay day tomorrow, there was little he could do about it.

The Lamb and Flag was packed as he might have expected, but Moll grinned at him as he entered, showing yellowing teeth, but the kindly glint in her eyes was a beautiful sight to Harry and his empty belly. She was the wrong side of forty and her voluptuous charms were not what they'd once been, but her heart was as wide as her girth for those she liked. There were few in the world who'd do a fellow a favour and expect nothing but a kind word in return, but Moll was a good sort. Of course, Harry knew she was sweet on him, but she never pressed him for anything more than a smile and he counted her a friend of sorts.

Settling himself down in a quiet corner, he murmured his thanks as Moll passed him a bowl of stew and a hunk of bread destined for another table with a wink, and sashayed off again.

Too hungry and intent on wiping the bowl clean with the last of the bread, at first Harry didn't notice the disturbance at the bar. It was only when Moll cried out in distress that Harry looked up. There was raucous laughter and to his dismay, Harry saw some devil had caught Moll by the arm and was twisting it. By the distress in Moll's eyes, he could tell she was frightened, and there was little that frightened the woman who'd presided over The Lamb and Flag and its rough clientele like an empress all these years.

Looking around, it was clear that no one else was willing to intervene. The fellow holding her was big and angry and clearly in his cups. Sighing inwardly, Harry got to his feet.

"Let her go."

Harry was rewarded by a look of deep gratitude from Moll, but the fellow holding her so tight didn't move, didn't even turn, at first, and the tavern fell silent. The expectation of a fight hung over the room with the inevitability of the space between one heart beat and the next.

And then the man turned.

For just the briefest moment Harry was eight years old again and screaming in agony as Uncle Joe held the burning poker against his shoulder. The eyes were the same, full of spite and malice, if older and more bloodshot.

"Outside. Now." The voice was Harry's, though it seemed to come from a long way off, and he didn't really remember saying it at all. He barely registered the protests from Joe that he'd only been messing about. As ever, the man's swift and familiar switch to blind drunken anger appeared fast enough when Harry would not be swayed.

A cold, dark rage swept over Harry as he stripped off his coat and shirt and handed them to Moll to keep, unwilling to ruin his only decent shirt on filth like Joe.

He stared back at the lumbering drunk and remembered the scrawny lad he'd been at the hands of this monster. The idea of using his own hands to beat a child made Harry physically ill, and the scar on his shoulder seemed to burn anew at the horror of it.

Joe would pay now.

He'd pay for the days of fever that Harry had been grateful for, as he'd dreamed of a mother long-dead to him. He'd pay for his life on the streets that had begun the moment he was strong enough to leave his bed and drag his trembling bones as far from Joe as he could get.

He'd pay for it all.

The fight was short and brutal. Joe might be big, but he was a drunkard and no match for Harry's youth and vigour. With fury, Harry realised that even the satisfaction of beating the man bloody was lost to him, as he found no respite from his anger in a man that was no match for his heavy fists. With a last, frustrated punch, Harry hit him, breaking his nose and hoping to lay him out cold. Let him spend the night freezing in the gutter and see how he liked it. But Joe stumbled on the wet cobbles, his eyes rolling back into his head as he slipped sideways. With a sick feeling in his stomach, Harry watched as the man fell, a dead weight, and could do nothing as his head hit the pavement with a nauseating smash.

The crowd who'd been jeering and cheering and taking bets fell silent once more as blood pooled between the cobbles, leaving little rocky islands in a dark, dark sea.

Joe wasn't moving.

"Go," Moll hissed, thrusting his shirt and coat into his hands. "You need to get out of here, Harry. You'll get the rope this time, never mind transportation."

Harry just stared at her, clutching his clothes, too numb to do anything.

"Go!" she said, her eyes frantic and glittering with tears now as she gave him a hard push. "Get as far away as you can, Harry," she said, her face full of misery. "And don't come back."

***

There was a cockerel crowing. The sound penetrated Harry's brain and brought him back to life, if that was what you called it. He was frozen to the bone, his guts so hollow his belly must be fused to his spine. Three days since he left London. He'd hitched a ride on a cart and walked until his legs felt like they would buckle, hardly daring to stop and sleep. Exhaustion had pulled him down in the end and he'd crept into a dilapidated barn. It was no warmer in the dusty darkness than in the frigid landscape outside, velvet white with hoarfrost, but at least it was out of the wind.

Harry hauled himself to his feet, his protesting limbs aching and sore, his hands and feet so cold that the pain was sharp and pulled at his empty belly. How long must he keep walking, he wondered, how far should he go? He couldn't keep this up for much longer at any rate. He needed to eat. The idea that his wages were waiting for him back in London was an added torment. His pockets were empty, and with no job, he'd not find food anytime soon. His only hope was to find temporary work on a farm or estate in return for a meal at least. He was fit and strong, when he wasn't about to faint from hunger, and he could do the work of two men, at least. That ought to be obvious. Perhaps he'd get lucky.

He snorted, the freezing air billowing around him in a cloud.

Luck.

If luck existed, it had a decided antipathy towards Harry Browning, he thought with chagrin. Except he could no longer be Browning. Not that it bothered him. He'd always hated the name, Joe's name. He'd choose a new one.

Thompson, he decided for no reason in particular as he tramped out of the barn, his worn soles sliding on the frozen muck of the lane as he set off. Thompson was a lucky name for sure. Yes, Harry Thompson was a lucky fellow who always fell on his feet, he assured himself, knowing he was being idiotic. It must be the lack of food making him delirious.

He paused, stopping in his tracks and staring at the sun as it glittered on the horizon. The landscape spread out before him, stealing his breath and making him wonder for the first time in his life if there really was a God.

Harry had never seen the countryside before, never seen anything beyond the filth and the stench and the bustle of the slums of London. Yet this ... this was beautiful. Frozen to the bone, sick with hunger, and with no prospects of any kind, Harry looked at the world anew. This world was clean, the air was sweet, and it was full of beauty. Not that he was some romantic fool. A landscape like this was designed to be every bit as cruel and hard as those he'd left behind if there was no work, no food, no roof over your head, and yet despite everything ... he began to hope.

Want more Emma?

If you enjoyed this book, please support this indie author and take a moment to leave a few words in a review. *Thank you!*

To be kept informed of special offers and free deals (which I do regularly) follow me on *https://www.bookbub.com/authors/emma-v-leech*

To find out more and to get news and sneak peeks of the first chapter of upcoming works, go to my website and sign up for the newsletter.

http://www.emmavleech.com/

Come and join the fans in my Facebook group for news, info and exciting discussion...

Emmas Book Club

Or Follow me here......

Emma's Amazon Author page

Emma's Amazon UK Author page

Emma's Twitter page

About Me!

I started this incredible journey way back in 2010 with The Key to Erebus but didn't summon the courage to hit publish until October 2012. For anyone who's done it, you'll know publishing your first title is a terribly scary thing! I still get butterflies on the morning a new title releases but the terror has subsided at least. Now I just live in dread of the day my daughters are old enough to read them.

The horror! (On both sides I suspect.)

2017 marked the year that I made my first foray into Historical Romance and the world of the Regency Romance, and my word what a year! I was delighted by the response to this series and can't wait to add more titles. Paranormal Romance readers need not despair however as there is much more to come there too. Writing has become an addiction and as soon as one book is over I'm hugely excited to start the next so you can expect plenty more in the future.

As many of my works reflect I am greatly influenced by the beautiful French countryside in which I live. I've been here in the

South West for the past twenty years though I was born and raised in England. My three gorgeous girls are all bilingual and the youngest who is only six, is showing signs of following in my footsteps after producing *The Lonely Princess* all by herself.

I'm told book two is coming soon ...

She's keeping me on my toes, so I'd better get cracking!

KEEP READING TO DISCOVER MY OTHER BOOKS!

Other Works by Emma V. Leech

(For those of you who have read The French Fae Legend series, please remember that chronologically The Heart of Arima precedes The Dark Prince)

The Regency Romance Mysteries

Dying for a Duke

A Dog in a Doublet

The Rum and the Fox

Rogues & Gentlemen

The Rogue

The Earl's Temptation

Scandal's Daughter

The Devil May Care

Nearly Ruining Mr. Russell

[One Wicked Winter]

[To Tame a Savage Heart]

[Persuading Patience]

[The Last Man in London]

[Flaming June]

[Charity and the Devil]

[A Slight Indiscretion]

[The Corinthian Duke]

[The Blackest of Hearts] (December 28, 2018)

The French Vampire Legend

[The Key to Erebus]

[The Heart of Arima]

[The Fires of Tartarus]

[The Boxset] (The Key to Erebus, The Heart of Arima)

The Son of Darkness (TBA)

The French Fae Legend

The Dark Prince

The Dark Heart

The Dark Deceit

The Darkest Night

Short Stories: A Dark Collection.

Stand Alone

The Book Lover (a paranormal novella)

Also check out Emma's regency romance series, Rogues & Gentlemen. Available now!

The Rogue

Rogues & Gentlemen Book 1

1815

Along the wild and untamed coast of Cornwall, smuggling is not only a way of life, but a means of survival.

Henrietta Morton knows well to look the other way when the free trading 'gentlemen' are at work. Yet when a notorious pirate, known as The Rogue, bursts in on her in the village shop, she takes things one step further.

Bewitched by a pair of wicked blue eyes, in a moment of insanity she hides the handsome fugitive from the local Militia. Her reward is a kiss that she just cannot forget. But in his haste to escape with his life, her pirate drops a letter, inadvertently giving Henri incriminating information about the man she just helped free.

When her father gives her hand in marriage to a wealthy and villainous nobleman in return for the payment of his debts, Henri becomes desperate.

Blackmailing a pirate may be her only hope for freedom.

Read for free on Kindle Unlimited

The Rogue

Lose yourself in Emma's paranormal world with The French Vampire Legend series..... Book 1 is a FREE download on Amazon....

The Key to Erebus

The French Vampire Legend Book 1

The truth can kill you.

Taken away as a small child, from a life where vampires, the Fae, and other mythical creatures are real and treacherous, the beautiful young witch, Jéhenne Corbeaux is totally unprepared when she returns to rural France to live with her eccentric Grandmother.

Thrown headlong into a world she knows nothing about she seeks to learn the truth about herself, uncovering secrets more shocking than anything she could ever have imagined and finding that she is by no means powerless to protect the ones she loves.

Despite her Gran's dire warnings, she is inexorably drawn to the dark and terrifying figure of Corvus, an ancient vampire and master of the vast Albinus family.

Jéhenne is about to find her answers and discover that, not only is Corvus far more dangerous than she could ever imagine, but that he holds much more than the key to her heart …

FREE download

The Key to Erebus

Check out Emma's exciting fantasy series with hailed by Kirkus Reviews as "An enchanting fantasy with a likable heroine, romantic intrigue, and clever narrative flourishes."

The Dark Prince

The French Fae Legend Book 1

Two Fae Princes
One Human Woman
And a world ready to tear them all apart

Laen Braed is Prince of the Dark fae, with a temper and reputation to match his black eyes, and a heart that despises the human race. When he is sent back through the forbidden gates between realms to retrieve an ancient fae artifact, he returns home with far more than he bargained for.

Corin Albrecht, the most powerful Elven Prince ever born. His golden eyes are rumoured to be a gift from the gods, and destiny is calling him. With a love for the human world that runs deep, his friendship with Laen is being torn apart by his prejudices.

Océane DeBeauvoir is an artist and bookbinder who has always relied on her lively imagination to get her through an unhappy and uneventful life. A jewelled dagger put on display at a nearby museum hits the headlines with speculation of another race, the Fae. But the discovery also inspires Océane to create an extraordinary piece of art that cannot be confined to the pages of a book.

With two powerful men vying for her attention and their friendship stretched to the breaking point, the only question that remains...who is truly The Dark Prince.

The man of your dreams is coming...or is it your nightmares he visits? Find out in Book One of The French Fae Legend.

Available now to read for FREE on Kindle Unlimited.
The Dark Prince

Acknowledgements

Thanks as always to my wonderful editor for being patient and loving my characters as much as I do. Gemma you're the best!

To Victoria Cooper for all your hard work, amazing artwork and above all your unending patience!!! Thank you so much. You are amazing!

To my BFF, PA, personal cheerleader and bringer of chocolate, Varsi Appel, for moral support, confidence boosting and for reading my work more times than I have. I love you loads!

A huge thank you to all of Emma's Book Club members! You guys are the best!

I'm always so happy to hear from you so do email or message me :)

emmavleech@orange.fr

To my husband Pat and my family ... For always being proud of me.

Made in United States
North Haven, CT
14 September 2022